ISBN 1-903110-37-8

1 3 5 7 9 8 6 4 2

Cover Illustration and Design by Owen Benwell

Printed and bound in the UK

**Published in 2006 by
Wrecking Ball Press
24 CAVENDISH SQUARE • HULL • ENGLAND • HU3 1SS**

Acknowledgments

"I acknowledge with gratitude the help I have received from Professor David Richardson, University of Hull, and from Mitch Upfold, and from my secretary, Mrs Liz Aydon."

Richard Adams

Daniel

WRECKING BALL PRESS

To Juliet, with much love from Dad

PART I

In the half-lit, foetid shack the new-born baby, slippery with blood and with part of the caul adhering to its head, was received by grimy hands and laid down, wauling, among the rubbish on the earth floor – vegetable peelings, a rag damp with dirty water, a few crushed insects, an old, shredded blanket, and the entrails of a drawn fowl.

From outside came faint sounds of splashing in the trench that ran the length of the hovels' backs, where a boy was stabbing with a pointed stick at the floating body of a rat. From further off sounded, for a moment or two in the still air, the falling twitter of a gaze-finch perched on a clump of laurels. Nearby, a tethered horse continually tossed its head, tormented by the flies. In the blazing, noonday sunshine, a sudden gust of wind stirred the glossy laurel leaves and slammed to and fro the shack's broken shutters, banging them against the unglazed window frames.

On the floor where the baby had been born, black bodies, both men's and women's, lay this way and that; mostly alive, and a few dead, while some, blinking and twitching, might have been either dying or recovering, there being no one near enough to tell which; or care, for the matter of that. Some backs and shoulders were marked with weals of whipping – good for the flies, these – while others, sweating and unscarred, shone smooth as the laurels.

The baby wauled again, an angry, frustrated cry. The same dirty hands picked him up and dandled him back and forth for a few moments.

"*Ay boom-a-boom, Ay boom-a-boom, baby.*

"*Dis baby gwine to live, gwine to live, boom-a-boom.*"

9

"How you tell? Mostly dey dies. You knows dat."

"Ay boom-a-boom, Ay boom-a-boom" – pause.

Then, "Hey, Missus Mudder, here he is, yore baby boy. You take him now."

Speechlessly, straining, the mother half-raised her gaunt body, bending forward clumsily; her skeletal arms took the baby and pressed his mouth to a dry nipple. She wept, trembling. One of the two women beside her was just in time to snatch the baby as the mother fell backwards.

"No milk?" The other woman nodded corroboratively and then called, "Sam! You Sam!"

Outside a boy, aged perhaps eight, came running, pressed his shoulder against the door which grated across the threshold, stepped over one body, then another and took the baby as the first woman held it out to him.

"You Sam, you knows Missus Ethel?" (She pronounced it "Heffle".)

He nodded, wiping the baby's sticky body with an open hand.

"Know where she at?"

He nodded. "She work, dey all workin' tobacco."

"You take baby. Ax Massa Janny, say O.K. she give the baby milk."

"Miz Heffle gettin' milk?"

"Ay does she." The woman gestured impatiently. "Go 'long now."

Sam spat on the floor, split his black face in a grin of white teeth and was gone.

Outside, among the short shadows, the boy in the trench had succeeded in spearing the dead rat and waved it triumphantly at Sam as he jumped across. Sam paused.

"Gwine eatim?"

"Cookim. Beamy Boy gettin' fire dis evenin', let me cookim."

"No eatim now?"

"Beamy Boy got knife. 'E skin 'im, cut off no-good bits. Den

10

cookim 'e good."

Sam nodded and began pushing himself a short cut through the laurels in the direction of the dirt path leading to the tobacco fields. The boy shouted after him, "Snake in dere!"

"Fuck snake."

"Maybe snake fuck you."

Without replying, Sam dragged himself forward, clutching at the laurels, and at length emerged on the open path. From here he could see the tobacco fields and the long line of slaves, each with a wicker basket on his arm, stooping to tug at a bush, then straighten up and drop his handful into the basket. They worked deftly, with a weary, practised skill.

The baby was still crying; a good sign, thought Sam. He splashed into a narrow stream, stooped to drink, and then began to run towards the white overseer, hoping to give the impression that he had run all the way. As he came up, the overseer turned to face him, one hand on the leather whip at his belt.

"Whose baby is this?"

"Miz Barb Brown baby, Massa."

"She still alive?"

"'Tink so, Massa. Only she sick very bad. No got milk. Missus Kathy at infirm'ry, she tell me tote baby 'ere, say Miz Heffle got plenty milk." He fidgeted with his bare feet. "I go now and ax her, Massa?"

The overseer made no reply. He took the baby from Sam, silenced it by giving it a finger to suck and then turned it round and upside down, examining it from all sides.

"'E big fine baby, Massa Janny, sir! He gwine make you damn' good nigger."

Johnny nodded, returning the baby.

"O.K., you take him to Missus Ethel. Not take too long time, tell her." Again he put his hand on the whip.

"When baby finish feed, Massa, I take 'im back 'ome?"

"No, he'll sleep. You keep him in the shade, under those trees."

11

He pointed. "I'll tell you later when Miss Ethel's to feed him again. You watch baby and you work, see? You know how to plait thin sticks for baskets?"

"Yes, Massa."

"There's a pile of thin sticks under the trees. If I see you not working, I'll whip you, understand?"

"Yes, Massa."

Sam carried the baby to Miss Ethel in the line. She saw him coming and, guessing the nature of his errand (to which she was not unused), put down her basket and opened her torn, dirty blouse. No other slaves stopped working.

"Massa Janny, he say O.K. for milk?" She grinned.

"He say you milk not too long. Den I keep him here for next time milk."

Miss Ethel put the baby to her breast. "Massa Janny must reckon baby make damn' good nigger, else he not say do dis."

A sudden thought struck her. "Who mudder?"

"Miz Barb Brown."

Ethel stared, wide-eyed. "She not near time. Baby come too quick?"

"Not know, Missus."

"No one tell you?"

"No, Missus."

The sweat stood on Ethel's forehead and across her broad face. Great drops ran down her breasts in runnels and fell to the ground. There was a long pause, as though the heat had struck them both voiceless. Finally, as though with an effort, Ethel said, "Miz Barb Brown – she die?"

"Not know, Missus. But she lookin' terrible bad."

The silence returned, until the overseer shouted angrily across to them. "Ethel, if you don't want a damn' good whipping, you get back to work."

Sam took the baby, asleep now, and carried him across to the dark shade under the trees. Here he found two stacks of wide, flat baskets, covered with cloths; the slaves' evening meal.

There was a smell of warm, ground maize. Sam's mouth began to water. Looking carefully all about him and making sure of a tree trunk between himself and the overseer, he pushed his fingers under the nearest cloth, drew them back covered with maize mash and quickly sucked them clean. Then, making a show of searching here and there for the best spot, he laid the naked baby in a hollow in the thin grass, picked up a handful of withies from the nearby pile and set to work plaiting, only pausing now and then to brush away the flies.

* * *

Baby, Thou Child of Joy! My heart is at your festival. It is only a few hours since your sleep and your forgetting. Before, you were one and indivisible with God, in that imperial palace whence you came to us, trailing clouds of glory. Those clouds are still about you. They envelop you; my eyes cannot pierce them. I see only the clouds and must believe that you lie at their heart.

What are these trailing clouds, Baby, lingering, leaving their traces, their wisps from the centuries behind as you are pressed helplessly forward, drawn second by second into your life, your indiscernible future? Among them, as they momentarily part, are revealed glimpses of what once comprised reality – all manner of folk, creatures and material things inhabitant of the past; your past, Baby, whence you have so newly come.

Between the clouds for an instant is revealed one Antam Gonsalves, a Portuguese of long ago, a captain who captured some Moors and was ordered by Prince Henry the Navigator to return them to Africa. In exchange he received not only gold but also ten black men. They, as it turned out, were forerunners. Portuguese forts sprang up along the coast of Africa, whence consignments of blacks were brought into Spain and Portugal, the nucleus of a new trade to the western colonies, where many were set to work

13

in the mines.

The clouds merge, the disclosure vanishes. Baby, we peer into thick darkness. Some huge, amorphous bulk is coming to birth, obscene and vile, dispersing the clouds, blotting out all but itself.

O Cruelty, impregnable, all-conquering, be thou adored for ever! Already we had perceived thine envoys here and there about the world; but they were mere trifles. How could we have conceived of Thee? O Evil supreme, now Thou art come Thyself! In thy train follow Agony, Grief and Misery omnipotent! Nothing so vast, nothing on Thy scale was ever known in the world until now. By what Name are we to worship Thy divinity? By what Name shall we adore Thee?

"I AM THE AFRICAN SLAVE TRADE."

Ah, Master, by Thee we know now that Socrates was a fool, Marcus Aurelius a dunce, Jesus Christ a trickster and a liar. No man can serve two masters.

"I AM ULTIMATE EVIL. FALL DOWN BEFORE ME. THERE IS NO CRUELTY GREATER THAN MINE."

The clouds roll together once more: we can no longer see Thee whole, but we can hear Thee, O Master. Those are Thy flames roaring through ransacked villages, Thy mothers bereft, Thy silly, defenceless victims screaming, Thy whips striking home.

And those are our ships, fit to sink with gold, O generous Lord, their prows indistinct once more in the clouds, but visible enough to us, Thy faithful followers. They are our reward for serving Thee.

* * *

My real mother died when I was born – in the year 1759 – and from all that I was ever told, I'd probably have been left to die too if it hadn't been for Missus Kathy taking a fancy to me when I was nothing but a new-born baby. Missus Kathy was a nurse – or what they called a nurse – in the slaves' infirmary on the estate. It seems that my poor mother – Miss Barb Brown she was called –

14

was ill and weak even before she bore me, and Missus Kathy, who delivered me, was much surprised when she saw that I was such a fine, healthy baby. Slave babies without mothers were mostly left to die, and probably, as I say, I'd have died myself without Missus Kathy. She was a good, kind-hearted lady.

Missus Kathy's abode – she always called it that and wouldn't let any of us call it anything else – was a wooden hut like all the others, just a short way from the infirmary. No doctor, no trained nurses, hardly any beds; just a few good souls like Missus Kathy who were ready to do what they could to help. Of course the white men, Massa Reynolds and his two grown sons, never gave her any money for what she did, but all the same she got some good of it, because if it hadn't a' been for her being "on infirm'ry", as they called it, she'd have been in one of the labour gangs working on the tobacco, out on the plantation. A lot of niggers didn't last long at that. "Field niggers", as they were called, were roused at first light and worked till midday. Then they got the first meal of the day, and what they got was ground maize. Then they worked till sunset, when they got their second meal of maize and apples. They only got the apples to stop them getting scurvy and to clean out their bowels and that. There were plenty of women field niggers as well as men. The huts where they lived were always dirty, stinking and full of rubbish – terrible places, really – because after a day's work they were too tired to clean them, and anyway most slaves didn't care whether their huts were clean or not. They'd never lived any different.

Missus Kathy always kept our abode clean. She made us help with cleaning it, too, and wouldn't let us act untidy with our clothes or leave rubbish on the floor. It was an earth floor, of course, like all the others, but the way Missus Kathy went on you'd have thought it was polished parquetry.

I dare say that if you've followed me this far, you're puzzled that here's a plain nigger talking to you like he was an educated man. Well, just stick around – that's to say if you want to – and you'll learn how this came about.

Missus Kathy was forever rubbing it into us that we were what she called "a family" and a good cut above the harum-scarum niggers who lived all over the estate like a bunch of cockroaches. For one thing, we had a father; or anyway she had a husband, kind of style. Who my "real" father was I never had any notion and didn't care either. Precious few niggers knew who their fathers were. If anyone said "That man's my brother", the next question he got was "Same father, same mother?" If he said "Yes", he could pass for respectable. If he said "Same mother, different father", that was tidy. But "Same father, different mother" was no relationship at all, and you let him know he'd have done better to keep his mouth shut in the first place.

I always kept mine shut, for of course I couldn't boast of any real parents at all, but for practical purposes we had got a father, and a good 'un, too. His name was Josh and he most certainly wasn't a cockroach. He had a regular, skilled job in the stables, looking after the white men's horses. There were seven or eight of them altogether, known as "grooms". And you'd better believe it when I tell you that the white men chose the grooms carefully and set a lot of store by them, because for the most part precious few niggers knew anything about horses. No experience, you see.

Taken altogether, there were about as many skilled workers on the estate as there were field niggers: bakers, tinkers, leather-workers, cobblers, tailors, blacksmiths, coopers and so on. In fact, not counting the profits from the sales of tobacco, the estate was just about self-supporting. And it was self-supporting for population, too. Our women had plenty of babies and there were always children old enough to work. They started work when they were six; toting water, picking up trash and so on. I don't remember that we ever needed to buy slaves straight off the ships. Just as well, too, because new slaves were that ignorant they were useless even when they'd been whipped; and quite a few just used to lie down and die.

But to go back to our father. I never really got to know anything about Josh; I mean, where he'd come from or whether he'd grown up on the estate; how he'd come to know so much about horses and horsemanship (for he could ride as well as any white man and

16

better than most) and how he knew such a lot about sick horses and doctoring them. Massa Reynolds thought highly of him and often used to take him along when he went to horse sales or to meet someone who was offering a horse for sale. Josh was even allowed to ride by himself into the nearby town to do errands for Massa Reynolds and his family.

One thing Josh never thought of trying to do was to get a better abode for Missus Kathy and our family. He told Missus Kathy – and I was there when he told her – that he somehow felt in his bones, as he put it, that Massa Reynolds didn't like the notion of him having a wife and family. He didn't want to know that Josh had a finger in any pie except himself and the horses. Josh told Missus Kathy that he couldn't say how he knew, but he was sure that if he said anything to Massa Reynolds about her or about us children, he'd fall out of favour and probably lose his position. And Missus Kathy accepted this, partly because she knew that Josh loved her and never even looked at another woman, and partly because he brought home so many "perks" as he called them: lamb and pork, baskets of eggs, butter and cheese and the like, which Massa Reynolds used to give him whenever he worked extra long hours; and sometimes when Josh had given him good advice about a sale or a purchase or about a winner at the local races and all such things as that. For Josh got to learn inside talk from black grooms in other stables; things that white men didn't usually get to hear at all. He used to say to Missus Kathy that we had a fine position on the estate and we should always take care not to do anything to spoil it.

I was the one who stepped out of line, though I never knew – never have known – what happened to the family, or whether anything did. But I tell you, I still wouldn't act any different now from what I did.

And what was our family, over which Josh and Missus Kathy took such a lot of trouble? There were three of us altogether, two boys and a girl. The eldest was Tom. Tom was eight years older than I was. When I came as a baby, he'd been working for Mr. Tosser, the head cooper, for nearly a year past – a place that Josh had found for him, of course. He'd set himself to learn and work hard, and was beginning to be really useful to Mr. Tosser. He was quiet and obedient in his ways and never gave Missus Kathy any trouble. In fact, I sometimes thought that Missus Kathy (who was his real mother) sometimes wished that he would bust out a bit, like some of the other local lads we knew. But Josh, who seemed to be always very much aware that our good situation was poised on a balance, always said that he'd be happy to see Tom go on with Mr. Tosser until one day perhaps he'd become the Master Cooper himself. Tom was always kind to me. We seldom quarrelled.

The next eldest was Doth. O my dear, my darling Doth! How I loved her! Doth was five years older than me, and even at thirteen was a big, strong, handsome girl. Oh, yes, it was easy enough to feel struck on a girl like Doth just by looking at her, and there were plenty who did. But to me she was far, far more than a fine-looking sister, one to be proud of. I've told how Missus Kathy saved my life as a new-born baby, because I looked good and she couldn't bear the thought of leaving me to die in the rubbish on the floor. I believe she must have saved Doth too. Even as a baby, Doth must have looked too good to waste.

She was everything to me. When I was little she used to wash and dress me and give me my breakfast. And then she'd take me with her to work. She worked in what they called the Make-and-Mend shop, right over the other side of the Slave Village. So the two of us got to pass the time of day with a number of people, coming and going as we did. As I got older, a lot of her friends and acquaintances became mine as well, and they'd have a word or two for me as well as for her. "Hello, young Dan'l," they'd say: "Mind and take good care of your big sister, now, won't you?" and all such teasing things as that. While I was still little I had the notion that I really was looking after her, and I used to answer "Yes, ma'am, let me alone for that." And then they'd laugh and say to Doth "Getting a big boy now, ain't he?" or any old nonsense that would do for a laugh or a joke. And I'd sit up comfortable in the Make-and- Mend shop and watch Doth patching and darning, and gossiping away with the other girls.

18

Doth used to tell me stories, too, and I'd ask her to tell me this one or that one again, the way little kids do. "Long ago," she'd say, "we weren't slaves: nobody was a slave, everybody was free. And in those far-off days there was a girl who kept cows for the king. Now one day," and so on. I could have listened for ever. "What's a slave?" I asked once and Doth said "A slave's someone who can't do what she wants for herself; 'cos she belongs to someone else and always has to do what they say." Of course that didn't really mean much to me at that age; but one day, going home a bit early, she took me out to the tobacco field and made me have a good look. "See," she said, "those are slaves. They've got to do that all day, because the white men say so." "And shall I have to do that?" I asked. "Not if I can help it," said Doth. "I love you too much. You're my very own Dan'l." And that was quite enough for me. I believed every word she said. Once, when I was taken badly sick, Doth begged Missus Blatch, who was boss of the Make-and-Mend, to let her off for two or three days so she could look after me. Well, you see, Missus Blatch knew me, and she told Doth to take real good care and make me better. I believe Doth saved my life that time. I remember once I woke in the middle of the night, taken awful bad, and she was awake and holding me in her arms.

Our white masters, Massa Reynolds and his two sons - of course I hardly ever saw them – I reckon they weren't too terrible hard on us, as masters went in those days. What the masters wanted was the crops – the tobacco and the rest. That was where their money came from. The crops were desperately hard work and the field hands were driven to it with whips by the white overseers. A lot of field hands, both men and women, broke down and died; but field work was never allowed to stop or fall behind. Other slaves were found – even skilled workers pulled out of the shops – and had to work in the gangs until they dropped.

A lot of estates favoured Creoles and Mulattoes – thought they were quicker to learn than us blacks – but Massa Reynolds didn't like them, except he used them in the big house, for domestic servants. What I heard was that he didn't want a third class between masters and slaves. As far as he was concerned, all black people were slaves and all white people were free. But as the estate became bigger, the number of slaves to work it had to grow and the new lots usually included a fair number of Creoles, whether Massa Reynolds liked it or not. The only alternative was slaves off the ships, and as I've said, that wouldn't have done for us.

I remember how I first realised that Creoles were different. A boy I knew had died and was to be buried. I had permission to go. Only white men had marked graves. Slaves were buried in pits, whether it was one or two or however many there might be, and the grass grew over them. No memorials were allowed. Slaves couldn't have paid for them anyway. The day I went, there were several to be buried, and one or two were Creoles. Of course, their families were there and while the burial was taking place they began making trouble, saying their people ought to have proper, individual graves. All that happened was that one of the white overseers who was there told them to be quiet or he'd take his whip to them. They obeyed him, but as I watched them, I felt that that wasn't going to be the end of it. Still, I never heard whether anything happened later.

That was how I came to meet Reverend Foster – at a burial. Doth went to this burial; a girl who'd been a friend of hers was to be buried, and I went with her. When we got there the first person we saw was this clean-shaven white man – dressed all in dark clothes – a stranger to us – standing with Massa Reynolds's son William. As we passed close by, this stranger suddenly took a step forward and put his arm round my neck. He began asking me questions; my name, how old I was, what work I did and so on. And then he asked me whether I knew about Jesus. I had no idea what he meant and I said "No, sir." "Well, you ought to," he says, but then William stepped out and spoke to him, and he let it go at that.

Thanks chiefly to Doth, to Missus Kathy and Josh, I had a happier childhood than most slave children. This was partly because I was fed better than most of the slave children on the estate, who had to keep going on the ever-lasting maize, black bread and potatoes which were doled out to their families; but also because, unconsciously, I knew that I was loved by Doth and Missus Kathy. They gave me affection and attention. They talked to me. What I felt really mattered to them. Missus Kathy's "Don't do dat, Dan'l" was a long way better than being ignored; and Doth – well, I've told you how I felt about Doth.

Apart from the kids round about that I played with – when I had any time to play, that is – there were two people I knew. One was the white clergyman, Reverend Foster, as I was told to call him. Reverend Foster was a visitor – a guest of the Reynolds family – and I don't know how I knew, but I did, that he was only staying for a time; one day he'd be leaving. Massa Reynolds had told him that he was free to go about and talk to the slaves; he wanted them to become Christians – that was his religion, the religion of the white folks. I realise now, although of course I couldn't then, that Massa Reynolds didn't mind any of his slaves becoming Christians because it taught them that God wanted them to obey their masters and not to resent them or make any trouble. But as I've learned since, Massa Reynolds wasn't so keen on another Christian idea, that all folk are equal in the sight of God. Reverend Foster wasn't to teach them that: he only had to teach them that God loved all men, black and white, and that if they worked well and gave no trouble, God would take them to heaven when they died.

Reverend Foster took a liking to me. He used to come to our abode in the evenings and ask Missus Kathy's permission to take me for a walk, and of course she couldn't say No because he was a white man. We used to walk down to the stream or to the tobacco plantation and while we were walking he used to talk to me about Jesus Christ: and I used to listen and say everything I could to please him because he was a white man and used to give me candy. Besides, talking with him was better than working, or helping Missus Kathy to sweep the floor or chop the wood. "You're a real, true little Christian, aren't you?" Reverend Foster used to say, and I'd answer "Yes, sir. I'm a true follower of Jesus"; or anything that I thought would please him and keep me away from work a bit longer.

For I had work now, real work like other slaves. At the time I'm speaking of, I was nine and had been at work since I was seven. (It should have been six, but I didn't get ordered to work at six, and of course I didn't ask about it.) It wasn't hard work for a child slave. Of course it was Josh who had got me the job, and he told me to be sure and do it well if I wanted to keep it. If I did it badly it would be only too easy to drop me.

The job was Messenger Boy. It often happened in the course of the day's work that Massa Reynolds or his sons, or any of the three white overseers would need to send a message across the estate, either to one another or to a black boss of the tinkers or the blacksmiths or some such. Now there wasn't a black on the whole estate who could read or write, so written messages were no good, except from one white man to another. Besides, a lot of the time the message would just be "Come here, So-and-So, I want to talk to you." And this was where the messenger boys came in.

Every morning, as soon as work began on the estate, there would be seven or eight of us messenger boys ready and waiting in a particular shed back of the big house: and if one of the masters needed to send a message, he'd shout "Boy!" and then the one of us whose turn it was would run to him – and damn' fast, too. There was seldom a written message, and the boy had to learn the message by heart and tell it to the person at the other end. It sounds easy enough, but there could be complications. The person might not be where you'd been told to go, and you'd have to find him, or sometimes the message made no sense to him, because things had altered and weren't what the white man thought they were; and so on.

A messenger boy had to be a good runner and someone who had his wits about him; like, whether he'd do his best to find the recipient, wherever he might have got to, or whether it would be better to go back and say he couldn't be found. Or he might have to take another message back in reply. One way and another, there was quite a lot to learn.

And there could be trouble, like I'll tell you now. I told you I knew two people. The second was a young man called Flikka. I suppose Flikka might have been about nineteen. He had red hair – well, sort of tawny – the only person on the estate who had; and he was cross-eyed, and had a birth mark on his right cheek. He never seemed to have any work to do, but wandered about the place as he chose. Nobody liked him; at least, he never seemed to have any friends. What I think now is that he was the bastard son of some white man and a black girl on another estate, and they'd dumped him on our estate and forgotten him.

Flikka took a dislike to me; I've no idea why. But whenever he saw me he had a spiteful word or, worse than that, he tried to do me harm. "Daniel," he'd say, "why don't you wash your goddamn face?" or "Daniel, everybody knows your mother works in the infirmary so she can steal things from sick people too weak to stop her."

Once he stopped me when I was running a message and asked me who it was for. I told him "Mr. Henderson", one of the overseers. "Well, you're going the wrong way," he said. "He's over on the tobacco; I've just seen him." But when I got round to the tobacco, Mr. Henderson wasn't there and I finally found him where I'd first been told. I was lucky not to get into trouble. The next time I ran into Flikka, I told him he'd misled me and I reckoned he'd done it purposely. "Oh, I'm always ready to oblige you," he said. "I'll knock you down if you like."

Another time I was running together with another of the boys, a lad called Moses who was a bit older than me. We met Flikka and for once he let me alone. When we'd passed him, Moses turned round and spat. "I'd like to strangle that swine," he said. "Well, I'd gladly help you," I answered. "I hate him. I wonder why he never seems to have any work to do." "Why," says Moses, "don' you know what he do?" I said I'd no idea. "The white men on other estates round here," he says. "He gets girls for dem – black girls. He make deal with a white man and then he bring him girl, one of ours. If she no want to go, he threaten her, frightens her. He done get paid, but I don' think the girl get a thing." "But where does he take them?" I asked. "Up on hill over dere," says Moses, pointing. "He no want Massa Reynolds or his sons to know, you see. They'd soon put stop on him and his white customers; they no want girls to be seen doin' it on their premises. Dere's few folk go up hill." Our ways parted just after that and I soon forgot what Moses had told me.

It was some time after that, that I happened to run into something I'd give anything to forget; something that's haunted me all my life. It was a blazing hot afternoon, and I was lying half asleep in the messengers' shed, when I heard Massa Reynolds shout "Boy!" It was my turn and Moses got me on my feet double-quick. I ran to Massa Reynolds, who was standing by the outside door, tapping his foot with impatience. Before I'd even reached him he called out "You, Daniel! Do you know where Mr. Henderson's at?" I answered, "No, Massa, but I'll find him real quick." "Good boy!" he said. "Well, you run and tell him I want to see him here right this minute."

Before I'd even run out of his sight I was pouring with sweat. When I got as far as the Carpenters' shop they were working on some sort of big trestle they'd dragged out into the open, and they weren't best pleased when I asked them to move it a fraction so's I could get by. "Who are you looking for now?" asked the carpenter Boss. "Message for Massa Henderson from Massa Reynolds," I said, and at that the Boss picked me up bodily and threw me over the trestle. I grazed my knees, but I got up and ran.

I crossed the stream and then I saw a crowd of slaves and Mr. Henderson in the middle of them. You could always pick him out, even at a distance, because he was very tall. I ran up to them, calling "Massa Henderson, sir!" He turned round, and I saw he had his leather whip in his hand. On the ground in front of him was a slave, a big man, lying on his face. He looked to be unconscious and his bare back was covered with great, bloody weals, a terrible sight.

"What do you want, boy?" asked Henderson. I told him the message and he pushed me aside before turning back to the slave. He hit him across the back and shouted, "Will you get up, you dirty nigger bastard?"

24

The slave never moved. The other field hands were gathered round, all bare to the waist, sweating. There were two or three women kneeling in front, crying bitterly and trying to help the slave as best they could. "Oh, Jeckzor, Jeckzor" one of them kept crying. "Oh, please, Massa" (to Henderson) "let us help him." "No way, no damn' way," says Henderson. But then he seemed to have second thoughts. "I'm going to see Massa Reynolds," he says to them. "Get back to work, all of you. If I see anyone not working when I get back, they'll be whipped as bad as him." And with that he turned and stalked off the way I'd come, without looking to see whether they were going back to work or not.

They weren't going back. The girl who'd been calling to Jeckzor flung herself down beside him, put her ear to his mouth and listened. Then she looked up at the others and cried out in some African tongue. They all began moaning, and jabbering away to one another in the same language. One of the men knelt down and listened the way the girl had, but evidently he too could tell the man wasn't breathing.

The girl looked at me and pointed to the sun. Then she shut her eyes and shook her head. One of the men said to me in English "Massa Henderson always hate Jeckzor. Jeckzor big man with us, always try help us. Massa Henderson want him dead; whip him, kill him." They all nodded and murmured. A lot of the men were crying now, same as the girls.

Then two-three of them got down and lifted Jeckzor up onto their shoulders. I couldn't bear to look at his back, he'd been whipped so dreadfully; just a great mass of blood and those terrible weals all across it. You couldn't see it had ever been a man's back.

The man who'd spoken to me pointed to the shed under the trees, the shed where they kept the tools and all the other tackle for the tobacco: and they all set off, men and women together, and a great crowd of flies buzzing over them as they went.

I ran all the way back to the messenger room. The carpenters had left the path clear by now, but I knew I'd lost time and I reckoned I might have been missed. But I hadn't. Moses was still waiting, next boy to go, and there were two or three others. I lay down to rest, but as often as I shut my eyes I saw Jeckzor – Jeckzor's back – and I'd start up again and clutch at the water-pot or the bolt for the shutters – anything that was real, anything that could tell me I wasn't in that tobacco-field.

"What's the matter?" asked Moses. "Something troublin' you? Come on, tell me. It'll help to put you right."

I started to tell him, but then I couldn't go on. I kept hearing the women crying. Finally Moses, good friend as he was, went up to the captain and told him I'd been taken bad with the sun and could he walk me home. When we got there, Missus Kathy was still out at the infirmary, and only Tom was in. Moses told him I'd had some sort of a bad shock and then he went back. I lay down on the bed and Tom held my hand. It must have been best part of an hour before Josh came in. Tom told him as much as he knew and Josh took over sitting beside me.

It was reassuring to have Josh there. He didn't ask me what the trouble was, and he didn't show the least impatience. He just held my hand and from time to time he gave me some water. It was warm, of course, but I kept on sipping it, just to please him, really. After what seemed a long time, Doth came in. As soon as I saw her I began to feel better.

"What's the matter, dear one?" she asked me at once.

"I'll tell you about it," I answered, "you and Dad."

"Well, take it easy," said Josh. "No hurry."

I began telling them; but when I got as far as the blood and Jeckzor's back, I stumbled in my words and then I choked and buried my face against Doth's arm. Neither of them said anything and after a minute or two I was able to go on.

"It was Henderson you said, wasn't it?" said Josh, when I'd finished. I nodded and he went on, "I would have known anyway."
"How?" I asked, but for quite a while he didn't reply.

At last he said, "There are some white men who hate slaves – hate black people - so much that they'll contrive almost anything to hurt them. If they haven't got a reason they'll find one - make

26

one up. And it comes cheap. 'Kill a nigger, get another. Kill a horse, you got to buy another.' It's like a madness, really. They'll ignore opportunities to make more money or get easier work. They'll decline promotion. They prefer to stay where they can go on terrifying and hurting niggers. It's like taking to drink: I've seen it more than once; and the only chance a nigger's got is somehow to keep away from men like that. One way's to find and stick close to some white man who values you enough to protect you. I've stuck close to Massa Reynolds these ten years and more. I don't think Henderson would be likely to try anything on with me. And I reckon he's done himself no good, whipping Jeckzor to death. Jeckzor was a good man. Other field hands respected him and took his advice."

"But how can you tell these cruel men?" I asked: for what he'd said had frightened me very much and in my mind's eye I kept seeing Henderson and his bloody whip.

"You have to keep your wits about you," replied Josh. "Ask your friends; and always watch the white men. Those who worship cruelty, they get so you can tell them. That's what it means to be a slave. Sometimes a white man may free a slave, but it's seldom."

Just at that moment Missus Kathy came in. Josh told her I'd been bullied by Henderson and he thought I ought not to talk about it any more for now; he'd tell her himself later. Then he produced half a ham that Massa Reynolds had given him, and after an unusually good supper I felt a long sight better.

Next day, I had several messages to run about the village and the plantations. The news of Jeckzor's death seemed to be known to everyone, and a number of people, who'd heard that I had seen Henderson kill him, stopped me and made me tell them what exactly had happened. It was clear that Jeckzor had been widely regarded, not only by the field labour gangs but also by the slaves working as craftsmen and by Massa Reynolds's domestic servants. He had been greatly respected as a man who'd been tireless in doing all he could to improve conditions for the slaves. He was the only black man who had sometimes been allowed to speak to Massa Reynolds face-to-face. More than once he'd spoken up for slaves in trouble, usually on account of misunderstandings between themselves and the white overseers. He had even – or so ran the rumour – refused his freedom; and not only that, but at his own request he had remained among the field labourers, saying that he could not leave the people whom he thought of as his closest friends. This, so I learned, was what had really led to his death. Henderson, who had always hated him, had ordered him to get on with his work and stop helping a woman whose labour pains had come on unexpectedly. When he would not leave her, Henderson had beaten him to death. The final moments of this cruelty were what I had seen.

All over the village I was stopped and made to give my account yet again. It was in vain that I protested I was a messenger on duty for Massa Reynolds. Since I was only a boy facing grown men, there was nothing I could do if they wouldn't listen. At last I became so agitated and weary that I sat down beside the track, and rested my sweating face between my drawn-up knees.

I was beginning to recover myself when I was kicked from behind. Struggling to my feet, I found myself facing Henderson. Several passers-by had stopped and were watching us.

I was about to go on running when Henderson spoke.

"Stay where you are."

"Massa, I running a message –"

"Shut up!"

There was a pause as he stared me down. I waited with averted eyes, half-expecting a cut of the whip.

At length Henderson said, "What's your name?"

"Daniel, Massa."

"And you've been talking about me, haven't you, Daniel?"

"Massa, I only done answer questions when folk ask."

"And what do you answer, Daniel?"

I could find no reply.

"Come on, nigger boy. You're so good at answering questions, you can answer mine, unless you want to be whipped."

28

"Massa, dey ask me tell 'em what done happen yesterday in de tobacco field."

"And what do you answer?"

"Massa, I just tell 'em about – about Jeckzor."

"And what about Jeckzor?"

"That you beat him, Massa, and, and –"

"And what?"

"He die, Massa."

"And you say I killed him, don't you?"

"No, Massa, I not say dat."

"Oh, that's interesting, Daniel. You say he died and you don't say I killed him. What do you say?"

"Massa, I say he fall down and you tell him get up and he no get up and so you whip him. And den – den he dead."

"Lie down, Daniel. No, right down flat, on your belly. Stretch out your arms. I want to see your back."

"Massa, I ain't done nothin'."

"Shut up!"

"Massa, I –"

But at this moment a third voice spoke, from the other side of the track.

"Please, Massa, is dat Daniel you got dere?"

Henderson made no reply. I called out, "Yes, I'se Daniel!"

"Where you bin, Daniel? I done look for you ebbrywhere. Massa Reynolds, he want see you now. I take so long find you, you best run all de way."

It was Moses. I got up, and once more stood facing Henderson, who said nothing, while I waited for him to dismiss me.

At last, when I was about to ask him, he said, "Why are you standing there? What are you waiting for?"

"Please, Massa, for you tell me go."

Almost before he had snapped his fingers and pointed, I was

running with Moses beside me.

"What for Massa Reynolds want me?" I panted.

"No say. He shout 'Boy' and when I come he tell me fetch you quick."

It was seldom indeed that Massa Reynolds talked directly to a black, except his own servants. I had never heard what followed on these rare occasions, but felt sure it could be nothing good. As we got nearer to the big house I could see Frederick, Massa Reynolds's butler, waiting on the path that led round to the messengers' shed. As soon as he saw us he called out "You, Dan'l, come quick!"

I couldn't run any faster. Half a minute later I fell panting in the sand at his feet. He dragged me up by a hand half round my neck and held me at arm's length. "You need washing," was all he said.

He dragged me across to the pump, held my head down and fairly drenched me. I actually felt better for the cold water, and shook myself half-dry like a dog.

We were at the threshold of the back door when Reynolds himself appeared, meeting us.

"Is that the boy, Frederick?"

"Yes, Massa."

As Reynolds looked me up and down I felt ready to faint with fear. My bowels moved and spittle gathered in my mouth.

He turned on his heel and said to Frederick, "Bring him in here."

We crossed the kitchen, went up a short passage and turned into a small, bare room with a stone floor – the first stone floor I had ever seen. The only furniture was a plain wooden chair and a table. Reynolds sat down on the chair and gestured to Frederick to leave us and shut the door.

I realised I was trembling. "You'd better hold on to the table," said Reynolds. "Come on, boy, pull yourself together; I'm not going to hurt you."

This at least was some relief. After a short pause he looked me very straight in the eye and said "You were in the tobacco plantation yesterday, weren't you, Daniel?"

"Yes, Massa."

"Why were you there?"

"You send me, Massa, tell Massa Henderson you want see him quick."

He nodded. "Now tell me what you saw when you found Mr. Henderson; and don't leave anything out."

I'd given my account so often that day that I could repeat it without hesitation. Reynolds perceived this. "How many people have you told that to today?"

"Massa, lots of people stop me, make me tell 'em."

"You're a messenger boy, aren't you? Have you been telling that all over the village?"

"Massa, people make me tell. I say I'se running a message, no can stop. Dey grab me, say we make you stop, make you tell us about Jeckzor."

"And how many times has that happened today?"

I shook my head. "Not know, Massa; many times."

"You're sure you haven't been telling a lot of people without being asked?"

"Certain sure, Massa. I not tell only dey make me."

He took out his pipe, filled and lit it, pressing the tobacco down with his thumb. At length he looked up once more.

"And has Mr. Henderson spoken to you today?"

"He gwine speak, Massa, but den message come you want me quick, so not speak more."

"I see. Well, Daniel, now you listen to me. You're not to speak of this any more at all, even to Mr. Henderson. If anyone tries to make you, you refuse and tell them that those are your orders from me personally. Do you understand?"

"Yes, Massa."

"Right. Get back to work."

I ran without looking behind me. Of course the other messenger boys pressed me to tell them what had happened, but when I said that Massa Reynolds had ordered me to say nothing, they let me be.

As twilight fell we were dismissed and I went home. Tom had got hold of an old pack of cards from somewhere, although neither of us knew the first thing about playing. But when Doth came in she soon put us to rights, and we were all three happily playing Beggar-My-Neighbour when Josh came back. He cast a knowledgeable eye over us, sat down and taught us Blembil, the slaves' gambling game. Of course we hadn't any money, but each of us gathered a handful of pebbles, which we found quite as good for winning and losing by candlelight.

After supper (and a frugal one it was, that evening, I recall), Josh went out for a while. When he came back it was to tell us that he wanted all of us to come for a stroll. It was seldom we all went out together (leaving nothing worth stealing) and we wondered what Josh could have up his sleeve. None of us asked him, however. I was a little surprised that there seemed to be so few people about, especially since it was a beautiful, warm night, with a full moon that made even our tumbledown hovels look less sordid than usual.

We had sauntered perhaps half a mile when Josh stopped, putting an arm round Missus Kathy's shoulders. The three of us looked at him enquiringly, but he only smiled, cupping an ear with one hand as though he was listening. Each of us did the same and after a moment we heard the sound from some distance away; the sound of people singing.

"Let's go and see what they're up to," said Josh. We walked on beside him as he left the track and led the way between two huts and across a patch of rough ground beyond. We came to a little copse, and as soon as we reached the other side we could hear the singing clearly. It was here that I became aware that whoever they might be, they were not singing in English – not even in slaves' English. The tune – for there was a tune – was full of pauses and strange intervals, like nothing I had ever heard before. Yet it attracted me strangely. I responded to it involuntarily; I wanted it not to cease.

"Who are they?" asked Missus Kathy in a low voice.

Instead of answering, Josh took a few steps forward, and as he did so I saw a man coming to meet us through the long grass. A moment more and I knew him for Martin, a neighbour of ours, who worked in the carpentry shop. As the singing ceased, he came up to Josh and greeted him without speaking. He paused, as though weighing his words. Then, hesitantly, he said, "I'm afraid that – that you may not be welcome, Josh. They'll think you're too close to Reynolds."

"Well, go and ask them," replied Josh. "We'll wait here. I shan't say anything to Reynolds or to any of the white men, and nor will any of my family here."

"I believe you," replied Martin, "but will they?"

We sat on the ground to wait as he turned and went back as silently as he had come.

It was some time before he returned, nodded reassuringly to Josh and gestured to us to follow him. His coming and going had made a narrow track through the long grass and this we followed, at length rejoining him at the top of a kind of shallow pit, which sloped away below us in a rough half-circle. In the moonlight I saw, with quite a shock, a crowd of slaves sitting silently on the grass. Evidently these had been the singers. They stared up at us, but none moved or spoke. We sat down where we were and I felt free to look about me.

At the foot of the slope was a flat space, where the long grass had been trodden down. At its centre was what appeared, by its size and shape, to be a grave, covered over with green branches laid across it from side to side.

Although the whole place was silent, it seemed full of tension and expectancy. Everyone appeared to be waiting. Beside me, I could feel Doth trembling.

Suddenly, from among the trees on our left, a harsh voice broke

33

out in clamour, and was answered by a voice from the opposite side. Although plainly a ritualistic question asked and answered in a foreign tongue, to me the mere vehemence seemed savagely minatory. From among the assembled people came cries of dread. As they died away, out of the gloom beyond the flat space came two men and two women, pacing side by side. Between them they carried a rectangular wooden box resembling a coffin. Casting aside the green branches, they lowered it into place in the grave. Then, standing back, all four called, "Jeckzor! Jeckzor!"

The cry was taken up by the whole crowd and continued until, as though in answer, there bounded out from the undergrowth a naked man, painted from head to foot in spirals of yellow, red and green. As he raised his hand in salutation to the people, they fell silent. He knelt beside the grave, stretched down his arm and, with a cry of disgust, drew out and brandished what everyone saw to be an overseer's whip. Among curses and cries of hatred, he broke it across his knee in the same moment that a tall, handsome girl appeared near us at the top of the pit, carrying a flaming pine torch. She, too, was naked and painted. Step by step through the staring people, she made her way down to the Painted Man, knelt and handed her torch to him. Amid a storm of elation, he set fire to the two pieces of the broken whip. They must have been smeared with grease or fat, for they flamed until he tossed them aside.

The four bearers now gathered up the green branches and strewed them into the grave, covering the coffin; and, as the Painted Man embraced his Torch Girl, the celebration became orgiastic. Men and women threw themselves into one another's arms and sank down on the grass. None showed any shame as they coupled side by side. To them, this was an act of worship, of homage to Jeckzor, a deed of harmony and concord, a witness to God of their indestructible humanity.

Josh drew Missus Kathy down beside him, clasping her closely. Tom, Doth and I drew a little apart and happily kissed and fondled until Missus Kathy, all smiles, appeared to beckon us to come home.

34

None of us spoke until, as we came back into the village Josh broke the silence, saying, "I'm glad for them all. They've honoured Jeckzor, and that lifts their spirits and makes them happy – for a time at any rate."

"What was the language?" I asked, for my head was still full of the strange singing.

"It's an African tribal dialect," answered Josh. "A lot of the slaves speak it naturally. It came over with them, like their tales about Spider and their pebble games. Those who don't know it soon pick it up."

"And the white men don't stop it?" I said. "All that ritual, I mean; like burning the whip?"

"No. They know that it – well, it comforts the slaves, you see, puts a bit of heart into them and can't really do any harm."

"Doesn't it ever make some of them want to run away?"

"Oh, no. Not here. There's nowhere they could run to, you see, they don't know the first thing about the country. They wouldn't know which way to go. And they haven't any money; and no food, either."

"You mean no one ever runs away?"

"Very seldom; and if it does happen it's nearly always some wretched man who's gone crazy and hardly knows what he's doing. I've known them come back, after starving in the woods for a day or two."

"Did you know that meeting was going to be held tonight?"

"I was fairly sure. But that was why I went out by myself earlier this evening – to make sure it was tonight."

The whole happening had left me excited and on edge. In my own mind, I could still hear the barbaric chanting and see the Painted Man bursting out through the bushes; and I could tell that Doth was moved in the same way. Neither she nor I were able to concentrate on our game of cards.

After a few hands Josh perceived this. When he suggested bed we all felt ready enough. But I was still restless and lay awake for some time. If I had known what the next day held in store, I would probably have copied the poor, crazy slaves and run away to nowhere.

In the morning, Missus Kathy went off early to the infirmary. She had left us a loaf and half a dozen apples, so we did at least have a few mouthfuls before separating to go to work.

It turned out to be a slack day for the messengers. The next-to-go was a boy named Matt, and he wasn't called until late in the morning, just before we got our midday meal. This left me to go next, but it was getting on for halfway through the afternoon before Frederick came into the room and said he wanted someone to go to the tobacconist's for two dozen clay pipes.

"And mind you carry them carefully, Dan'l," he said to me. "Those clays break easily. They're not required urgently, so you'd better walk with them on the way back. Oh, and four ounces of Sailorboy snuff, tell old Benjy, and just you mind he keeps his thumb off the scales."

Since it was quite a way to the tobacconist's, I set off at an easy jogtrot, keeping a sharp lookout for Henderson. I knew where he ought to be – in the tobacco plantation – but where he was concerned you could never be sure.

Since Frederick had said there was no hurry, I thought I'd go round by the Make-and-Mend Shop, and perhaps – if they'd let me – spend a little time with Doth. I turned into the track and I suppose I might have been about a stone's throw from the shop when I saw that something was wrong. Several women were gathered together outside. They were clearly protesting, waving their arms and clamouring. As I ran towards them I recognised Flikka, conspicuous by his red hair, and there was Doth herself, struggling in his clutches: between the two of them and the women stood two rough-looking youths armed with cudgels, who were threatening the women and keeping them back.

Flikka was twisting Doth's arm behind her back. She caught sight of me and screamed "Daniel! Daniel!"

Without weighing my chances and, to tell the truth, in such a rage that I hardly knew what I was doing, I leapt at Flikka and managed to get a grip of his throat. He flung Doth to the ground, snatched my hand away and gave me a blow that knocked me clean across the track. I staggered and fell backwards into a pile of rubbish.

"Piss off and don't come back!" shouted Flikka, and turned his attention once more to Doth.

"Now!" he said, slapping her face. "You come up the hill with me or I'll really hurt you."

Something was pressing painfully into the small of my back. As I struggled to get up, I pulled it out and saw it was a hollow length of iron piping, about as long as my forearm and fairly heavy. At one end the edges of the hole were bent and ragged, where it must have been clumsily cut. The other end was smooth.

I gripped it and got to my feet. Flikka was facing me. I swung back the piping and hit him as hard as I could. It caught him above his ear and he went down like a stone. Before his two mates could reach me I hit him again. I felt his skull crack and blood poured out. Both of them turned and ran, leaving Doth to me and her friends.

I supported Doth back into the shop and helped her into a wicker chair. Flikka was still lying where he had fallen.

The next thing I remember is Clarice, one of the girls, shouting, "Daniel! I think he's dead."

I followed her outside, where people were already crowding round. I stooped down and felt for his heart. He was dead right enough.

I asked two of the bystanders to help me to carry the body indoors and lay it out on one of the tables. I covered the face with some sort of garment lying nearby. I felt faint and it was only by an effort that I was able to keep my self-possession.

Missus Blatch was standing in the doorway, repelling intruders. I joined her.

"What ought we to do now, Missus, do you think?"

She flung her arms round me, shedding tears. "Oh, dear Daniel, dear, dear Daniel! Well done! You saved us from those horrible men!"

"But listen, Missus; Flikka's dead and his friends – helpers – whatever they were – they've cleared off! What ought we to do now?"

She made no immediate reply and I could tell that she felt almost as dazed and uncertain as I did.

At length she said, "No help for it; we'll have to find one of the white men to take charge."

At this moment, as it fell out, one of the overseers, a young man named Otway, appeared at the far end of the track. Seeing him, the bystanders melted away, leaving Missus Blatch, four or five of the girls and myself to wait as he came up to us.

Missus Blatch told him what had happened, emphasising that I had had to hit Flikka to stop him brutalising and abducting Doth. Otway heard her out without interruption and then went inside to see the body. It was here that Doth joined us. Otway questioned her closely, asking whether she had ever had any kind of relationship with Flikka. Could he have acted out of jealousy or because she had provoked him in some way? Reassured about this, Otway turned to me again.

"You're not denying that you hit him with an iron bar and killed him?"

"No, massa, but I didn't mean to kill him, only stop him hurting my sister and taking her away."

"You say you hit him twice on the head with an iron bar, and yet you didn't mean to kill him?"

"Massa, I only meant stop him taking my sister away."

"Why should he take her away? Where to?"

I told him what I knew about Flikka and what he did with girls. I could tell that although initially he was sceptical, at length he became convinced of the truth of my account. When I had finished, he said, "Well, this is a very serious matter. I shall report it to Mr. Reynolds at once. You, Daniel, and your sister here, both of you come with me."

We waited outside the door while Otway went in to speak to Reynolds. Doth did her best to reassure me, but I couldn't help feeling terrified: I knew that white men had a short way with slaves who gave trouble. I had killed another slave and probably that was all that Reynolds would bother himself to hear.

When Otway called us to come in I was startled to see the Reverend Foster sitting in one corner of the room, reading a newspaper. When he didn't look up, I realised that Reynolds had evidently not thought it necessary to ask him to leave the room while he dealt with us.

Reynolds was seated behind a big desk and gestured to us to stand in front of it. Then he said to me, "I know you, don't I? You're one of the messengers."

"Yes, massa."

"And you've killed a man by hitting him over the head with an iron bar?"

"Yes, massa. To stop him hurting, taking away my sister."

"You're the sister," he said to Doth.

"Yes, massa."

"This man was threatening you. Why?"

"Massa, he make black girls go up de hill for white men. He try to make me do dis, but I not go."

"For prostitution, you mean?"

"Yes, massa. He do dis to many girls here. Ask dem, dey all tell you de same."

"And he was forcing you – struggling with you – when your brother killed him?"

"Yes, massa."

Reynolds shrugged his shoulders and turned to me. "As a rule, a slave who kills another slave is hanged and no two ways about it. But now that I've heard what you and your sister have to say, I shan't hang you. You can't stay here, though. Everyone would know that you had killed another slave in a violent attack and weren't sentenced for it. You'll have to be sold."

At this moment, the Reverend Foster spoke. "Mr. Reynolds, sir, may I say a word? You've been very kind to me during my visit here. I've made several good friends among your slaves and as it happens this boy is one of them. I know him well and I'm happy to say that he has all the makings of a good Christian. I'd like to ask you of your generosity to let me take him back to England with me. In that way no one anywhere in this country will hear of this unhappy business."

While Foster was speaking, Reynolds had plainly been becoming more and more impatient. Now he said, "Very well, Mr. Foster, I agree to what you ask. Now, Mr. Otway, please leave and take these slaves with you. They've wasted enough of my time already."

Even now, many years after, it still distresses me to recall the grief I felt in leaving the estate – the only "home" I had ever known – and of parting from my family. Even Tom shed tears, while Missus Kathy seemed almost out of her mind. As well as she could for weeping, she told us yet again how she had been determined to save my life and to adopt me from the very moment that I was born. Doth, of course, already knew what Massa Reynolds had decreed. Her anguish went too deep for tears. I held her in my arms as she laid her head upon my shoulder, saying again and again that she couldn't bear the thought of living without me. Even Josh, though he didn't weep, remained silent for some time after he had heard the news. Doing my best to find some comfort for them, I said that the whole village would surely feel glad that Flikka was gone for good, and that the Reverend Foster's kind intervention assured me of one friend at least. Being able to count on his protection meant that I might be able to build up the kind of relationship with him that Josh had with Massa Reynolds. Probably, I said, this change, which seemed so unhappy now, would turn out in time to have been all for my good, for my future prosperity. One day, perhaps, I would return and share that prosperity with them. Reverend Foster, I pointed out, was a minister who had come here on purpose to find black people to convert to Christianity. Well, he had found me, hadn't he?

Thus I did my best to put on a confident front and cheer them up. And before I had finished, I had convinced myself, at any rate, that as my future unfolded I would be sure to find good opportunities for advancement. In time I would surely be granted my freedom and no longer be a slave. Josh joined in, saying that that was the right way to look at my situation. He had personally known more than one slave who had gained his freedom. My best course was to make myself useful to Reverend Foster; but to be patient and not expect too much too soon.

Talking in this way, the two of us succeeded in comforting Missus Kathy and Doth a little, and everyone lay down to sleep in an easier frame of mind. Next morning, we were all pleasantly surprised when young Mr. Otway came in to wish me luck. He was sure I would do well, he said; I had his blessing.

Such warmth and approval from a white overseer was unusual, to say the least. He shook hands with me and went on to tell Doth that, having made some enquiries, he felt as glad as she did that Flikka was out of the way; and if she came in for any more of that kind of thing, she was to let him know at once.

No sooner had he left than the Reverend Foster appeared. He gave Missus Kathy two newly-baked loaves and a pound of butter, and then told me that he had what he called "a horse and cart" waiting, and hoped I was ready to set out.

Of course there were more tears, which Foster did his best to staunch. Then, as resolutely as I could, I walked away with him, compelling myself not to look back.

PART II

I had never in my life been outside the estate before. Now, perched up beside Mr. Foster, I felt almost afraid to look about me. Keeping my eyes down, I glanced to one side; there was grass growing beside the dusty road. It was the same on the other side, too. Rather timidly, I raised my head but saw only the road stretching in front, bordered by the grass and here and there a few trees. In one of these a mockingbird was singing.

In the distance I saw a group of houses. They didn't look like any kind of building on the estate. For one thing, all the windows I could see had glass in them; one flashed in my eyes and then, as we moved on, another. A door opened and out came a man – a white man – who stood still for some moments, looking up at the clouds in the sky. Then he walked down to the road and turned in our direction. He was wearing a sunhat and carrying a tool-bag on a strap over his shoulder. As he drew nearer he stared at Mr. Foster and myself sitting side by side. His expression was unmistakably hostile. I felt nervous and looked down to avoid meeting his eyes. Foster wished him a good morning. He did not reply, but passed us in silence.

All that morning we jogged easily along, past cornfields, cottages and woodland. We met with few fellow-travellers and stopped only to rest the horse and let it drink from any convenient creek along the way. Once we came upon a gang of blacks who were stripping the branches from felled trees and burning them on a bonfire beside the road. Our horse fidgeted and refused to go near the crackling and the smoke drifting into its eyes. Lacking all experience, I felt uneasy, trying to lead it forwards; however, one of the workmen, with a friendly grin to me and a few respectful words of greeting to Foster, took the bridle and, speaking quietly and reassuringly to the horse, at length succeeded in coaxing it past the fire. Although I had occasionally seen horses at work on the estate, I had never seen anything like this before, and thought it well worth the penny that Mr. Foster gave the man.

It must have been a good two hours into the afternoon before Mr. Foster said it was time for a halt and a meal. He went on to explain to me that according to the strict rule in American society, he and I would have to separate to eat and drink. Being used to this rule on the estate – where only house-slaves ever saw white men sitting down to a meal – I said I'd be happy to do whatever he wished. When we reached a tavern in the next village, he brought me out some bread and cheese, two apples and a pot of beer before disappearing indoors for his own victuals.

While he was gone and I was wolfing down the bread and cheese, three or four black lads of about my own age came drifting down the street and stopped to talk to me. When I told them I was travelling with my white master, they naturally asked where we were going. When I told them that my master was an Englishman and that we were going to sail to England in a ship, they were visibly impressed. One of them said he'd never heard of England and where was it? I told him that I didn't know any more than he did, but my master was a minister and actually lived in England. "So you nebber been dere," said another of them. "Where he get you, man, where you from?"

I told him my master had taken me away from a tobacco plantation. He said that was lucky for me: tobacco plantations were terrible places, he'd heard, where a slave could die of the work in seven years or less. I told them about Jeckzor, whipped to death by a white overseer for helping a poor woman in labour. At this one of the boys, who had not so far spoken, said that black people weren't going to submit to this kind of cruelty forever. One day they'd rise up and put the brutal white masters to death. Why didn't I join them, instead of cringing and grovelling before white men for a few handfuls of food a day? This stung me, and I began to tell them how I'd killed Flikka for what he was trying to do to my dearest Doth.

In the middle of this, out came Reverend Foster, wiping his mouth with the back of his hand. "Hallo, lads," he greeted them amiably. "Been having a chat with my friend Daniel? Why don't you come to England with us? Black people get better treatment in England, you know."

At this one or two of them grinned sheepishly: 'said I'd told them it was far off across the sea. Their parents wouldn't like them to run away. Anyway, the white men, for whom they did night work, would be sure to catch them; they had horses and big dogs.

Foster gave them a farthing apiece, wished them luck and said that now he and I had to be getting along. They trotted beside us for a little while, calling out farewells and good wishes. I felt I was luckier than they were, and this added a few sparks to my self-confidence. If I had only known, they were premature.

Later that afternoon the road led through several miles of woodland. We were proceeding at an easy jogtrot when suddenly two rough-looking men, both carrying guns over their shoulders, strode out from among the trees and stood facing us in the middle of the road. Naturally, Foster pulled up. Before he could speak, the older of the two men levelled his gun at me and shouted, "You goddamn two-bit nigger, d'you want me to blow your black balls off right where you're sitting?"

As Mr. Foster began to speak, the man shouted, "Shut your fucking mouth, nigger-lover!" And then to me, as he pointed at the road, "Get down outa there, sharper than shit, unless you want a taste of lead."

Terrified, I leapt into the road, falling painfully on my knees, and remained crouching.

"Stand up! Come here!"

I took two hesitant steps forward. "Fucking quicker than that!" he yelled. "Run, blast you!"

45

Hardly knowing what I was doing, I stumbled forward and stood in front of him.

"It's not healthy for a nigger-boy to sit next to a white man," he said. "Know why, do ya?" and as I answered nothing, "Well, speak up, do you, hey?"

"No, no, sir." I gasped breathlessly.

"Why," he said, "he gets wet." And thereupon he opened his breeches and pissed over me, gripping my shoulder to hold me still. After a few moments his companion copied him.

Foster said never a word, but only cowered in his seat as they finished and turned towards him. They stared at him silently for a while, as though to satisfy themselves that he had nothing to say. At length the older man said, "Best not stay here, nigger-lover. It ain't the best spot. Drive on!"

Foster opened his mouth. "But – but –"

"Drive on, preacher-man, I said!" And he brandished his gun.

Foster paused a moment, then took up the reins, joggled them up and down along the horse's back and clicked his tongue, at which it started forward. The two men turned and watched as the distance grew between Foster and themselves. I had never felt so frightened in my life, not even when I had lain at the feet of Henderson.

Suddenly, when Foster had gone perhaps a hundred yards, the younger man, going behind me where I stood, gave me a tremendous kick and shouted "Run, nigger! Run all the way to hell, damn you!"

Foster, hearing him, turned his head and stopped. As I caught up, he said, "Perhaps you'd better sit at the back, Daniel."

I could scarcely draw my breath. Sobbing uncontrollably, I knelt in the cart, clutching the rail for support. At length Foster said, "Well, it's over now. I'm sorry, Daniel. I'm very sorry."

I made some reply and we drove on in silence.

Soon I saw that we were nearing a town – after all these years its name escapes me – and Foster said we would stay there for the

46

night and go on in the morning to the port, where we were sure to find a ship going to England. I asked him what he meant to do with our "horse and cart", and he replied that it would be easy to sell, as long as we didn't ask too much.

We never spoke, then or later, of what had happened in the wood.

Foster arranged our night's lodging with no trouble at all; the small hotel where we enquired had separate (and cheaper) arrangements for black servants – grooms, drivers and so on. As luck would have it, I saw an old pair of trousers lying on the floor in the black servants' dormitory, and was glad enough to change them for my own.

As soon as he had seen and approved his quarters, Foster told me that what he meant to do now was something he felt sure would agree with me very well. He wanted me, he said, to do him credit when we found our ship, met the captain and so on; and he was going to buy me a new suit of clothes, a couple of shirts, a good, thick seagoing jersey, a pair of stout shoes and woollen stockings to go with them.

Naturally, I was overcome by this generosity. I began to feel better at once and could hardly find words to thank him. He replied that it was for his benefit as much as mine. It wouldn't look well tomorrow if his servant were wearing dirty old clothes. I told him I'd never worn shoes or stockings in my life and he said that at that rate we could think about them later, when we'd got to England.

It became an exciting and enjoyable afternoon, the only drawback being that I was quite unused to wearing clothes like these; and I felt odd in them. The tailor, however, assured me that they were a very good fit, and that I would soon get used to them. He suggested that I should go outside and stroll up the street and back. (My master was a minister, so he knew we were trustworthy, he said.)

When I got outside, I was sure that I must look as odd as I felt. But my timidity vanished as I walked on amongst both black and white people, who were plainly indifferent to my appearance, although one stout white man, striding along, deliberately jostled me into the gutter. All the same, I was finally convinced when I met two young black girls who were idling along, looking in the shop windows. Both of them looked at me with obvious admiration, and when I said "Good afternoon", they broke into happy smiles but could find no reply. I returned to the tailor and told him he had persuaded me. Foster paid him in cash and he called his boy to carry the parcel to our hotel.

The following morning, I dressed in my new clothes and as soon as Foster and I had finished our respective breakfasts, he tipped the ostler to bring our "horse and cart" from the stables, and off we set for the port and the sea.

I had formed no mental picture of "the sea", and as Foster pulled up at the top of the hill overlooking the harbour, I was fairly trembling with excitement. Below us lay the town, with its roofs and streets. Its further edge was made up of anchored vessels large and small; and beyond lay the sea.

As I sat staring at the expanse of blue water shining under the morning sun, I realised that apparently it had no further edge. The sky met the sea. And beyond that? Presumably more sea, more sky. Then my eye fell upon a moving object coming towards us, floating on the water, and men standing on it. Why didn't it sink? And we, Foster and I, were intending to travel on a floating thing like that, all the way to England, wherever that might be.

Foster must have read my thoughts. "You needn't be afraid, Daniel," he said. "You'll be quite safe. Ships really do float. And they go along, too, with the wind in their sails to drive them. We'll go down and make their further acquaintance."

He got out and fitted an iron shoe to one of the wheels, explaining that this would slow us down and make the descent easier for the horse. Then we slithered down the rather steep hill and having arrived at the foot, pulled up for a rest while Foster explained to me why ships didn't sink. We drove on, stopped at the first inn we came to and paid them to put up our "horse and cart" and take care of our luggage (such as it was) until we came back for our midday dinner.

48

"Where are we going now?" I asked, as we crossed the road to the seaward side.

"To find our ship," replied Foster. "The first thing we'll do is pay a visit to the harbour-master and see whether he can give us any useful advice."

The harbour-master's office, we were told, was about half a mile along the seafront. Foster said there was plenty of time, and we dawdled beside the moored boats and ships, while I asked scores of questions and Foster answered them as well as he could. Once we stopped to watch while several loads of crates and heavy boxes were winched across to the open hold of a ship and lowered down. I admired the skill and confidence of the man working the crane.

"Well, he gets plenty of practice," replied Foster. "It's highly-skilled work, of course, and no doubt he's paid accordingly. If he accidentally let one of those crates drop on a man's head, he'd be in trouble."

"So would the man, I expect," I answered. "Does it ever happen?"

"Not as far as I know," said Foster. "But I don't know much about matters of that sort."

We didn't have to wait long at the harbour-master's office, where there were two or three young clerks on duty, all with various papers piled up in front of them. Foster explained that we were bound for England, and if possible would like to travel as passengers on some merchant ship. We would, of course, pay the captain accordingly; we weren't out to drive a bargain, and we didn't mind how long the crossing took.

The young man conferred with one of his colleagues. As he did so he nodded in our direction, and I formed the impression that once again Foster's being a minister was telling in our favour. At length he returned and said that he could tell us of something suitable, although of course we would have to work out the terms with the captain. His name was Captain Longside, and he was well known to the harbour-master as an honest man and a thoroughly reliable sailor. His ship was a brig, the *Robin Hood*, lying at Berth 23. If we were going to see him, we should tell him that we had seen himself, Mr. Dearing, and that he had recommended us.

Money changed hands, but I didn't look to see how much.

Berth 23 turned out to be only a short walk away, and we stopped to admire the *Robin Hood* before looking for Captain Longside. Knowing nothing whatever about ships, I thought she looked very attractive. Her decks were clean and she had a neat, trim appearance that made me want to sail away on board her as soon as we could.

A gangplank was in place and Mr. Foster went on board, while I followed two or three yards behind, at what I hoped was a properly respectful distance. We had hardly stepped down onto the deck before a man in overalls came up and asked our business. Mr. Foster said that if it was convenient he would like to have a word with the captain; whereupon, the man told us to wait while he went to see whether the captain was on board. After a short time another man appeared who, from his clean clothes and air of authority, I guessed could only be the captain. He wore a peaked cap, was smoking a pipe and had about him a certain look of scepticism, as of a man not much given to smiling. As he came up to us he did not offer his hand to Foster, and the way he glanced at me made me move still further off.

He spent a considerable time in conversation with Foster and I could see that he was asking questions. More than once Foster shook his head emphatically.

Finally, he turned and beckoned to me to join them. I ran up but kept my eyes on the ground.

"What's your name?" asked the captain.

"Daniel, sir."

"How old are you?"

I had never been at all sure about this, but I replied with an age that I thought must be about right.

"Do you want to go to England? Won't you be leaving a lot

50

behind?"

"No, sir. I'm well off as a servant to Mr. Foster."

We followed the Captain down a companion ladder to the lower deck, where he opened the door of a cabin containing two bunks.

"Thank you, Captain," said Foster. "I'm sure we'll be very comfortable. Shall I pay you now?"

The Captain replied with a nod, and Foster followed him (as I guessed) to his office. Their business was soon done, and the two of us went ashore for dinner.

When we came back that evening, there was a note in our cabin from the Captain, asking Foster to dine with the mate and himself, and adding that he was sure I would be well looked after in the fo'c's'le by Mr. Miles, the Bo'sun.

I unpacked and stowed our stuff as Foster directed. When everything had been done to his satisfaction, he washed his hands, combed his hair and left to join his hosts.

Sitting alone in the cabin, the excitement that I had hitherto felt at the prospect of sailing to England drained out of me and I began to think realistically of what I was leaving behind. While it was true that Foster had saved me from being sold by Mr. Reynolds into slavery in some remote place I did not know, the melancholy truth remained that I was now to be taken away from Doth, from my family and the estate, the only place familiar to me, the only place I had ever dwelt. The future was unknown and I felt ill-equipped to encounter it. I was about to be setting off to a distant country, and perhaps would never return to America. Of England I knew nothing, but I had no alternative. Like waves breaking over me, things were happening now over which I had no control.

After a depressing half hour's meditation, I followed Foster's suggestion and made my way forward into the fo'c's'le, where I found the Bo'sun and four or five of the crew. When I explained that I was servant to Mr. Foster, who was sailing to England on the ship, Mr. Miles told me to sit down, make myself at home and have a drink. He was a big, burly man with a shock of black hair and rolled-up sleeves showing hairy forearms. The drink was whisky, which I had never tasted in my life. I couldn't imagine how anyone could drink it for pleasure.

"There's fifteen crew altogether," said Miles. "Eight or nine of us are English, sailed with the ship quite a few times. The rest have signed on just for this trip. They're new boys, like yourself."

This seemed a reasonably good start, and I kept silent and listened to the conversation, which seemed to be largely about horses. The remainder of the crew arrived in the course of the evening, four or five together and the rest one by one. One of them was black, and we caught each other's eyes and smiled as he passed me.

Supper came in: an excellent beef stew, followed by treacle tart. But here I was embarrassed: everyone except me had his own knife, fork and spoon. The cook lent me a set out of the galley, but I felt silly and out of countenance, especially when I realised that I wouldn't be able to buy a set until we reached England.

"Never been to sea before?" someone asked, and when I admitted it and explained that I was no sailor but Mr. Foster's servant, he went on "Then you'll find there's a lot to learn, Darkie."

Miles told the crew that we were to sail with the tide at three o'clock that morning. I would have liked to watch us sail away, but thought I might only be in the way, and decided to go on making myself as unobtrusive as possible. I went back to our cabin and, finding Foster not yet returned, went to bed and soon fell asleep.

When I woke next morning, I was immediately conscious of the movement of the ship. She was rolling from side to side and it cost me an effort to stagger forward to the fo'c's'le, where the kindly cook gave me a substantial breakfast.

Having eaten, I went up on deck. It was a fine day, the sun shining and not a cloud in the sky. It excited me to see the spread sails and the ship's white wake, and to look back at the town we had left growing smaller and smaller in the distance. I had left Foster asleep, but when I went back to our cabin I found him dressing and plainly in good spirits. While he went off to breakfast, I made the beds, swept the floor and generally tidied up.

It was quite some time before he reappeared. I had stayed in the cabin in case he might want me for anything else. However, he only complimented me on what I had done, and said he was now going to teach me what he called "one or two things I needed to know".

We began with "telling the time", which I found easy enough once I had got the hang of it. Foster said I was a quick learner, and we went on to reading. The alphabet I found much harder, although Foster was patient and seemed positively to enjoy explaining the letters and sounds as many times as I asked. When I spelt out "c", "at", "cat", he clapped his hands, said I was beginning very well and that that would do for one day. He put an arm round my shoulders, pressed me to himself for a moment and planted a quick kiss on my forehead. I thanked him for the trouble he'd taken and, as he settled himself with a book, asked permission to go back on deck.

For some time I stood watching the sailor at the wheel. I could grasp that there must be a connection between the binnacle and the slight movements of his hands, but I couldn't understand why the binnacle seemed to play so large a part in the business of steering. And again, how did the ship respond to the wheel? What was the secret of steering? I didn't dare to ask questions, not even when the sailor turned his head and gave me a friendly wink.

I felt a tug on my sleeve and, turning, found the young black sailor beside me.

"How are you getting on?" he asked. I told him I thought I was settling in quite comfortably. I asked him several of my questions about the ship, and in the light of his replies I began to understand a good deal.

"What's your name?" he asked.

"Daniel," I replied. "And yours?"

"Bernard Watney. But folks mostly call me 'Snowball'."

"Do you mind that?"

"Oh, no. It's friendly, after all."

"Are you English? Do you come from England?"

"Well, I was born there. But when I was seventeen I ran away to sea and I've been a sailor ever since; here, there and everywhere."

"No wife? No children?"

"Lord, no. They'd only cost money and get in the way. I'm hoping to be taken on as first mate before much longer. I've served with several captains I reckon might not be sorry to take me on as mate."

"Does it hinder you, being black?"

"Not at sea it doesn't. That's partly why I've stuck to the sea. America's not a good place to be black, you know."

"What about England?"

"It's patchy, really, is England. There's some good places and some bad. But tell me about yourself. Anyone can see you're no sailor; so what are you?"

"I'm a slave. A 'nigger'."

"You mean, born a slave?"

"And grew up a slave." I told him about Massa Reynolds's estate, and about the slave village and the field work. Then I told him about Missus Kathy and our "abode". I told him about Henderson and how he murdered Jeckzor. And finally I told him about how I had killed Flikka, and come away with the Reverend Foster, to go with him to England.

"And do you like that idea?"

"Yes, I think I do. Foster's been kind to me. If I hadn't become his servant, I'd have been sold a slave."

Bernard was silent. He seemed to be deliberating with himself whether to speak again. At length he asked, "Had you ever seen Mr. Foster before?"

"How could I? I told you, I'd never been outside the plantation in my life."

He said no more, but I felt curious. "How d'you mean? I *couldn't*

54

have seen him before, could I?"

Hesitantly, he replied, "I – *I've* seen him: *I've* seen him before."

"What? How could you have? In England, do you mean?"

"Yes. In England."

"But where, for goodness sake?"

After another pause, he asked, "Are you sure you want to know?"

I frowned in perplexity. "Well, yes, of course. Why shouldn't I want to know? Where have you seen him before?"

"I've seen him – er – in prison."

"You wouldn't be pulling my leg, by any chance?"

"No, Daniel, I'm not. I've seen him before, in England, when we were both in prison, in a town called Winchester. But we didn't meet then, didn't know each other."

I said nothing, but waited.

"When I was sixteen, I was sent to prison for three months, for stealing from shops. That was why, when I came out, I ran away to sea."

"And you say Foster was there too?"

"Yes, he was. I was in a group of young, short-sentence prisoners. Our lot were taken out to work separately. Sometimes we had to wait in the courtyard until the two prison guards who took us out were ready; and that's where I saw Foster more than once, in another gang. I'd know him again anywhere."

"Bernard, are you quite sure? I mean, if you had the least doubt, you would tell me, wouldn't you?"

"I can't be in any doubt at all. We never spoke to each other, but more than once I was near enough to hear his voice; that's how I was sure when I heard it here, on the ship. When I felt certain it must be him, I hung about, pretending to be busy with a rope, while he was talking to the Bo'sun on deck."

"Do you know what he was sent to prison for?"

"No. But of course you'll realise it wouldn't be any good to bring it up now. He's done his time and now he's as free as we are. But if he's really a clergyman, then I'm St. Peter."

"What do you think I ought to do? Or ought I to do nothing?"

"Daniel, if I were you, I'd avoid arousing the least suspicion – on his part, I mean – until we're paid off at Bristol; and then I'd find a way to leave him – some way, any way."

"But I've got no work in England. I don't know anyone; and I don't know the country at all."

"Well, I can't be of any help to you there, because I mean to sign on with another ship as soon as I can. But if you can't come up with something, you're not the lad I took you for. Let's go and have dinner."

That afternoon I had another reading lesson with Foster. Later, I went back to the fo'c's'le, where I watched two of the crew playing chess. One of them good-naturedly offered to teach me and by the time he had to go on duty I had become altogether taken with the game.

That same evening I had an accident. I still wasn't entirely used to the movement of the ship; and crossing the deck I slipped and fell, getting a blow on the head. Mr. Miles happened to be nearby and saw me fall. He came over at once, pulled me up and supported me while I did my best to collect my wits.

"That was a nasty bang, lad," he said. "How do you feel?"

"Not too good, sir, but I suppose it'll pass off."

"Well, if I were you, I'd go and lie down for a bit. If you don't feel like coming along to supper, I'll ask Cookie to bring you something in your bunk; a drop of brandy wouldn't hurt you, either. You just hop into bed, now, and I'll bring you a tot."

His sympathy made me feel better, but I was shocked and dizzy, and glad of his arm back to the cabin. Foster wasn't there, and the kindly Bo'sun, having brought the brandy, made me drink it off neat. With his great topknot of hair and his hirsute arms, he rather resembled some large, hulking animal tending its offspring. He saw me between the blankets and tucked me in, so that I wondered whether he hadn't got some children of his own back home.

56

"Now you just shut your eyes and have a good sleep, young fellow," he said as he left me.

And sleep I did, almost at once. The cook, rather than disturb me, must have come and gone. When I woke, I found Foster kneeling on the floor beside my bunk. He was stroking my forehead and then, seeing that I was awake, leaned over and kissed me on the lips. As I turned my head away, he said "Oh, my darling, dear boy Daniel, we both know now, don't we, our true feelings for each other? I love you with all my heart."

I felt bewildered, and unable to make sense of what he was saying.

"Oh, my sweetest, most precious lad," he went on. "You're all the world to me, but you must have known that already. Known that I love you very dearly." He slid one hand beneath my averted head, turned it to face him and kissed my mouth again. His hand prevented me from turning my lips away, and I felt his tongue thrusting between them. Then, groping, he pushed his other hand down beneath the blankets.

As I tried to struggle in the narrow bunk, everything fell into place: our evening walks down to the stream; his asking Reynolds to let him take me away; his lavish expenditure on smart clothes for me; his bargaining with Captain Longside for a single cabin for the two of us. And – ah, yes! – waiting to show what he really wanted until we were out at sea, bound for England, with no more than twenty-five other people aboard, none of whom would be likely to pay much attention to anything a black nigger boy might say. For what, might one guess, had Foster been sent to prison? And why did it suit him now to pretend to be a clergyman?

All this passed through my mind as I gave in to what he was doing. If I were to take a stand against him, not only would it get me nowhere on board the *Robin Hood*, but once we were ashore I would have destroyed any chance I could expect of help or support from him – and there would be nobody else to turn to.

Foster was so sharp set on what he wanted that he evidently did not perceive that he was getting no response from me. It didn't take him long to gratify himself and then, after a few more perfunctory endearments and caresses, to go to his own bunk and sleep.

I lay awake, partly because my head was throbbing and painful, and partly because I needed to think. After much pondering, I decided that I would not only have to accede to Foster's wishes, but actually to convince him that I felt as he did. At all costs, I must retain his friendship and willingness to help me when we had landed. But how to part from him when the time came? That would have to remain a matter of opportunity.

In the morning I felt feverish and told Foster that I thought it best to stay in my bunk for the time being. The Bos'un, when he looked in, said he would send Snowball along with some bread and a bowl of soup. The soup made me feel better, but Snowball, seeing that I was still poorly, said he would leave me to rest and come back in the afternoon.

The last days of the voyage remain among my worst memories. Doing the best I could to convince Foster that I felt for him as he did for me was a continual strain, of which gratifying his lust was the most disgusting part. It was fortunate for me that, despite his continual protestations of love, his natural disposition, (of which I believe he was quite unaware) was altogether selfish: he really thought that what he did was as enjoyable for me as for himself. I don't think it ever occurred to him that if I felt as he did, I would want to play a more active part. My passivity suited him and he looked no further. For me each time seemed more repellent than the last, and the thought that I was going to have to accompany him when we landed often brought me close to despair; to thinking that I would never be able to get away from him. For I had no money and where could I go?

There was one circumstance that, I thought, offered some vague grounds for hope. This was the discovery that Foster was, to use a plain word, stupid. He was not ignorant: I myself had ignorance enough for twenty boys. No; what he revealed, as we talked, was a kind of slow-minded obtuseness, an inability to perceive that one thing followed from another. One day, for instance, when Snowball had remarked casually, in the course of conversation, that the world took twenty-four hours to revolve on its axis, it became plain that for Foster this had no connection with the sun or the time of day, although he himself had taught me to tell the time by the clock. Nor had it ever occurred to him that times by the sun differ simultaneously in various parts of the world. Another day he showed that he had never realised that sound takes time to travel and that this is demonstrable.

Both Snowball and I were always careful to avoid any insistence or argument with him. Our toleration, while not, of course, making his company more pleasant, allowed me to hope that in some way or other his muddy mind might lessen the difficulty of escape if opportunity offered.

About six o'clock on a fine morning we duly sailed into harbour at Bristol and moored the ship at a quay convenient for unloading. The Captain went ashore to report at the harbour-master's office and to collect the money to pay off the crew. When he returned, they gathered on deck and he paid them one by one, sitting at a chair and table brought from his office.

Once paid, they were free to go ashore and most did so immediately. The Bo'sun, however, remained on deck, and the Captain asked Foster, Snowball and myself to do the same. Foster showed some impatience at this, and finally asked the Captain whether he and I were not now free to go. The Captain did not answer him but, turning to me, said, "Daniel, you are under arrest. Go below to my cabin and wait for me there."

Before I could say a word, Foster broke out angrily, "What do you mean, Captain, by saying Daniel's under arrest? What for? And by what authority are you acting?"

The Captain replied that aboard his ship he had power of arrest. He then turned to the Bo'sun and said, "Mr. Miles, please take Daniel and Watney below to my cabin and wait with them until I join you."

All three of us, of course, obeyed him, so that I did not hear what Foster said next. As we entered the cabin, Snowball turned to me with a broad smile. I saw nothing to smile at, and was trembling with apprehension when Miles put a hand on my shoulder and said, "Don't worry, Daniel. You're not in trouble, so calm down."

He, too, was smiling, so I did my best to do as he said. We had not long to wait until the Captain joined us. His first words were, "Mr. Foster is waiting on deck, unless he's gone ashore, which he's free to do if he wishes." Then, looking at me, he said, "Daniel, you're not under arrest. Just keep quiet and listen. Watney, tell Mr. Miles and Daniel what you told me yesterday."

"Well, sir," answered Snowball "during the crossing I became friendly with Daniel, and he told me that Mr. Foster had begun treating him in a way he didn't like; a dirty way, sir. He'd been using him, sir, for, well for –"

"Buggery?" said the Captain.

"Yes, sir, that and – and, well, messing about with him and making him do nasty things and that."

"Did Daniel tell you he didn't like it?"

"Yes, sir, he did. But he said he was afraid to tell you or Mr. Miles, because he thought you wouldn't – well, wouldn't want to listen to him."

"And you thought the same, didn't you?"

"Yes, sir. Well, you see, sir, I've had some experience, and I know that many captains and bo'suns think that such things are no business of theirs; that they're quite normal among sailors on ships at sea. And then what with Mr. Foster being white, sir, and me and Daniel being black –"

"You changed your mind, didn't you?"

"Yes, sir."

"Why?"

"It was when Daniel told me that Mr. Foster meant to keep him with him, sir, after we were ashore, and he didn't want to stay with Mr. Foster, but he had no money and no work and he didn't know England at all, and he had no friends he could go to, so he couldn't run away from Mr. Foster."

"Daniel, is that true?"

60

"Yes, sir."

"And so, Watney, you decided to tell me after all?"

"Yes, sir. You and Mr. Miles, sir."

"Well, Mr. Miles, knowing you and your moral principles as I do, you no doubt feel that you want to help Daniel, get him away from Foster and perhaps find him a roof over his head and a job to go to?"

"Yes, Captain, sir," said Miles.

"He behaved well on the voyage?"

"Yes, sir; he did. All the lads took a liking to him. No one interfered with him, though, not like Mr. Foster."

"Well, please call Mr. Foster in."

When Foster came in, the Captain said, "Now, Mr. Foster, before you say anything, just listen to me. First, Daniel doesn't want to stay with you. He wants to leave you. Mr. Miles and I think that by law he's free to do so."

"But, sir," broke in Foster, "he is my protégé."

"He is not a slave. Not in this country. He is free to leave you. Where he decides to go is no business of yours."

"But, sir –"

The Captain held up his hand. "We also know that during the recent crossing, you have abused him in filthy ways. You buggered him several times. That is against the law."

"Sir –"

"We also know that you have been in prison in Winchester. We don't know for what, but that will be on record. We also very much doubt whether you are in holy orders. Now, have you anything to say to us?"

"I – er – I shall take you to law, Captain. You will hear from my lawyer in due course."

"My name and address are written on this piece of paper," said the Captain. "Now take your luggage and leave the ship."

* * *

I disembarked from the *Robin Hood* in the company of Mr. Miles. When I tried to thank him for all he had done to help me, he cut me short, saying that he had been only too glad to show up Foster for what he was and to get me away from him.

"He's a villain, sure enough," he said. "We could probably get him put back in prison if we wanted, only 'twould be too much trouble. He'll likely get himself back there in time."

The docks were crowded, but no one seemed to think it unusual to see a black lad walking side by side with a brawny white man. There were several black men working in the gangs among the piled crates and roped bundles, none of whom bothered to take the least notice of me as I carried one of Mr. Miles's bags, accepted a quid of his tobacco, spat it out on the stones and chattered with him.

"You've nowhere in particular to go, have you, Daniel?" he asked me; and when I replied that that was so, he went on, "Well, you'd better come home with me for the time being. I've got a notion I may be able to help you and perhaps myself at the same time. Can you keep a secret?"

"Oh, yes, yes, sir," I replied, agog with expectation.

"So can I," he chuckled and vouchsafed nothing more as we left the docks and came out into the bustle of the workaday city.

Bristol, capital of the west of England, the only big town to which I had ever been, overwhelmed me with its noise, and I could only stare about and holler one question after another as we made our way up the street, past the shops and counting houses, half-deafened by the hooves and wheels thundering over the cobbles. We stopped at a tavern for bread and cheese and beer, and again no one seemed to think it unusual that we sat down together. I was the only one surprised. I thought it best to stop bothering the good bo'sun with more questions, and kept quiet as he finished his quart and read the newspaper he had bought from a lad at the door.

"It's good to be back home," said he, as he folded it up and put it in his pocket. "There's nothing better than English draught beer. You'll soon acquire a taste for it, my boy."

I smiled and nodded, and after a pause he went on, "You'll be welcome to stay with us for a few days. We've a girl and two boys in the family. Jim's the youngest. I guess you're probably about the same age as him. Can you sleep on the floor?"

"Yes, of course I can, sir."

"You're like the Irishman was asked could he play the fiddle. 'Said he was pretty sure he could, but he couldn't say for certain because he'd never tried."

"I'm sure sleeping on the floor's easier than playing the fiddle, sir."

"How about mice?"

"Oh, I simply dote on mice, Mr. Miles. American mice, you know."

"You're so sharp you'll cut yourself," said he, grinning. "Well, let's be on our way. The sooner we're home the better. It's a fair way out to Filton."

We reached Filton and Mr. Miles's home that afternoon. It was something like an abode, I thought, with its plot of smooth grass in front, its bright blue front door and pots of flowering geraniums in the windows. We went round to the open back door, where Mr. Miles whistled two or three notes which were evidently a personal signal, for his wife, almost crying with delight, came running out from the kitchen and clasped his huge bulk in her arms. I thought her a fine, handsome woman, but of course every woman looks her best when she's brimming with happiness.

"Jack, oh darling Jack," she kept saying, as she kissed him again and again. Although she took me in with a quick glance, it did nothing to interrupt her welcome, which continued for some while until Mr. Miles, kissing her hands and then holding her at arm's length by the shoulders, said, "Tea, lass, tea." Even then she paid me no particular attention as I followed the good bo'sun into the kitchen and stood by his chair as he sat down.

I realise now that she didn't question her husband about me because she knew that he would tell her in his own good time: and over the first cup of tea he did just that. Foster he simply described as "a bad master", going on to say that he didn't care for the notion of putting me ashore with no money and nowhere to go. She nodded her agreement.

"I've got a bit of a notion about young Dan'l," he said, "but it'll keep for the time being. Where's the children?"

"Ursula's gone to see Ellen," replied his wife, "and the boys have gone fishing. I take it Daniel will be staying with us until you've fixed him up? Have another cup of tea, Daniel, dear, and tell me about where you've come from."

I think she didn't say "about your home" in case I'd never had one. I felt shy and tongue-tied, but managed to tell her a little about my mother and Dorothy, and how sad we'd been to part when Mr. Reynolds had handed me over to Foster.

"I'll write to your mother," she said, "to tell her you're safe and sound. I'll send the letter to your Mr. Reynolds and ask him to see she gets it."

I couldn't help laughing at the thought of Mr. Reynolds being asked to pass a letter on to one of his slaves; but still, I thought, there was a chance that he might. Anyway, it was the only chance there was.

All this time I felt confused and bewildered at finding myself sitting with white people in these spotlessly clean surroundings, like nothing I had ever known in my life, and seeing on every side strange objects at whose use I could make no guess. Evidence of wealth beyond anything that I had ever imagined, they fairly nonplussed me. The fire, bright with flaming coals, seemed wonderful beyond belief; so did the painted china, the cushions on the chairs, and the curtains at the windows. They made me feel nervous. Mrs. Miles must have perceived my uneasiness, for she took my hand, saying, "Come along, Daniel; come out in the garden with me and look at the flowers."

Even the garden, of course, was unlike any place that I had ever seen; and I still could not relax. There was a seat under a cherry tree, to which she led me. After we had sat there together for a little while, she said, "Now you stay here in the sun, my dear, while I go and see to one or two things, and I'll be back quite soon."

Left alone, I flung myself on the grass and shed tears of homesickness and anxiety. I lay prone, my face in my hands, sobbing.

I was still crying when I felt a hand on my back, while a voice said, "Come on, old chap: it can't be that bad."

Raising my head, I saw two white boys kneeling beside me, plainly flummoxed by my presence in their garden. They were both carrying rods and one of them had three fish on a string through the gills.

"Have you been took bad?" said the one who had spoken. "Come on, tell us what's up."

I wiped my eyes with the back of my hand. "No, no," I said. "I'm all right. Your father's come home; he brought me with him. From America."

At this they both jumped up and ran indoors, shouting "Dad!" I scrambled to my feet and was about to follow them when Mrs. Miles came out, took me by the hand and led me back indoors. She was so kind and reassuring that I soon cheered up.

I have always remembered that evening; sitting on the arm of Mr. Miles's chair as he talked with the boys about where he had been and listened to all they had to tell him.

"You'll take me with you next time, won't you, Dad?" said Dermot, the older boy. "If you can take Daniel, you can take me."

"Well, I think Daniel may do better to stay here in England," replied Mr. Miles. "But when you've finished at school, my boy, if you've still a mind to it, you might come along and try whether the sea suits you."

Some time later, Ursula returned, laughed with surprise and pleasure to see her father and (this I have never forgotten) bent forward and gave me a kiss on the cheek by way of welcome.

I remember walking down the street with Mr. Miles, who persuaded the butcher to unlock his shop and sell us a leg of mutton for supper. I remember stripping with the boys to wash under the pump. As they knelt by their beds to say their prayers,

Jim put an arm round my shoulders.

"Look," he said to me, "I can imagine how strange everything here must seem to you, but nothing – nothing at all – is going to hurt you, all right? We're your friends." I shared his bed and slept soundly.

Oh, how often, during the years that followed, did I long to find myself back at home with that good Christian family! Although I could not know it, in all my life to come – until now, that is - I was never better off nor better treated than by them.

PART III

I suppose I must have stayed about a fortnight with Mr. Miles and his family. Yet in memory it always appears longer, so that I find myself unreflectingly thinking, "When I was with the Miles family we always used to 'do this' or 'do that'"; as though that "always" referred to a period of months. The fine summer weather, perhaps, had something to do with it, but far more the kindness with which they treated me. I had never been so warmly befriended nor enjoyed such consideration.

Of course they could have found fault with me on many a score; my table manners, my grubby hands, my illiteracy, my ignorance, my disagreeable habits, such as picking my nose, or spitting on my hands before setting about chopping wood or stooping to heave up a weight. But they never did. Suggestion or dint of example was the furthest they ever went, ("Want to wash your hands for dinner, Dan?") and they always behaved solicitously. At church on Sunday, when Jim saw that I couldn't understand the prayer-book the sidesman had given me, he shut his own and kept as mum as I did; and slipped me one of his own farthings to put in the bag.

Mr. Miles was clearly enjoying his holiday from sea. He dug vegetables in the garden, read the newspaper, painted the house here and there, sat in the sun, visited friends in the village, went to the tavern and brought back quarts of beer for supper, and in the evening read to us from *The Pilgrim's Progress* and *Robinson Crusoe*. He read well. This was a new experience for me and I enjoyed it.

On one occasion, he was away for most of the day "on business", as he put it. He arrived home shortly before supper and confessed to having walked "quite enough". The only one to know what he had been doing was Mrs. Miles, who asked him whether he had talked with "the lady" and hoped that all had gone well. In reply he tapped the side of his nose with his forefinger and said, "'Could have been worse." He ate a hearty meal and told us he reckoned he deserved it.

Later, instead of reading to us as usual, he asked me to come with him into the garden. I joined him on the seat under the cherry tree. When he had got his pipe going to his satisfaction, he said, "Well, Daniel, I've spent the day getting you what I hope will be a good job and a good place. You don't have to take it if you don't want to, but I reckon it'd suit you and you couldn't do better. I'll tell you a bit about it.

"A lot of rich ladies nowadays employ good-looking boys as their personal pages. A page has to attend on his mistress, you know; carry her things – her comb, scent, smelling salts, spare handkerchief – all that sort of thing, whatever she needs to have with her. Often he has to run errands, carry letters and so on. And to have a black page is considered very smart just now, because they're not too easy to come by; reliable, well-behaved black boys, that is. Often, they're dressed in smart uniforms. When a lady goes visiting, the page may be sent to wait in the servants' hall; or she may want him to sit quiet in a corner of the room, to show how stylish she is. If she has her portrait painted, she may very well want the page put in the picture too, or so I'm told. 'Suggests riches, you see.

"Of course, it can be hard work. The page may be kept up half the night when his lady's dancing or playing cards. But the thing is, it's clean work and if the lady's pleased with you, you may very well get a higher position as you grow up. What do you think of the idea?"

"Well, Mr. Miles," I said, "it sounds fine to me. The only thing is, I'm a bit of a rough lad, as you know, not used to fine people or fine ways. I can't even read or write, not properly –"

68

"That wouldn't matter," said he. "There's plenty can't – grown men, too. You could probably learn in your spare time. And if you take the trouble, you can soon mend your rough ways, as you call them. A cheerful, good-hearted boy, no fool, ready to take pains and set himself out to please; that's what they look for. It's well worth a try, anyway. And if you find it doesn't suit you, you can always come back here." He paused. " Well, Daniel, you think about it for a bit, while the Missus and I go out for a drop of beer. It's entirely up to you. If you don't fancy it I shan't mind."

When they returned, I told him I'd be happy to do my best. We went back to the seat under the cherry tree.

"The place I think I've found for you," he said, "is with Lady Penelope Marston. She lives about fifteen miles from here, not far from Bath. She's a wealthy widow. Sir James Marston died a year or two ago, and left her very well off. Her servants speak well of her – 'say she's a kind and not too-demanding mistress. Her housekeeper took me in to see her, and I thought she seemed a nice lady. I told her I'd bring you over this Thursday afternoon; that'll give us time to get you ready, trim that stylish curly hair, see to your things and that. You're all right for shoes, but you could do with another pair of stockings. A hat, too; you're not respectable without a hat. A clasp knife might come in handy, and we'll put a shilling or two in your pocket, just in case."

"Will the lady pay me?" I asked.

Mr. Miles chuckled. "About five pounds a year, if you're lucky. And that reminds me, Daniel. Never, never steal, d'you see? Never. For a servant in a rich house that's always a terrible temptation. There's servants been hanged for that. Well, you might not be hanged, but to be dismissed without a character, that's fatal, that's ruinous."

We talked on for a while, and Mr. Miles gave me a lot more good advice. "And be sure you don't quarrel with anyone," he finished. "None of the other servants, I mean. You'll almost certainly be the youngest, and you're black into the bargain. So you must keep quiet, only speak when you're spoken to and so on. Even if someone treats you badly, never show any resentment, and never make enemies."

When we came back indoors, Mr. Miles told the family what he'd arranged. No one had a word to say against it.

"But we're going to miss you, Daniel, that we are," said Jim. And Ursula reduced me to tears by insisting on giving me her own little cross and chain to wear round my neck. I've still got it, as you can see. I've worn it all these years.

"You won't forget us, will you?" said Dermot. And I never have.

* * *

I needn't tell of all the preparations that were made for me next day. I realised that Mr. Miles was spending money on my account as if I was one of his own sons; but as before, he made light of it.

"It's about time somebody laid out a few pennies on you, young Daniel," he said. (I knew, of course, that it must be far more.) "I'm sure that one day, when you're grown up, you'll be able to do us a good turn in one way or another. We shan't lose touch, you and I."

"Is it far to go tomorrow?" I asked.

"About fifteen miles at the most, I reckon," he replied. "Our neighbour Alec Williams is very kindly lending us his pony and trap. If the Lord only gives us a fine day it ought to be a nice little trip."

"I'm going to miss *Robinson Crusoe*," I said that evening, after he had read to us as usual. The truth was that I was going to miss a lot more than *Robinson Crusoe*.

"Only put your trust in the Lord, my boy," said Mr. Miles. "He's always with you, and if you'll only trust Him, He'll see you through thick and thin. You do believe that, don't you?"

"It's you that's helped me to believe it," I replied.

"Well," he said. "Mrs. Miles and myself, we've both got confidence in you. Else, we wouldn't be at the trouble; not that you've been any trouble, my lad. It's only just my way of speaking, you know. We've all been only too happy to have you here with us."

70

The next morning was as fine as anyone could wish. I put on the suit Foster had given me, and stood docile while the boys satisfied themselves about my hair, ears, fingernails and shoes. Mr. Williams obliged us by himself bringing round the pony and trap and after the most heartfelt thanks and farewells on my part, we drove away, with the family waving us out of sight.

Of course, this was the first time I had seen open country in England. What struck me most was its vivid greenness; the meadows on either side, with their placid, grazing cattle, interspersed with cornfields. In the distance lay the darker green of woodlands. Everything seemed peaceful, with a kind of stability and permanence. On me, it had a reassuring effect.

This, Mr. Miles told me, was the road to Bath, as old as the Romans of long ago. On this fine morning there was a good deal of traffic; carthorses pulling loaded wagons, horsemen riding clippety-clop and once or twice, lofty coaches, driven four-in-hand by imposing, top-hatted coachmen. It was exhilarating company.

A few miles outside Bath we turned off the high road and drove down dusty lanes, with leafy branches overhanging the way and here and there a ford where we stopped for our pony to drink. We passed through one or two villages, drowsy in the noontide heat, before pulling up at a tavern that met with the approval of the discriminating Mr. Miles. We took our bread-and-cheese and beer to a bench outside. There was hardly a sound except the pony's gentle tearing at the grass, and the song of a bird. A farm boy, passing by on a donkey, gave us a friendly wave and called "Na, Darkie."

"Not far now," said Mr. Miles, as we set off again. He let the pony amble, and after no more than a mile or two pointed to a church tower half-hidden behind a belt of trees.

"Here we are, my lad – Clepton Saint Peter."

We passed the church, and a little farther on, behind a pair of ornamental iron gates and a gravelled drive, saw facing us the most elegant house that I had ever seen. Its three storeys were built of dark-red brick, crowned by a cream-coloured cornice. On either side, lower wings extended slightly forward, so that they seemed as though guarding or attending upon the house itself. We turned first to the right, then left and crunched down a gravelled slope leading past one side of the house into a stable yard. Here I begged Mr. Miles to pull up.

"This isn't – this surely isn't – where we're going, is it, Mr. Miles?" I was trembling.

"It certainly is, my boy," he replied. "Clepton House."

"And – and the lady lives here?"

"Lady Penelope Marston. She does indeed."

"But you never told me." I was panic-stricken, close to tears of dismay. "I never dreamt – it would be – be so grand; so far above me."

"You've nothing to worry about, Daniel. I've been reliably told that the lady and her servants are good-hearted, decent people. They won't treat you high-and-mighty. We're not on your tobacco plantation now, you know. This is England. Come on, give me a smile. Think of your dear Dorothy. You and she both stood up to Reynolds, didn't you? And these people are much, much nicer than Reynolds, believe me."

I managed a lopsided smile.

"I got this opportunity for you because I know you can bring it off. You've been blessed with a nice disposition, Daniel. Give it a chance. Just be yourself."

His warmth and kindness, and the thought of all he had done for me suppressed, if they did not altogether disperse, my trepidation.

As we got down a boy came running, took the pony's head and led it away to a drinking trough in the shade.

Mr. Miles was about to knock when the door was opened by a plump, smiling woman, who evidently remembered him.

"Good afternoon, Mr. Miles," she said, shaking hands. "So you've brought the young lad. Come in and sit down a while."

I followed Mr. Miles into a bright, spacious kitchen.

"Sit down, both of you," she said, pulling out a bench from

under the table. "I expect you'll be glad to cool off after your drive." She brought each of us a glass of beer. "I expect you could eat a slice of plum cake, couldn't you, young man?" she said to me.

"Thank you very kindly, ma'am," I replied.

It was a generous slice, and I was barely halfway through it when a stout, sedate personage entered the kitchen, closed the door behind him and, as we both rose to our feet, looked at us in a grave, taciturn manner.

"Who are these people, Mrs. Beddoes?" he asked.

"This is Mr. Miles, a seafaring gentleman, Mr. Graydon," she answered. "Mr. Miles, this is our butler, Mr. Graydon. Mr. Miles spoke with her ladyship on Monday while you were out visiting the wine merchants. He's brought this lad he thinks may suit her ladyship as a page."

"Ah, yes," said he. "Now I recall her ladyship mentioning the matter. She has a visitor at the moment, but I'll inform her that you're here."

As he left the kitchen, Mrs. Beddoes opened the door to the scullery. "You'll want to have a quick wash, my boy." She filled a bowl and gave me soap and a towel. I had just finished when the butler returned.

"Her ladyship wishes you to remain here," he said to Mr. Miles, "while she talks with the boy. As for you, young fellow, come with me."

I hadn't been expecting that Mr. Miles would not be included, but there was no help for it. I followed the butler up a short flight of stairs, through a green baize door and along a corridor. At the further end he opened another door and took two or three steps beyond. I followed.

"This is the boy, your ladyship."

He stood aside and gave me a gentle push forward.

The room was the largest I had ever seen in my life. In those days I didn't know the words "palatial" or "overpowering", but that was its effect on me. I don't know how long I stood, struck dumb and bemused, before being led by the hand to a chair beside

73

an open window.

Here, recovering my senses, I looked up, to find myself face-to-face with a gentleman who was looking at me with an amused but not unkindly expression. After a few moments he turned his head and said to someone behind him, "Well, that's a fair start, anyway, Penny. He's a good-looking lad. His appearance wouldn't discredit you."

He moved a little to one side, disclosing his companion beyond. She, I knew at once, could only be Lady Penelope Marston.

Just as I had said to Mr. Miles, my first feeling was that this was a person immeasurably far above me. I had never seen any woman like this before. Unconsciously, I had formed in my mind a picture of an elderly lady, grey-haired and rather severe-looking. So I was startled, for I could not have been more mistaken. In those days I had had little or no practice in guessing ladies' ages; but at least I could see that this lady was young – twenty-six, perhaps, if that, and very good-looking. Her dark hair, falling to her shoulders, framed a most pleasant face: oval, with large, brown eyes, a rather long, straight nose, lips which lay slightly apart and an expression the very opposite of severe. Discriminating, certainly, but – what? Tolerant? Kindly? Something more, perhaps. Compassionate? What I mean is that as she looked at me I felt that in some extraordinary way she had absorbed my own feelings of nervousness and tension and dissolved them, as it were, in herself. Of course, I am speaking with hindsight, for I was to come to know Lady Penelope Marston almost as well as I had once known Doth or Missus Kathy. Yet now, even at this first look, her appearance reassured and calmed me. In a word, she put me at my ease.

"You're not afraid of me, are you?" she said, smiling. "I don't look frightening, do I?"

I could only smile and shake my head. She took a plate of sugared biscuits from the tea-table at her elbow.

"Have one of these and tell me your name."

"My name is Daniel, your ladyship." I ventured a bite at the

74

biscuit.

"But have you another name? A family name?"

"I'm afraid not, your ladyship. Slaves don't have family names."
(Crunch, crunch.)

"You've come from America?"

"Yes, your ladyship; from a big tobacco plantation in Virginia."

"Mr. Miles and I had a talk the other day. He spoke well of you."

"He's been very kind to me, your ladyship."

"And you want to be my page?"

"Very much, your ladyship." (It seemed easy, now, to talk to her.)

"Have you had any experience of being a page?"

Suddenly, I had an inspiration. "Well, on the plantation, your
ladyship, I worked as a personal messenger for Mr. Reynolds, the
plantation owner."

She smiled. "He was the big boss, was he?"

"Yes, your ladyship. It was a large place; a good mile across or
more. Sometimes Mr. Reynolds would want a note carried to one
of the other white men, or sometimes he just wanted me to tell
one of them to come and talk with him."

"Why do you want to be my page?"

"Well, Mr. Miles has told me all about the work, your ladyship.
I like the sound of it and I believe I could do it to your
satisfaction."

She turned to the gentleman. "What do you think, Francis?"

"I suggest you take him for a week or two on trial, Penny. But
look, my boy, you do understand, do you, that you have to be
entirely committed to this job? All day and all night, if it's
required of you. Now, have you ever been in any sort of trouble?
Been punished for doing wrong? It'll be better if you tell the truth
now. Have you ever stolen, for instance?"

"Never, sir. Mr. Miles will tell you the same. I've never been in
any sort of trouble for wrongdoing."

"How soon can you start?"

"At once, sir. I brought my clothes and things with me."

He smiled. "Did you indeed? Well, Penny, I suppose you'll tell Graydon to look after him till tomorrow." She nodded.

Less than half a minute later the butler returned. It seemed like magic. Of course, I knew nothing of bells in those days, and hadn't noticed the gentleman pulling the bell-cord.

There is little more to tell of that day. Mr. Miles was sent for. Lady Penelope spoke graciously to him and said she would be happy to send him five pounds if I proved satisfactory. Then he and I parted, without showing our emotional feelings before the company, and the butler took me in charge.

I spent the evening carrying in logs and splitting them for burning. After supper Mrs. Beddoes took me up to my attic room, where I stowed my belongings, climbed into bed and slept at once. The day, I felt, had gone well.

I might mention one other trifle. I had fallen head-over-heels in love with Lady Penelope Marston, and wished only to serve her to the last drop of my blood.

I was up betimes, or so I thought. But the other servants had already dispersed to their work and in the kitchen I found no one except Mrs. Beddoes and the scullery maid. I had just finished a generous plate of eggs, sausages and bacon when Mr. Graydon came to summon me to Lady Penelope in the morning room. She was writing at her desk, and looked up as I came in.

"Daniel," she said, "I've sent to the tailors in Bath. Two of their people will be here early this afternoon to measure you for your uniform. Until then, Mr. Graydon will give you some useful work to be getting on with." She turned back to her writing and I bowed and withdrew.

I spent the morning polishing silver and replacing the burned ends of candles in the candlesticks about the house.

The tailors arrived soon after servants' dinner. Lady Penelope received them in a small parlour off the drawing-room. They were so extremely deferential that I was hard put to it not to smile.

"Of course it will be our great pleasure, your ladyship to fit the

76

young man out completely in accordance with your esteemed wishes. We have brought several samples of our latest and most genteel uniform materials and we hope you will be graciously pleased to inspect them and give us your highly-valued instructions."

Lady Penelope took her time in looking at the various materials and patterns, while the tailors took my measurements.

At length she selected two; a plum-coloured velvet and a royal blue corduroy. A coat, cap and breeches were to be made from each, the coats to have silver buttons, with collars and cuffs embroidered with silver thread. On the lapels and on the left breast were to be small emblems in the form of silver dolphins

Having settled all this, Lady Penelope disconcertingly went the length of asking me whether I agreed with her choice. Of course I expressed warm approval.

"No criticisms?" she said, eyebrows raised in a smiling pretence of surprise.

I returned her smile. "Not one, your ladyship."

Finally, she told the men to return with the clothes ready for a fitting at the same day and time next week: she trusted there would be no delay. ("Oh dear no, your ladyship; it will be our pleasure to be entirely punctual.") Mrs. Beddoes was summoned and told to give them a meal before they left. I joined them below stairs and sat not far away, polishing shoes. They had nothing to say to me; I received the impression that they found Lady Penelope's schedule distinctly exacting, though this they kept to themselves.

Earlier that day, at dinner, (when I was sitting, of course, at the extreme foot of the table), Mr. Graydon had briefly told the other servants that I was on approval for the post of page to her ladyship. No one had anything to say to this (such as that I was black), and I kept my eyes down and concentrated on my plate of Irish stew and greens.

I was beginning to grasp that a major reason for Lady Penelope's servants to feel contented was the quantity and quality of the victuals. This dinner, like many others I was later to enjoy, fully deserved our concentration and there was very little talk.

As I settled into my humble position in the household and began to take notice of the surroundings and the company, I came to understand the hierarchy and those of whom it consisted. By the standards of those days it was not a large establishment, and this was tacitly reflected in the demeanour of its chief, the butler. Mr. Graydon was not exacting in handling his people. The reason, as I came to realise, was that he was not happy in his situation, and accordingly remained somewhat detached from it. He was self-seeking, and thought his talents made him worthy to head a bigger household. So while he took care always to appear correct and diligent, he felt that he was not living the life to which he aspired. His heart was not in what he was doing; and although he supposed that his discontent lay concealed, in fact it was apparent. The servants exploited it. They were often negligent, and sometimes guilty of liberties for which even I could see that they should have been taken to task.

Grace Hobden, Lady Penelope's personal maid, and I were under her direct orders, and in this position of being "among them yet not altogether of them", I was well placed to observe the community. It seemed to me that the two footmen, Hayward and Lister, must have opted for domestic service primarily to keep themselves off the land. They did as little as they could get away with; and since they were tall young men of good appearance, they passed muster easily enough. Lister found time to teach me to play cribbage. He and Hayward talked of little but their sexual exploits, which I reckoned existed largely in their own heads.

There were two parlourmaids and two housemaids, all engaged, it seemed to me, on the strength of being what are called "steady girls". With two of them, Mary and Edith, I became in time quite friendly. I was their "little blackamoor", and they used to make my bed and wash my shirts and stockings.

Mrs. Beddoes was the best cook I have ever known and well aware of her gift. Of course, everybody took care to keep on the right side of her, and her popularity made her amiable and good-tempered. "Come on, young Dan'l," she would say. "Do a bit of churning for me and you can have a lump of butter on the new bread, 'soon as I've baked it." During all the time that I was in that household I never had a bad meal. Even Lady Penelope herself sometimes deferred to what Mrs. Beddoes thought would comprise the best menu for a dinner party.

Mr. Hodges was the head stableman and coachman, with two grooms under him. He and his wife lived in a sizeable cottage adjoining the stable-yard. Their infant daughter, Marian, had been born about two years before my arrival. Their firstborn, a son (as I was told) had died some years before. I, of course, had little to do with Mrs. Hodges, but whenever I spoke with her she was always kindly and agreeable.

Naturally, being in constant attendance on Lady Penelope, I saw a good deal of the horses, of which there were six altogether. In spite of Josh, I have never known much about horses, but I do know that Lady Penelope's were widely admired.

Miss Osborne, the housekeeper, was a warm and kindly soul. She knew how to make people work for her, and was sometimes not above lending her girls a hand; or even, on occasion, deputising for Mrs. Beddoes.

I need not describe every member of the staff – the gardeners, bootboy, scullery maid and so forth, except to say that they went to make up what seemed to me a comfortable society. Lady Penelope, though not indulgent, was not an unduly exacting employer and in any case (as I shall relate) she was away from home a good deal. She certainly made good use of me. On occasion, as when she went out for the evening and came home late, my work could be onerous indeed, but with health and energy on my side – plus my adoration of Lady Penelope - I could just about contrive to cope with it.

The principal feature conditioning my life was simply that I was black. This put me in an ambiguous position. On the one hand, although it was not so humiliating as being a slave in Virginia, I knew that these white people, lenient and restrained as they were, in their hearts looked down on me as one of an inferior race. As long as I behaved respectfully and took care to be deferential they had nothing against me; but sometimes the mask slipped. "Get out of the way, you bloody nigger!" gasped Hayward one morning, when he was struggling to carry indoors a heavy sack of potatoes. Another time, when Mr. Graydon asked who had left the back door wide open to an east wind, Lister replied that it was that confounded page boy, who needed his black arse kicked. I felt this kind of contempt keenly, but I knew better than to complain. If insults were the common lot of black people, at least there was some compensation for me personally.

The compensation lay in the fact that Lady Penelope plainly thought of me as a valuable possession, rather like a diamond ring or a gold watch. Just as Mr. Miles had told me, my mere presence contributed to her self-esteem and her elegance. Though demanding, she was not inconsiderate; and besides, what mitigated her most peremptory demands was that in my eyes she was a demi-deity. I thought the world of her and considered myself lucky indeed to be her bedizened attendant. My flamboyant uniforms were a delight to me and even when I was almost dropping with weariness I never forgot that I held a unique position in her regard. I was hers as the other servants could not be.

One morning, when I had been in the household for about six weeks, she told me that she was going away on a visit and I was to come with her: we would be starting early in the afternoon. It wasn't, of course, my place to ask where we were going or how long we would be away. I did up a couple of clean shirts, two pairs of stockings and a few other things in a bundle and was waiting with Mr. Hodges beside the light carriage and pair half an hour before she joined us, attended by Grace Hobden.

My seat was beside Mr. Hodges on the box, my uniform swathed in a light cloak against the dust. "But if it comes on to rain, Daniel," she said, "you're to come inside. If you want to pass water, go and do it now, before we start." This was typical of her straightforward altruism and candour.

So away we went. It was a beautiful afternoon, the sun glinting

80

on the leaves as we passed the woodland on the further side of the house. I thought it best to keep quiet and leave it to Mr. Hodges to speak first if he had a mind to. It was some time before, having spat out a mouthful of tobacco, he said, "So 'ow d'you like your job, boy, eh?"

"Very much, sir, thank you," I replied.

"Your first job, is it?"

"First in this country, sir."

"Ah," he said, and relapsed into silence.

After a good hour – as it seemed to me – we came to a ford and he stopped to let the horses drink. As they finished he called "Log on" and they pulled us out on the further side, up a gravelly slope to a crossroads. He pointed with his whip at the signpost. "What's that say, boy?"

"I'm afraid I can't read very well, sir."

"Then you'd best set to and learn quick as what you can. 'Can't get far in life without you can read and write, you know."

"I know the letters, sir. But there's no one to teach me the rest, you see."

"Why don't you ask her ladyship?"

"You don't mean, ask her to teach me, sir, surely?"

"No, no, but to tell summun off to do it."

"Well, I'd hardly like to ask even that, sir. I don't think it would really be my place to do that."

"You can leave it to me, boy. I'll ask her."

"Thank you very much, Mr. Hodges, sir. That's very kind of you."

He said no more, and after some time we came to an inn, where we stopped to change horses. Lady Penelope got out, gave me her bag and strolled a little way up the road. I followed behind.

"Oh, the heat," she said, to no one in particular. "Daniel, give me my fan."

She leaned on a low wall, fanning herself, yawning and closing her eyes.

Presently she said, "Go and ask them for a glass of milk, Daniel, the colder the better."

They gave me a glass straight from the dairy and she drank most of it without pausing.

"You finish it, Daniel," she said, handing it back to me with a smile. I thanked her and did so.

Resuming our journey, we hadn't gone far before Hodges said, "You know where we're going, boy, I suppose?"

"No, sir, no one's told me."

"Guildford, that's where." He paused. "But we won't be going into the town. Her ladyship's friend lives a mile or so outside. We'll be staying two nights. She told you that much, I suppose?"

"No, she didn't, sir. I'm glad to know."

Some time later he once more broke silence. "I reckon she ought to get married again, fine-looking woman like 'er. 'Tain't in nature, like, 'er living alone. Ah." He seemed to be hesitating. Then he said, "You know what I reckon?"

"No, sir."

"I reckon she wants keep her own 'and on 'er money, that's what. 'Can't say as I blames 'er altogether, eether."

To me it seemed a long journey. We changed horses again and the day was beginning to cool when at last we turned off the road, drove up a short avenue and stopped in front of a handsome house all of grey stone, its walls covered here and there with purple-blooming creeper. Lady Penelope alighted. Grace and I fell in behind her and Mr. Hodges, going ahead, was about to knock on the door when it was opened by the gentleman who had been with her on the afternoon when I had come to be engaged as her page.

"Penny!" he cried delightedly. "I was watching out for you! I hope you had a pleasant journey."

"Hot, but otherwise quite enjoyable, dear Francis," she replied, put an arm round his neck and kissed his cheek.

The butler was hovering in the hall. He took charge of Grace and of Lady Penelope's luggage, leaving Hodges to drive round to the stable-yard. I followed Lady Penelope into the drawing-room and went to stand at the farthest end. On a nearby writing-desk I noticed two opened envelopes and just managed to puzzle out that one was addressed (in block letters) to "Francis Hardwick, Esquire."

"So you kept your black page?" he asked her. "He suits you all right, does he?"

"Oh, yes," she answered carelessly. "Francis, will the architect be coming?"

"Yes, tomorrow morning. John Stedman. I think you'll like him. Good reputation, and very keen to take on the job."

When they had settled themselves in the armchairs, I sat down in a bay window. A tea-tray was brought in and the maid brought me a glass of water, which I was glad to accept.

Mr. Hardwick and Lady Penelope fell into lively conversation, to which I was careful to be seen to pay no attention. For the matter of that, I wasn't interested. What little I couldn't help hearing seemed to be about some sort of building, but I was content to watch the starlings running on the lawn and the cat absurdly trying to catch them. After some time, Mr. Hardwick suggested a stroll in the garden, and Lady Penelope dismissed me below stairs. The two or three girls in the kitchen had apparently never seen a black person before, and remained virtually tongue-tied as I did my best to talk to them, getting very little for my trouble beyond silly giggles and embarrassed Yes's and No's. After a while I went outside, sat in the sunny stable-yard and watched the martins building under the eaves.

That night I found my bed comfortable enough. After a meagre breakfast next morning, finding the servants' company no more friendly than the evening before, I went out again into the yard. It was some while before the butler summoned me to join Lady Penelope and Mr. Hardwick at his carriage. I sat with the coachman, of course. We drove through the city of Guildford and stopped somewhere on the further outskirts. As I was climbing down, Mr. Hardwick put out his hand and helped me, smiling as he did so.

"Do you like looking after Lady Penelope, Daniel?" he asked.

So he had actually taken the trouble to learn my name! I could hardly look him in the eye. Still, I managed a smile as I answered. He seemed about to say more, but then turned his attention to a smartly-dressed young man carrying a portfolio, who came up to us, took off his hat and bowed to Lady Penelope.

"This is Mr. Stedman, the architect," said Mr. Hardwick. "Mr. John Stedman, Lady Penelope Marston." While they shook hands and spoke together, I slipped away a few yards and stood waiting.

"You've been told what I have in mind, Mr. Stedman, have you not?" asked Lady Penelope.

"Yes, your ladyship," he answered. "It's greatly to your ladyship's credit, if I may say so. I've brought a few outlines – just initial sketches, you know – to show you. Mr. Hardwick has already seen them and been kind enough to give his approval."

"And this is the site?" she asked, turning to look at the open field a little to our right.

"Yes, your ladyship."

"Daniel, go and open the gate."

I held it open as they walked into the field.

"And I own this?" she asked.

"The conveyance only needs your signature, Penny," said Mr. Hardwick. "The land's all yours down to that little stream at the bottom."

They strolled away and I followed behind. There was much pointing here and there, discussion and display of the contents of the portfolio. After a little it was borne in upon me that what they were talking about was building in that field. Lady Penelope had a great deal to say and was evidently questioning Mr. Stedman closely. His answers apparently satisfied her for as he spoke she nodded agreement more than once.

They spent a considerable time walking round the field and when at last we returned, it was to find the coachman leading the restless, unharnessed horses up and down the road. Lady

Penelope seemed in excellent spirits.

"You'll let me know about the money, won't you?" she said to Mr. Stedman. "I'll let you have whatever you need now by way of an advance. Francis, you say the mayor and the town clerk are dining with us?"

"Yes, at four o'clock, Penny," he replied.

"And Mr. Stedman is coming too?"

"Oh, yes, of course."

On our return, Lady Penelope sent me into the town to buy her half-a-dozen handkerchiefs, two oranges and a bottle of smelling salts. When the party sat down to dinner, I took up my place behind her chair, doing my best to ignore two spaniels which kept sniffing round my ankles.

The mayor, an elderly but handsome man, and the town clerk were plainly delighted to meet Lady Penelope, and listened respectfully as she and Mr. Hardwick talked about her intention to build on the land we had seen that morning. They stayed a good while after dinner and by the time they and Mr. Stedman left I felt desperately hungry. It was late when Lady Penelope was ready to go up to bed, and returning to the kitchen, I was obliged to ask for the meal that no one had offered me. What they gave me was bread and cheese and pickle with a couple of apples (and those they seemed almost to grudge). I ate everything voraciously, but no one offered me any more.

It was no better at breakfast next morning; a poached egg with two thin slices of brawn, and the remains of the porridge-pot without milk or sugar. The tea was milkless, too, as well as tepid. I asked for blacking and brushes, polished my shoes, washed my hands and went upstairs to wait for Lady Penelope. She ate a good breakfast and I could have cleaned up her plate, bacon rinds and all.

Before we set off for home in the early afternoon, I made bold to ask for a snack and was given a chicken carcass to pick over, some stale bread, a little butter and a pot of small beer. My thanks remained unspoken, and I went out to join Hodges and the horses.

85

As we were about to set off, Mr. Hardwick gave me a shilling and wished me luck. He didn't wait for my thanks, but turned away to speak with Lady Penelope. "I'll give instructions to my bank," she said to him as she got in. "Let me know how things go on, won't you?"

"I'll engage the builders straight away, Penny," he answered, kissed her hand and stood back as we drove off.

We were just turning into the high road when Hodges said, "So you stood by yesterday, young Daniel, did you, and watched 'er waste 'er time and money?"

"I couldn't make head nor tail of it, sir," I answered. "Is she going to build herself a new house, to come and live here, or what?"

"Not a bit of it," said he. "You 'aven't 'eard what she means to build, then?"

"No, sir, I've no idea."

"Almshouses, that's what."

"What are almshouses, sir?"

"Why, 'ouses for cadgers and spendthrift sods 'oove never saved a penny and turned beggars in their old age, that's what. She thinks it's Christian charity to build 'ouses for the likes of them to live in when they've grown too old to go on cheating and stealing." He spat in the road.

"You mean she really pays her own money to put up houses for people like that?"

"Yes, that's what I mean. She calls them the deserving poor. I calls 'em dodgers and loafers. When the 'ouses are built, that there mayor and Mr. 'ardwick, they'll pick out all the shiftiest wasters in Guildford to come and live there for nothing."

"But why does she do that?"

"To save 'er soul on Judgement Day, that's why. She's reckoning on going to 'eaven, like. Oh, she's got a kind heart, sure enough, 'as Lady Penelope. But if old Sir James was still alive, 'e'd soon put paid to such foolishness."

After a pause, he added, "She's got a great idea of 'erself as a ministering angel to the poor. And there's those like 'erself who push 'er on, tell 'er she's 'oly saint, like."

"But – er – do all the servants know this, sir?"

"'Course we do. She treats us well, I'll say that for 'er. Plenty to eat and Graydon lets 'em down easy. Goose that lays the golden eggs, that's what she is."

This gave me a good deal to think about. Until then I had thought of my employer as a miraculous wonder, far above any such mean notions as work or occupation. But in this, it seemed, I had been mistaken. Her riches put it in her power to do good, to relieve suffering. This was her work. Knowing her as I did, I could not, like Mr. Hodges, see her as a soft touch for malingerers who imposed upon her. I knew she was discerning and shrewd. Furthermore, in all probability I had myself lived upon a lower level of poverty than ever Mr. Hodges had. I had known what it was to be short of food and clothing, to live in squalor and to fear remedyless disease as a killer. I knew that in the world everywhere there were deserving poor in dire need of relief. If Lady Penelope chose to spend money, intelligence and energy in helping them, then I had even more reason to love and revere her.

As spring advanced into summer, still with sunny days and fine weather, Lady Penelope made frequent expeditions, always attended, of course, by her black page. Most of these I enjoyed, being treated hospitably and given enough to eat; though there were still one or two houses where a black lad seemed to be a sort of freak. However, I became more practised in breaking the ice below stairs and even made friendly acquaintances among the servants from whom I was sorry to part. Almost always, the servants I met were curious to learn about Lady Penelope, about my work for her and what it was like to be black among white folk. On this last I was always ready with a few conventional and unrevealing replies. As a rule, I could not help being struck by the narrow outlook and lack of ambition of most of the servants. They knew their own world and looked no further. On matters of which they had heard little or nothing they were inclined to be touchy. I came to grasp that to them I was the queer one for being bent on advancement; for I had notions of rising above this lowly society and even of coming one day to rub shoulders with people like Francis Hardwick. A black man to reach such a position? Yet all the same I entertained it seriously. If Josh had virtually succeeded, so could I.

We went to towns where Lady Penelope had a finger in all manner of charitable pies. Several of these involved almshouses, but sometimes she also visited prisons, and in these she always required me to attend closely upon her. As a rule I was disgusted and sickened by the vile conditions in these places and by the state of the inmates, some of whom seemed actually dying of one or another untreated disease. In a prison, my vital duty was to guard Lady Penelope from assault, for not infrequently there would be one or two deranged persons at large among the prisoners, with no distinction made by their gaolers between half-wits and the so-called sane.

Nothing, however, deterred Lady Penelope, who remained self-possessed in situations from which, without her, I myself would have thought it no shame to cut and run. In these circumstances it is hardly surprising that my feelings for her remained little short of adulation. I kept the smelling salts handy, but she never asked for them. Often, she would sit down and converse with some demented wretch as though the two of them were on equal terms. Afterwards, when she made her conclusions known to local magistrates or other civic dignitaries, I would stand apart, but it was clear enough that they found themselves unable to regard her as a mere sentimental meddler. I remember once some young fellow attendant upon the mayor, with whom she was deep in conversation, took the opportunity to ask me whether she really was personally acquainted with John Howard. I knew nothing whatever about John Howard, but I told him without hesitation that she certainly was. I never saw anyone treat her disrespectfully: there was that in her manner which put paid to any ideas of that sort.

The servant appointed to teach me to read was none other than Mrs. Beddoes. She made our work positively enjoyable, and I used to look forward to the lessons. She made me compose sentences and then do my best to write them down, and when I complained that this wasn't reading, she would refer me to yesterday's or last week's sentences and ask me to read them out, mistakes and all. After some time I came to realise how much I'd learned – reading and writing too. When I asked her whether this was how reading was taught in schools, she said that it wasn't, but it ought to be. She should have been rewarded, she said, for inventing it.

It amused me to see that during these sultry midsummer weeks, windless, still and anything but conducive to industrious energy, the pace of the whole household slackened; heavier tasks remained tacitly left on one side, while sweeping, dusting, cleaning windows, polishing silver and the like were done with a kind of absent-minded detachment, rather like the diminishing pace of a horse between the shafts when its driver has become too listless to urge it on. As Lady Penelope's personal servant I was, strictly speaking, exempt from this sort of work, but I was canny enough to do what I could to seem busily occupied; cutting fresh flowers for the drawing-room vases, emptying wastepaper baskets (including those I had already emptied), topping up inkwells, brushing the dogs' coats, making sure the shutters and window-blinds worked properly and anything else I could think of. Graydon, I knew, was not likely to drop on me, and anyone else seeing me apparently busy at a job would suppose that another of the servants must have told me to do it.

One close afternoon, while ostensibly checking the bedroom wainscots for mouse-holes, I came upon Lister in bed with a girl who must have slipped in unseen. I was out of the room like lightning and next day felt some slight satisfaction that Lister (who, of course, never breathed a word), evidently felt confident that he had no need to ask me to do the same.

Lady Penelope seemed for the most part unaffected by the weather, carrying on her work as usual. She wrote to a great many people in connection with her philanthropic work, and paid close attention to incoming letters, making jottings for reply in the margins. She read literary reviews in newspapers and almost every week bought books, sending me on foot to Bath with orders for her bookshop; and hot work it was, I may say, tramping there and back in the sunshine. Books weigh heavy; but I was happy to do it.

In the afternoons, she would as a rule sit in a shady part of the lawn and read for a good two hours or longer. She often invited friends to dinner, for she loved conversation, with or without contention. Usually she would require me to attend upon her when she was a guest elsewhere. If, after dinner, the company played whist or backgammon, she would sometimes dismiss me below stairs, or again, when the fancy took her, would tell me to stand behind her and watch the game.

Whist I could never understand, but after a time I acquired a fair grasp of backgammon. I always took the greatest care never to presume upon my place. I was not to be drawn into conversation. Sometimes I was offered a glass of wine, but always I declined it.

"Poor lad," she once said to her hostess, "he can't be expected to sit like a graven image with no diversion all the evening. Besides," she added smilingly, "he's my luck. Black people always bring luck with them, don't you know?"

I know – I know for certain – that no one ever suspected her, as a young widow, of impropriety, for she was not only well-liked but greatly respected, partly for her warm and friendly personality, but also for her benevolence to the poor and needy of the neighbourhood.

Now that I had been in her service for several months and (as I hoped) had shown myself undeterred by any number of demands, Lady Penelope took to giving me, now and then, half a day's holiday, during which I was free to spend my time as I pleased. What was more, she would sometimes give me as much as a shilling to put in my pocket; and none of the other servants to know of it, of course. On these days I would change my uniform for rough clothes and set out to stroll in the open country. I kept to the roads and paths, and if I happened to meet a farm labourer or the like I would speak, pass the time of day and explain that I was in the service of Lady Penelope Marston, and enjoying half a day off. Once these people were satisfied that I was not up to mischief, they usually became friendly enough, and sometimes asked me to lend them a hand with their work. I made several acquaintances, and did my best to learn a few skills, such as hedging and ditching, or using a scythe.

People used to laugh at my clumsiness, but no one seemed to take against me for my colour, and I was always careful not to let anyone guess that I was carrying more than a penny or two. I think that one reason why they were friendly was that they knew I was in the personal employ of Lady Penelope. Quite a few locals had good reason to feel well disposed towards her.

One fine evening in early autumn, I was walking home through Clepton St. Peter. As I drew near the village tavern I was surprised to see three black people, two young men and a still younger girl, sitting on the grass verge beside the road. Their clothes were dirty and they themselves looked dismal and impoverished; a sight to make anyone feel pity.

I sat down on the grass beside them. I was about to speak when a cart passed by, driven by a farmhand with whom I was acquainted. He gave me a nod.

"'Ullo, Darkie. 'Ow yer gett'n on, then?"

"All right, Bob," I answered. "'Ow's yerself?"

"All right, Darkie."

This concluded the conventional courtesies and on he went. I turned to the strangers.

"Nice to see you," I said. "How d'you do. 'Don't see many black people round here, more's the pity."

They answered me not a word, and none of them looked at me.

"Are you staying round here?" I asked.

One of the black lads raised his head and muttered, "We b'long Mr. Grench."

"I see," I replied. "And where's he? You're waiting for him, are you?"

The other boy jerked a thumb at the tavern behind us.

"Mr. Grench eat. We wait."

"Better him not see you talkin' us," said the first lad.

"Why ever not?" I asked. There was no answer, and I went on, "Why shouldn't I talk to you? Do you mean he'd try to stop me?"

"Better you go," whispered the girl. "No good he see you. Beat you, maybe."

"Beat me?" said I. "Why the hell should he beat me? Why shouldn't I talk to you?"

None of them replied. I had a sudden gleam of inspiration.

"You mean he's a white man and you're his servants?"

"We'se slaves," said the girl. "Mr. Grench tell us no talk anyone."

At this moment a burly, rough-looking man − a white man − came out of the tavern door. I stood up and faced him. He looked hostile and angry.

"You bloody nigger!" he shouted at me. "You let my slaves alone and get your black arse out of here, d'you see? Go on, bugger off!"

"I'll see you flat on your white arse first," I replied.

At this he began to rage like a madman, waving his arms and cursing and swearing. "I'll beat the hell out of you, you bastard nigger!" he shouted. Clenching his fists, he strode forward. I stood where I was and he stopped, face to face with me.

"You heard me!" he yelled. "Are you going to f- off or not?"

People were coming out of the tavern and others out of their cottage doors. A small crowd gathered. Mr. Randall, our village blacksmith, laid a hand on Grench's wrist.

"Listen, Mister," he said. "That young fellow works for Lady Penelope Marston. You just let him alone now, and be on your way. We don't want no trouble round here."

Grench made no reply, but aimed a blow at me. By now I had realised, of course, that he was the next thing to drunk. His punch was meant to hit me in the face. I stopped it with an open hand and hit him on the jaw as hard as I could. At the same moment Mr. Randall hit him in the stomach and he went down, winded and gasping. The three black youngsters had stood up and drawn

92

away into the road.

Grench got unsteadily to his feet. He was evidently not beat yet. It was at this moment that I heard a light, quick clopping of hooves, and looking behind me, saw Lady Penelope's pony and trap approaching. Hodges was driving and Lady Penelope, dressed for an occasion and wearing a light cloak, was seated behind him. At sight of the villagers Hodges pulled up.

I went quickly round behind the trap and opened the door.

"If you please, your ladyship," I said, pointing to Grench, "that man has attempted to attack me. He says that those young black people are his slaves and that Mr. Randall and myself are to let them alone."

A silence fell. I gave Lady Penelope my hand and helped her down. Without the least hesitation she walked up to Grench and looked him in the face.

"Is that correct?" she asked, in a calm, level voice. "Are you saying that those young black people are slaves? That they are your slaves?"

Grench, though obviously disconcerted, pulled himself together.

"Yes. Yes – er – ma'am," he said. "They're my lawful property. I'm going to take them away with me, now this minute. 'Don't want no trouble."

Lady Penelope answered him not a word. She turned and walked over to the black youngsters, who cowered before her, whimpering, and smiling, she took one of the lads by the hand.

"You needn't be in the least afraid of me," she said. "Now listen, all three of you. There are no slaves in England. That is the law. You are not slaves and that man cannot take you away with him against your own wishes. If you want to leave him, I will look after you myself. Now calm yourselves and answer me. Do you want to leave that man or do you not?"

The girl burst into tears. "Oh, lady," she sobbed. "We want go 'way, but we 'fraid he beat us."

"No, he won't," said she, and turned to Hodges, who all this time had been holding the pony's head.

"Hodges, take these young people back with you now. Tell Mrs. Beddoes I want her to let them wash and to give them a meal. Then let them sleep in the hay loft."

She turned to Randall. "Mr. Randall, will you be so good as to see them into the trap, and make sure that that man lets them alone?"

She turned to me. "And you, Daniel," she said, "Go at once, explain to Dr. Vernon what has happened and tell him that I will be with him and Mrs. Vernon quite soon."

With that she went into the tavern and shut the door behind her. I ran at once on my errand. When I returned the crowd had dispersed and there was no sign either of Lady Penelope or of Grench.

Mr. Ward, the innkeeper, came out and told me that Lady Penelope had set off to walk home, having firmly declined his offer to put his horse to and drive her himself. ("But she wouldn' 'ave it no ways.") I felt shocked to hear this and ran after her. However, I didn't succeed in overtaking her, and got home to find her supervising Mrs. Beddoes in looking after the young blacks.

When she had seen them fed and taken in charge by Hodges, she told him to tell one of the stable boys to turn to and drive her to Dr. Vernon's. As for myself, she said that we would talk next day.

In the morning I was up and dressed earlier than usual, but rather to my surprise on going into the yard, I met Hodges coming out of the stable door. Before I could speak he remarked sourly, "And what the devil you up to, Darkie, eh?"

"I was wondering, Mr. Hodges, about the – er – the people that Lady Penelope said were to be lodged in the hayloft."

"Oh - the people, huh – you was wonderin', was yer? Did she tell yer to come and ask me about them?"

"No, Mr. Hodges; she's not up yet, as far as I know. But last night she told me she wanted to talk to me about them first thing this morning, so I thought before I saw her I'd better find out what's what."

"What's what, eh? 'E'd be a good 'un as knowed that."

I waited silently while he scratched his neck.

94

"Well, I reckon they're animals, just about. Can't talk any sense, can't understand what they 'ears no more'n a dog. Tried to run away but I stopped 'en'. Anyways, they're up there now, you can tell 'er."

"Have they had anything to eat?"

"Not since last night they 'aven't."

"D'you reckon I'd best have a look at them before I see Lady Penelope?"

"Do as you like, boy." And he turned away with an air of irritated indifference.

Going into the stable, I saw at once why they hadn't run away. Hodges had taken down the ladder that usually led up to the hayloft and left it lying on the cobbles. With some difficulty I put it back – it was heavy – and climbed up.

In the loft there was no one to be seen and not a sound to be heard. I tried calling out in a friendly voice, but as this got no answer I had to search. They had hidden as best they could, but after looking up and down for a while I found the girl. I made no attempt to drag her out, but simply sat down nearby.

"Listen," I said, raising my voice so that they could all hear, "I'm the black lad you saw last night outside the tavern. I'm a servant of the kind lady who took you away from Mr. Grench and had you brought here. She's going to look after you now. She's sent Mr. Grench away and he's never coming back; never. She wants you to come down with me now and eat some food. Will you do that?"

She didn't answer, and neither did the boys. I tried again two or three times, but could get no reply at all. Finally I called out "I'm going away now, but I'll come back later. Try to understand that the lady's your friend and so am I."

With that I went down the ladder, took it down and returned indoors.

Lady Penelope was finishing breakfast. The door was standing open so I tapped and went in.

She smiled. "Good morning, Daniel. I can see you've been up in the hayloft. Are the young black people all right? Have you spoken to them at all?"

"They're still up there, my lady, but I'm afraid I couldn't get them to talk to me nohow. They seem to be terrified of everything and everybody. 'Won't speak; 'won't move.'"

She drank her coffee and paused, frowning.

"Do you think they understood you?"

"Yes, my lady, I'm sure they did, but I reckon they're more or less frit out of their minds."

"Ring the bell."

I did so and she stood up and went out of the room, gesturing to me to follow her into the garden as Lister came in to clear away. I placed a cushion for her on the seat under the silver birches.

"Well, Daniel," she said, "we obviously can't send them away while they're in that state. It looks as though getting across to them's going to be a long and trying job, wouldn't you say?"

"Yes, my lady, I would."

"Well, this is what I want done. Obviously you're the best person to gain their confidence because you're black. So, for the time being, you're to stop being my page and concentrate on getting them to see sense. Do you think you can do it?"

"Well, my lady, from what I've seen this morning, I honestly can't tell, but I'll do my best."

"Twenty-four hours a day?"

"Certainly, my lady, if you wish."

"Get some food for them from Mrs. Beddoes, and come and see me again this evening. If you need money, ask Mr. Graydon."

As I bowed and walked back to the house, she called after me, "And Daniel, don't hurt anybody and don't get hurt yourself."

I explained matters to Mrs. Beddoes, who cooked my breakfast and then gave me three or four generous hunks of bread and cheese and half a dozen apples. "Just you sit tight, Dan'l," she said. "They've got to eat some time. I must say it's a right old job Lady P.'s given you, but I reckon patience is the answer, same as

96

a dog or a cat, like."

I returned to the loft, piled up some hay and lay down.

"I'm the same fellow," I called out, "the lady's black servant. I've brought you some food, but if you want it you'll have to come here and talk to me. Just understand that I'm a friend. I'm going to bide here until you come."

So I bided. Yes, I bided all right, until the tedium seemed interminable. As I couldn't see the sun or even any shadows, I had no way of keeping count of the time. I could hear the stable lads below talking to each other and the horses stamping and blowing as they were fed and groomed. I heard two of them led out, but the lads didn't come back and virtual silence fell, except for the scuttering of mice and now and then the sharp caw of a jackdaw on the roof. At last I fell into an uneasy doze, troubled by the biting of ticks attracted, I suppose, to the warmth of my body.

After a long time I became aware of low voices not far from me. My companions – if that is what they were – were whispering to one another, but in their own lingo and not a word could I understand. The intonation, however, was more-or-less plain, redolent of exhaustion and desperation. Questions and answers were alike faint; but not the smell of ordure.

Still I waited without moving; but I had to breathe and somehow I felt that even this was being listened to and weighed in the balance.

Suddenly there was a sharp movement and one of the boys appeared, dashed up to me, grabbed a handful of bread and cheese and was gone.

I should have thought of that. I bundled the rest of the food together and enclosed it between my legs. After a little while the girl crawled out of the hay, trembling and weeping. Her words bubbled out through slobbering lips.

"No beat us, master. Pliss no beat."

"I no beat you," I answered. "No one beat you any more, ever. I want you come and eat food. Look, food here."

At this, all three of them came hesitantly towards me. As

though feeding half-tamed birds, I held out bread and cheese on the palms of my hands, to be snatched and swallowed.

At length, when all the bread and cheese was gone, not a core of the apples remained and all the water in my flask had been drunk, they looked at one another as though trying to decide whether to stay or go. Now that they were more-or-less close beside me, I could see that they were little more than children, and scrawny children at that, with thin arms and spindly legs. The girl, I thought, was about fourteen or fifteen.

I smiled at one of the boys and after a moment he returned my smile uncertainly. I said, "You know now, Mr. Grench gone away, him finish, you belong to the white lady, same as me."

They all three nodded and remained still as I stroked them, one by one, on the shoulders. "No one going to hurt you," I said, and then asked, "Where you come from? What country?"

"Not know," answered one of the boys.

"Where were you before you belong Mr. Grench?"

"Home," the other boy said. "White men come, take us away. We walk long way, go 'cross water, plenty white men, give us to Mr. Grench."

"He beat us," said the girl. Then they all began talking together in their own language which, it seemed to me as I listened, could only be some African tribal patois.

"Where you going yesterday, with Mr. Grench?" I asked.

"Not know."

They fell silent and I did so too. Suddenly one of the boys said, "Fah-dah, Fah-dah."

"What's Fah-dah?" I asked.

He put a hand on the girl's arm. "This Fah-dah."

I smiled at her – she was trembling, her eyes glistening with tears – and said, "Fahdah. Very good. The lady happy you come live with us. She tell me look after you, make you happy."

I thought she would be rather nice-looking, if only she was cleaned up and not so miserable.

The other lad began speaking once more in their language, pouring out a stream of frenzied talk, at moments tossing his head and clapping his hands as though for emphasis. As he continued Fahdah still wept, burying her head in her hands. When at length the outburst came to a stop, the first boy said to me, "You know what he say?"

"No," I replied.

"He say Mr. Grench treat her bad bad."

"What do you mean?"

To this he answered with a sequence of gestures which made his meaning unmistakably clear, while the wretched girl rocked herself to and fro, scarcely able to draw her breath for sobbing.

"She think this very bad bad," said the boy. "Think maybe you beat her. You want beat her?"

"No!" I shouted. "All bad finish now. You good all time now. Lady make you happy."

"You know," continued the boy, "you know long time off, we live in black people place, all black people, then bad bad come, white men come."

"Why you tell me this about Fahdah?"

"I tell you, maybe you say you no beat her. Then she no be afraid more."

"I see," I said. "Fahdah, you no bad. Here you good. No one hurt you. White lady say you good. You belong her now, like me."

Our jumbled talk ran on, but I gained almost nothing from it, except that they were brothers and sister. All the same, I went on trying to gain their confidence and, if I could, to make them feel more secure.

It seemed to me that my first task was to get them to come down from the hayloft and into the stable. After a long time, the elder boy ventured to follow me down the ladder; but no sooner had he reached the stable floor than he insisted on going up again to the loft. I restrained my impatience as best I could; and my restraint paid off, for it became plain that he had gone back to induce the other two to join him. After much talk in their own tongue, they all came down very hesitantly and stood side by side, looking at me and plainly wondering what I was going to require of them next.

It was obvious that in spite of Lady Penelope's instructions, they had not washed the previous evening. The relatively clear light of midday in the stable showed them covered in grime. To my surprise they followed me out into the yard and assembled round the pump. I stripped, went under the pump, soused myself thoroughly from head to foot and signed to the older boy to do the same. He took a good deal of coaxing but finally allowed me to help him off with his horrible rags and keep still while I drenched him. His brother followed his example and when I had thrown their clothes on the midden, both seemed content to sit in the sun to dry off.

Poor Fahdah resisted all my gentlest efforts to persuade her to undress, until finally I left her to her brothers and took a turn round the stable block, by way of implying that I was ready to indulge her modest scruples, if indeed they - and not fear - were really the reason for her reluctance.

As I was returning I saw the boys stripping off her wet clothes and settling her in the sun. Her back was turned towards me and it was now that I underwent a kind of momentary hallucination, inasmuch as in all honesty I thought I was looking at the surface of the moon. The illusion was gone in an instant. What were really confronting me were Fahdah's shoulders, back and buttocks. All were covered with great weals, the flesh barely resembling a human body. With a horrible shock I realised that this could only be the result of a brutality almost past belief. Between the ridges ran deep grooves, lined in places with dried blood. My head swam; why was the girl not dead?

She lay down in the sun while her brothers stood beside her to drive off the flies. As I came up to them I realised that I was trembling. I laid a hand on the elder boy's shoulder and pointed down at her.

"Mr. Grench, he do this to her?"

100

"Mr. Grench, he want fuck Fahdah. She say no and he beat her."

"All the time?"

"Many, many time. Stop only he no want her die."

My horror and revulsion were slightly mitigated by an inkling that the two boys were beginning to believe that they had nothing to fear from me and that I wanted only to help them. They might not understand all I said, but the mere sound of a kindly voice was no doubt reassuring. Relying on this, I took a chance, gestured to them to stay where they were, went back into the stables and helped myself to some swaddling clothes and a couple of horse blankets. These provided enough clothing for the time being, and all three seemed relaxed and calm. So I took another chance, went into the kitchen and begged Mrs. Beddoes for enough cold meat, cheese and bread for their second meal of the day. She was tickled.

"Gettin' 'em up together then, Dan'l, are you?" she asked.

"I hope so," I replied, "but it's no wonder they're all on the jump; and the wretched girl's as good as mad." Thereupon I proceeded to tell her about Mr. Grench and Fahdah's back. As I had expected, she was both horrified and indignant.

"You're goin' t'ave a bit of a job with 'er, then," she said. "Wait on, young Dan'l; I'll find 'em a drop of soup out of the stockpot."

By the time they had finished their meal, the boys were showing something faintly resembling human good spirits, and even Fahdah was at least composed and seemed to have ceased, for the time being, to look about her for the next infliction of ill-treatment. We were all sitting peacefully together when Hodges came into the yard. As he paused, looking askance at us, I went up to him.

"Mr. Hodges, sir, I've had a hell of a job to get them to come out of the hayloft and wash under the pump. They're warming to me a bit now, I think. I'd like you to come and have a look at the girl's back."

Despite himself, Hodges's reaction was not unlike my own.

"Christ almighty!" he said. "Who done that, then?"

101

"Their previous owner, the man you saw last night outside the pub. And I'll tell you why he did it, if you like."

As I told him, he hit his lip and clenched his fist. I followed up the advantage.

"Mr. Hodges, I'm trying to do what Lady Penelope wishes. I daren't leave them alone for the present; they might very well try to run away again. I know it's asking a lot, but could you please find Lady Penelope and ask her to come and see them?"

I kept silent while he demurred and then talked himself round. "Not goin' t'expect me to run up and down all day for 'en, are yer?"

"Oh, no, Mr. Hodges, sir. Believe me, it's only just this once."

As it happened Lady Penelope was not far to seek. She had evidently been reading on the lawn, and came out to us soon after Hodges had returned. I stood up and after a moment my three waifs followed my example.

"Well, Daniel," she asked, "How are you getting on?"

"It's early to say, my lady," I replied, "but I'm daring to hope they're beginning to trust me a little. They've had a very bad time, though, at the hands of that evil man you sent away yesterday evening."

As she looked at Fahdah's back, she closed her eyes and turned her head away. Then, as she bent down to embrace her, the poor girl started up and would have run away if I had not restrained her. Lady Penelope had to content herself with kissing each of the boys.

"Have you thought what you're going to do about them tonight, Daniel?" she asked.

"Well, my lady," I replied, "do you think we could make over one of the smaller rooms at the back of the stables for them to sleep in? And I'd like to sleep there with them, if you approve."

"Yes, Daniel," she said. "I think that's an excellent notion. You'll need some mattresses, and blankets too. I'll tell Graydon to start Lister and Hayward on getting them down now. Have you any other ideas?"

"Well, your ladyship," I answered, "I think they ought to be seen by an apothecary, especially the girl. She's in a pretty bad way, if I'm any judge."

"I'll get Dexter to come tomorrow morning. I'll tell Mrs. Beddoes about feeding them, too. Have you talked to her?"

"Oh, yes, your ladyship. She's been very helpful, thank you."

"Good. But what about clothes?"

"Well, your ladyship, I've thrown away the clothes they were wearing. That was the only thing to do. They may have been infested; I didn't look. Would it be possible to get them some more tomorrow?"

"Yes, of course. Can you see to that yourself?"

I had no idea how I was going to see to it, but I said, "Certainly, your ladyship. Shall I ask Mr. Hodges to come and see you now?"

"Oh, perhaps you can tell him what I want, can you?"

"Well, begging your pardon, my lady, but I think it might be better coming from you. I – er – well, I'm not sure that Mr. Hodges has quite – er – quite come round to them yet."

She laughed. "You mean he doesn't fancy hearing my orders from you?"

"Well, your ladyship, I'm anxious to keep on the right side of the other servants insofar as I can."

"Well, you stay here with your new friends, and I'll go and get hold of him. Oh, there's one of the stable boys. Boynton, tell Mr. Hodges I want to see him here."

I felt guardedly pleased with my first day in the new job. Hodges was still surly, although he clearly agreed that Fahdah was in need of help. The two boys actually came into the kitchen for their supper, although they were tongue-tied in the face of Mrs. Beddoes's kindly banter. But nothing could persuade Fahdah through the door, and finally I took her supper out to her myself, and more-or-less stood over her while she ate it.

Our sleeping quarters had been swept clean and tidied up, and I lay down contentedly on my mattress. I could hear a nightingale singing among the thick trees beyond the stables.

However, I had not hitherto understood how deeply Fahdah had been injured. Twice during the night she woke screaming and we could only get her to lie down again with her brother's arm round her. Even so, she babbled continually in her own tongue, and I was driven to wonder whether she ever slept soundly at all.

"Is she always like this?" I asked the boys.

"Yer. She 'fraid Mr. Grench come while she sleep."

In the morning, both the boys went into the kitchen for their breakfast, and I brought Fahdah's out to her in the yard. Dexter, the apothecary, arrived soon afterwards, thoroughly examined both boys and made up a liniment for their wrists and ankles, which had been painfully inflamed by Grench's chains. Apart from this, he said, he could find little the matter with them that could not be put right by plenty of good food, exercise and sleep. He thought that perhaps some light work might be helpful, by way of building up their morale and self-esteem.

When he came to look at Fahdah (whom Lady Penelope persuaded to undress) he was as deeply shocked as we all were. Having very gently felt her back, he said that no bones were broken, although her muscles were terribly damaged. Her kidneys, too, he thought, were probably affected, but only time could put this right. Told about her troubled sleep, he said that it was only to be expected and made up a soporific medicine, emphasising that the dose at bedtime must on no account be exceeded.

"She's in a bad state, your ladyship," he said. "I'll call again in a week's time to see how she's getting on. Meanwhile, she ought not to do anything at all strenuous or demanding."

After he had gone, Lady Penelope said to me, "I'll keep Fahdah with me today, Daniel. Take the boys into the garden and see whether Bennett has any little jobs they can usefully do."

"Certainly, my lady. But first of all, if you agree, I'll see whether Mr. Hodges can help me to find some clothes for them."

I found Hodges in the stables. "What yer after now, Darkie?" he asked. "Want something else for yer black riffraff, I suppose,

104

do yer?"

"They won't be riffraff by the time I'm through with them, Mr. Hodges. Lady Penelope wants me to put them on light work in the garden. Come to that, I can put them on anything you want done here. I've thrown away the clothes they had on when they came here, and about time too. I was wondering whether you might possibly have any old stuff they could wear. Just rough stuff, of course; only the boys. Mr. Dexter thinks the girl's in a bad way and Lady Penelope says she'll look after her for the present."

To my surprise, Hodges was quite forthcoming.

"Well, if they're going to do some honest work, that's different. I dare say there might be some old shirts and breeches what were going to the rag-and-bone man. I'll 'ave a look."

I wondered whether even the rag-and-bone man would want the things he came up with, but the two boys made no objection when I said they were to put them on. At least they were reasonably clean and fitted after a fashion.

"Well," said Hodges, looking them over with a semblance of approval, "now they can clean out the stables. The horses can be turned out into the paddock while they get on with it. There's the brooms, over there."

Although they had plainly never seen a broom in their lives, the boys were willing enough. I turned to and worked with them, and after an hour we had got on pretty well. They were ready enough to work, provided I was with them and they knew exactly what they were expected to do. Their only handicap was their ignorance of English, which made communication difficult. When we went in to the kitchen for midday dinner I told this to Lady Penelope, who said that I should give them some instruction every day. Fahdah she had put to bed in a room adjoining her own, and had apparently sat beside her all the morning, comforting her and answering her questions about what she had to expect in her new home. The great thing, said Lady Penelope, was that she now had a motive for recovering and taking a place in the household. From what little Fahdah had been able to tell, Lady Penelope thought that she and her brothers had probably been taken from the Bight of Biafra to be sold, but she had not pressed her to tell more, since the memories were so distressing to her.

In the afternoon the boys and I, instructed by Mr. Bennett, the head gardener, did some jobs in the garden, cooling off by plunging into the pool at the bottom of the big meadow. Then, as we sat in the sun, I did my best to help them to memorise the words for various familiar objects – gate, pump, stones, trees, hedge and so on. I turned it into a sort of game by making a "centre" of pebbles, from which each boy could draw one every time he remembered a word correctly. They made it into a competition and after half an hour the younger boy roared with laughter on finding that he had more pebbles than his brother, who took it in tolerably good part. They would have continued longer, but I thought it best not to overtax them and called a halt with a promise to do more tomorrow.

During the following weeks they made quite good progress in adapting to civilised ways, although there were features which they grasped only with difficulty and after some time. Chief of these was the ownership of private property. As far as I could make out, they had never had a notion of this. If they needed something for their work – an axe, say, or a knife or a gimlet – they would help themselves without asking anyone and as often as not forget to return it. This failing – though no failing in their eyes – applied not only to needful objects of utility, but also to more-or-less anything which took their fancy. Once, the whole household was in a great taking over the disappearance of a gold snuffbox, formerly a cherished possession of Sir James Marston, which had its place, together with a few other ornaments, on an occasional table in the drawing-room. It was some time before it was traced to one of the African lads. He had had no idea of appropriating it permanently for himself; he had pocketed it simply because it had taken his fancy. As soon as he was asked about it he readily restored it, with no sense of guilt and supposing that it must be needed for some sort of use elsewhere. As the boys had no possessions of their own, it was difficult to inculcate any idea of "mine not yours", and I'm not at all sure that

106

they ever did grasp it entirely.

The servants treated them with detachment, largely on account of their ignorance of English. They all knew, of course, that they were protégés of Lady Penelope and on this account stopped short of showing impatience or irritation. Like most working-class people, however, they didn't care for "foreigners", and none of them – not even Mrs. Beddoes – showed any attempt to make friends with them. Surprisingly, the exception was Hodges, who came round to them by slow degrees once they had convinced him that they could work hard. (I never put them on any work in the house.) As they became more practised and proficient, he became positively avuncular and was even, now and then, not above a few scant words of praise. Meanwhile Fahdah, with Lady Penelope's comfort and daily reassurance, made good progress, lost much of her obsessive fear and was beginning to feel more secure. Her improvement decided Lady Penelope to fulfil an engagement she had made some months before to pay a two-day visit to Cirencester, leaving Hodges in charge of the lads and Mrs. Beddoes to look after Fahdah.

It was Hodges, soon after our return, who put forward the notion that the lads and I might take on some local jobs beyond home ground and get paid for them. He had now, he said, got enough confidence in our work to make the suggestion. Lady Penelope approved of the idea, and a day or two later we found ourselves repairing fences for a farmer in the next village. This turned out a success, but the lads, who had never had any money in their lives, at first had no idea how to make use of their earnings. There was not, in truth, much that they needed; but at least they soon learned how to buy sweets at the village shop. I kept their money for them and doled it out on request. Later in the year they found that they had enough to buy clasp knives, and Hodges made sure that they understood that this was a just reward of honest toil.

I have nothing but happy recollections of the latter months of that year. The summer weather remained as fine as any of us could remember. Everything – so it seems in memory – went well for us, everybody, from Lady Penelope down to Jack, the backhouse boy. It was in September, as I recall, that two gentlemen came down from London to inform Lady Penelope that certain of her investments had proved highly profitable and had gained for her an unexpectedly large capital sum. Typically, her first step was to raise the wages of everyone in the household, while her next was to enlarge and improve the village school. It was at about this time that Lister left us, to take over from his father their small family business. His replacement, a young man named Paul Chester, was one of the most likeable and good-humoured people that I have ever known. We became friends and his company added a great deal to my contentment. Throughout these months – as was to be expected – Fahdah and her brothers became reasonably fluent in English and consequently much happier in their daily lives. Paul Chester was friendly towards them as though it had never occurred to him to be anything else.

One morning in February of the following year, I had just placed a bunch of snowdrops and aconites on Lady Penelope's desk when she came into the room and admired them as she sat down. Then, after a pause and with a kind of hesitation – almost uncertainty – she said, "Daniel, you've served me very well for a long time and worked hard. I shall always remember it." She broke off, fumbled with a drawer and took out, for no apparent purpose, a box of writing paper.

I hardly knew what to reply, but after a few moments I said, "That's very kind of you, your ladyship. I've been only too happy in your service."

"A page," she went on, "a page is – is a boy, Daniel. I'm sure no one can have been a better pageboy than you. But – but you're no longer a boy. You're a young man and tall for your age." She smiled. "Whatever that is."

I caught her drift now and waited in silence.

"I can't tell you how sorry I am to say this, Daniel, but I can't employ you as a page any longer. You see, you're well past the usual age and as tall as quite a lot of grown men. It wouldn't be – well, it wouldn't be fitting." She reached forward and took my

108

hand. "I'm very sorry."

"So – so this job's at an end, your ladyship?" There was a catch in my voice.

She bit her lip and nodded, looking down at the box of writing paper.

"Daniel, you don't have to leave the household if you don't want to. You can certainly continue in employment here. I'm not sure in what capacity, but I expect we could make an arrangement."

"You're very kind, your ladyship. May I think about it for a little while and tell you later?"

"Of course." She stood up, and went across to the window, looking out at the rain. "Now tell Fahdah to come here."

I went out, told Fahdah and then took a turn up the wet gravel slope, to collect my thoughts. The fact was – and at first I felt rather ashamed of it – that I would be glad not to continue as a page. It hadn't felt right for some time, but I hadn't recognised, hadn't admitted to myself, that this was so. What Lady Penelope had said was perfectly correct. I wasn't a boy now; I was a tall young man, and if I continued attendant on a good-looking widow like Lady Penelope, people would be bound to think nasty things. She'd avoided saying this, but it was the truth, nevertheless.

The next question was, did I want to remain in the household? The fact of the matter was that I didn't. I had always nursed the aspiration that one day, when I was old enough, I would enter upon the world and make money, would come to live on equal terms with white people. England offered a far likelier society for this than America, which offered nothing at all. So when was I going to start?

When coincidences occur, those to whom they happen often entertain a superstitious idea that they are somehow "meant"; that they are attributable to Providence or to some vaguely imagined transcendent power. Opportunities not infrequently seem to follow from coincidences. On the whole, people feel favourably about them. They are generally thought of as lucky rather than unlucky.

I left my thoughts in abeyance and said nothing to anyone – not even to Paul Chester – about what Lady Penelope had said.

It so happened that on the following day I was required to go to Bristol (driven by one of the stable-boys) to fulfil a number of commissions; in particular, to give an order to the wine merchants who had been favoured by Sir James and retained ever since.

I formed another purpose, one that I kept to myself. The trip seemed to offer an opportunity to find a profitable job – one that would constitute the beginning of my new, independent life. It occurred to me to confide in Lady Penelope, but upon consideration I decided to leave this until I had actually achieved what I was after.

Having finished what I had been told to do, and arranged with Boynton to meet him in the late afternoon for the return journey, I set off on my search. My idea was to offer my services to anyone who was ready to take me on. After four hours I found myself facing total disappointment. Butchers I had tried, fruit merchants, grocers, haberdashers, builders, corn chandlers, dealers in exports and three or four agents for rich, capitalist employers. None was ready to employ me at more than a starvation wage. I even approached a firm of moneylenders but they, naturally enough, wouldn't begin to consider me. Ingenuous as I was, it had not occurred to me to think about what I had to offer. I had no experience and no trained skill or vocation. The only reference I could provide was that of Lady Penelope Marston –whatever her social standing, no woman of business. I had no capital to contribute. Above all – no one said this but I could infer it – I was black. "Why don't you go to sea?" said one man. "That's a job you could be sure of getting and it offers opportunities."

It was a severe blow. I could not even make a start, so it seemed. For the time being I would have to remain with Lady Penelope. No doubt she would be glad to find me a situation, but in all probability it would only be in service, and it was this way of life from which I wanted to sever myself.

I was drinking a disconsolate pint in the same tavern to which I had once gone with Mr. Miles, when I felt a hand on my shoulder and, turning, found myself face to face with a stranger, a rough-looking but plainly self-confident man, aged perhaps forty-five. For all his coarse features he was smartly, even expensively dressed. Whatever his purpose with me, it was plainly not to beg.

"I'd like to talk to you," said this personage. "Kindly do me the honour of buying you a drink."

It so happened that the barmaid was standing more-or-less opposite, and before I could reply he had ordered two double whiskies, one of which he handed to me.

"We'll go over here," he said, and led the way to an empty table by the further wall. I found myself following him, and sat down.

"My name's Hawkshot," he said. "Captain Hawkshot, if you like. I don't know whether you're in work at present or not, but if you'll work for me for the next few months, when the job's done I'll pay you —" and he named a sum which took my breath away; a sum, in fact, which I could not credit. But he repeated it and added, "I'll write that down and sign it, if you like."

To me there seemed only one possible explanation.

"Is it criminal?" I asked. "Illegal?"

"It is entirely legal," he replied, "though it's certainly hard work. I shall be glad to take you on."

"In this country or abroad?"

"It's a commercial voyage," he said. "My ship's going to West Africa for slaves, then across to Jamaica to sell them and then back here. That's the full extent of the voyage, for which I'll pay you."

"How long will it take?" I asked.

"It might be twelve months or it might be more. One reason why you'd be useful to me is that you're black. You'd have a natural advantage in dealing with the slaves."

As I paused, he went on, "I already know something about you. I recognised you when you came in, but if you hadn't, I would have come over to Clepton to talk to you."

Rather startled, I asked, "Why, what do you know about me?"

"I know you've worked hard for some time as a personal servant to Lady Penelope Marston and apparently earned her approval. I happen to be acquainted with her coachman, Hodges, and he's told me enough about you to make me think you'd probably suit me."

At this time I knew nothing whatever about the African slave trade for, as I have recounted, Reynolds seldom or never bought slaves straight off the ships. He could afford acclimatised slaves. Even the field hands on his estate were mostly American-born, as I was myself. Hawkshot's offer of this very large – indeed, capital - sum, enough to set me up in business, was a true coincidence, being made to me at the very moment when my present job had come to an end. It seemed providential.

"This offer you're making," I said, temporising. "It's a large sum."

"Well, as I say, it's hard work," answered Hawkshot. "I'm not pretending it isn't. It's work that doesn't suit everybody. I pay well to attract capable people. What I'm offering you is the rate for the job."

As I still deliberated, he said, "Well, do you want it or not?"

"How soon would you want me?"

"We're sailing on Friday. I should want you aboard by Thursday afternoon at the latest."

"I'll take it." We shook hands, and he told me where to find the ship.

Scarcely able to believe what had happened, I made my way through the streets to rejoin Boynton, who had been waiting an hour and more.

It can only have been destined, I thought, as we left Bristol and took the Bath road. Some guiding power intended me to meet Hawkshot in that tavern this evening. It was meant, it was meant to be.

* * *

I need not say much about my parting from Lady Penelope and her household. Before I left, she spoke to me kindly, thanking me

112

for my help and hard work. When she asked about my plans, I simply told her that I was sailing abroad. As we parted, she gave me two guineas.

Hodges asked me whether Captain Hawkshot had spoken to me. I told him he had, and that I was considering what he had offered me. Hodges replied, "Well, if yer find yer don't care for it, I dare say 'er ladyship would employ you back 'ere." I thanked him for the good opinion of me that he had given to Captain Hawkshot, to which he replied, "Well 's'pose y'aven't bin so bad, for a darkie."

Fahdah and her brothers were waiting for me in the stable-yard. The dear girl had composed and memorised a little speech of farewell. "Dear Daniel, I want you have very good luck. I always remembering you. I hope one day you come back see us again."

I would have liked to take her in my arms, but remembered just in time that she didn't really care for embraces, with good reason. She didn't like anything pressing on her back. So I kissed her palm-pink hands and pressed them against my cheeks for a moment.

The only other servants to say more than goodbye to me were Mrs. Beddoes and Paul Chester. Paul was the only person I had told about what I was going to do. "Be careful, Daniel," he said. "I'm afraid it may be dangerous."

I told Paul how sorry I was to part from him, but that when I returned, I would come back to Clepton before going anywhere else. He wished me luck.

And so we parted and Boynton drove me back to Bristol.

* * *

After a two-way stroll down the harbour-side, I found Captain Hawshot's ship moored exactly where he had told me it would be. I had failed to notice it and walked past, for it did not in the least resemble the mental picture that I had formed. It looked as though it had had a hard life. From stem to stern it was battered and badly needed repainting. Although it was seaworthy and plainly capable of withstanding rough conditions, a smart appearance was clearly not something upon which the Captain cared to spend money. The only bit of new paintwork was the name, *Frisky Shark*, conspicuous on the bow.

I had spent a minute or two in looking it over, when a voice called, "'Ere, Blackie, you comin' aboard?" Looking up, I saw a bald-headed man staring down at me from the deck. He looked to be in late middle age and the lips of his brown, weather-beaten face were sucked inwards, presumably over toothless gums.

The gangplank was down and I was close to it, so without replying I went aboard. He met me on the deck: he was taller than myself, and spoke with an air of authority.

"You Daniel or Wilkins?"

"Daniel."

He took out a list and ticked it.

"My name's Jarvis: I'm the mate."

"Captain Hawkshot himself's in command, then, I take it?"

"Well, 'course he is. Don't be muckin' stupid."

"He didn't tell me when he took me on."

Without answering, Jarvis called to a man sitting near the wheel, smoking a pipe.

"'Ere, Jenkins, show this nigger where to stow 'is kit."

We were standing in the waist, and I waited while Jenkins – a hefty, muscular youth – came up to me. He gave me a nod but said nothing. I went forward with him and followed him down an open hatch that led directly into the mess-room. Here, with a bottle of whisky on the table, four more of the crew were playing cards.

"Another muckin' nigger, eh?" said one. "What's yer name?"

"My name's Daniel," I replied, "and it isn't 'nigger'."

The man stood up. He looked about forty, had a long scar down one side of his face and only one eye.

"You lookin' fer trouble?"

I leaned across the table, gripped his right hand in my own and

114

shook it.

"Not in the least," I said. "All I mean is that I don't care to be called a nigger."

"Why not? Aren't you one?"

I made no answer, but remained facing him across the table. The other three men had not moved.

"Oh, chuck it, Tom," said one of them. "If Jarvis catches yer fightin', Hawkshot'll 'ave yer put ashore." He looked up at me. "On board 'ere, yer've got to bunk down where yer can. Drop yer kit in the corner there. No one'll pinch it. Yer can sleep on the floor." And with this he turned back to the game.

During that evening I gradually learned how squalid conditions were on board the *Frisky Shark*. Everything was shabby; everything you touched made your hands dirty. And the conditions were in keeping with the crew. There was hardly one who would have seemed out of place among the convicts that Lady Penelope used to visit. It was plain to see what Captain Hawkshot looked for. All were big and strong, but besides this, they gave the impression of being rough, unscrupulous men, if not brutal yet certainly callous; strangers to probity and having little regard for it.

I went back on deck and returned to the waist. Four more men had come aboard and were being ticked off his list by Jarvis. Among these was Wilkins, the only other black member of the crew. Although I didn't altogether like the look of him, we shook hands and exchanged our names.

"Your first time on this trip?" he asked.

"Yes. Yours too?"

He nodded. "You English?"

"Well, born in America. But I count myself as English. I certainly don't mean to go back to America."

"'Think we're going to enjoy this trip?"

"I've no idea. But it's good pay, isn't it?"

"From what I've heard it'll need to be. What d'you make of that lot behind you?"

Turning round, I saw what I hadn't noticed before. Fastened against the wooden partition was a kind of hall-stand, with a double row of pegs, one below another. Across each of these lay a leather whip about three feet long from the leather-bound hand-grip to the tapered, waxed tip. With each lay a pair of handcuffs.

"Ready for use when required," said Wilkins.

Walking forward, we stopped beside a large pair of hatch doors. They were mounted on a wooden base, sloped somewhat upwards towards the port side and were closed together with a padlock and chain through their centre handholds.

"Hatch to the hold," said Jarvis, from behind us. "Tomorrow you'll be going below to have a look at it."

Later, while we were eating, Captain Hawkshot came down the hatchway into the mess-room. Most of the crew did not trouble themselves to turn their heads. I was, naturally, expecting him to come out with some sort of general greeting, such as "Hallo, there!" or "Glad to see you all." However, I was mistaken.

"Where's Jarvis?" he asked.

Jarvis appeared from the galley, where he had presumably been eating by himself with the cook.

"Here, Captain."

"Are all the crew aboard?"

"All but two, sir. Hulbert and Foster."

"As soon as they come, tell them to report to me."

"Aye, aye, Captain. What time are we sailing?"

"Six o'clock, with the tide. See all the crew are on deck."

And so saying, Hawkshot went back up the hatchway.

As soon as I had finished eating, I went on deck and found him in the waist, apparently about to go ashore.

"Excuse me, Captain," I said. "Can I -?"

"What do you want? Be quick."

"I've been told to sleep on the floor in the mess-room. Can I ask whether –"

"They've been making a fool of you, then. You should have realised that. Keep your wits about you. There are plenty of hammocks. See Jarvis."

There was nothing for it but to go back to Jarvis. Two or three of the crew, who had overheard me, didn't conceal their amusement; neither did Jarvis. However, he gave me a hammock and showed me where I could sling it.

As soon as four or five of the crew had turned in for the night, I followed their example. I felt only too glad to be bringing the day to an end.

I had never slept in a hammock before and found myself unable to settle comfortably. The man nearest to me was not only soon asleep but snoring loudly and steadily. Lying awake, I couldn't help thinking that I hadn't started off on the right foot and feeling apprehensive about the voyage ahead.

In a while I did doze off after a fashion. I was awoken by the clatter and commotion of men near me swearing, getting to their feet and putting on the clothes they had taken off for the night. Not wanting to find myself in trouble for lagging behind, I was following suit when my neighbour, the snorer, turned over in his hammock and said, "'Ere, darkie, you ain't crew, are yer?"

"We're all crew, aren't we?"

"Naow. Don't be so muckin' daft. Yer was took on as a slave-basher, weren't yer?"

"How d'you mean?"

"Oh, for muck's sake. Crew are seamen, lad, taken on to sail the muckin' ship. But there's ten or twelve, including you and me, as are taken on to get the slaves aboard and see to 'em on the way across. I know you're a slave-basher 'cos Hawkshot told me. I've done this trip three or four times before, and I"m senior slave-basher. You ain't never done it, 'ave yer?"

"No."

"Well, I'll keep an eye on yer. My name's Wain – Jack Wain. And to start with, yer don't 'ave to work with the crew. Yer'll 'ave plenty of work to do later, no muckin' danger. But for now, yer can

117

go back to kip."

There was no returning to sleep, but I lay in my hammock for the next hour or so, until I saw Wain turning out, whereupon I did the same. Two or three of the slave-bashers were already at breakfast in the mess-room and another four or five came in as we were starting on our meal. The ship was rolling – not heavily – but enough to trouble the stomach of a greenhorn like me. However, I managed to eat what I was given and kept it down.

The meal finished, Wain knocked on the table for silence. "Right, now; all the lot of yer. We're goin' down to 'ave a look at the hold. All right, Rawlings, Simpson, I know yer've done it before, but yer'll come with the rest, see?"

We went on deck and gathered in front of the big hatch doors. Wain took a key from his belt and fitted it to the padlock. Having drawn out the chain, he told four of us to open the doors. Even with two men to each side, they were almost too heavy to pull up and rotate back and down on their hinges. Peering in, we saw a steep flight of steps leading down into darkness.

"Right," said Wain. "Where are the old hands? Hickman, Shergold, follow me down."

Holding the rails on each side, he went backwards down the steps. The two men followed. We heard him call out, "Get the muckin' portholes open. You know where they are."

We heard Hickman and Shergold stumbling and cursing and then, with a metallic rasping and sounds of heavy slamming, the gloom below was dispersed – though not much – by daylight from four portholes. I was surprised to see how far apart they were.

"Bloody hell!" said Wilkins, craning his neck beside me. "It goes across the whole damned ship!"

"Right!" called Wain, now visible below. "Come down one at a time. Keep holding the rails. Anyone falls it'll be their lot."

No one was in a hurry to be first. Wain had to call "Right, Cooper, Limbrick, get on with it!" before anyone moved. I myself, going last, was scared to find the steps even narrower and further apart than I was expecting. Once I stopped, trembling, while

Wain swore at me from below. As soon as I was down, I became aware of a nauseating, mephitic stench that seemed to form part of the air I breathed. I choked on it.

Wain addressed the group. "Now, understand this, all of yer. This is the hold where the slaves are goin' and it'll be your job – your job and no one else's – to see they get here undamaged and in good condition. All right?"

"But where do we put them, Jack?" asked the gigantic youth standing at my elbow.

"Why, on the muckin' floor, of course!" replied Wain. "Yer can't 'ang 'em from the muckin' ceilin', can yer?"

The youth frowned in perplexity, but said no more.

"When yer done lookin', I'll tell yer 'bout 'ow yer goin' to do the job. And keep yer bloody wits together, cos it's important."

I took a look round. The first thing to strike me was that the place was not lofty, as it had seemed when we were peering into it from the deck. The misapprehension must have been due to the obscurity and gloom. In fact the planking of the ceiling was barely five feet above the floor, so that it was not possible to stand upright except in the space immediately below the hatchway where we were gathered.

What I next saw with surprise was the size of the place. Apparently Wilkins had been right: it seemed to comprise the entire space of the ship's lowest level. Around the whole interior, about two feet above the floor, was a stout shelf some six feet wide. Two wooden partitions ran across the deck, supported by fitting into slots on each side. They were thin and light – almost flimsy – and plainly easy to move from one pair of slots to another.

"Right," said Wain, having satisfied himself that we had all got the measure of the place, "Now listen to me carefully, even them as 'ave 'eard it before. This is where the slaves are kept during the crossing to Jamaica. It holds four hundred, although we'll be lucky to get that many. The first lot lie all round the bottom; that's to say, on the floor. Feet to point to the centre. It'll be your job to make sure they're stowed tight together. They 'ave to lie on their sides and not on their backs or their bellies. 'Ave yer all got that? On their sides, and as close together as possible. It's you that'll be seeing to this, not me, and it's important. And you'll manacle them together in pairs, left leg of one to right leg of t'other. 'Ave yer got that? It will now be demonstrated. You, Hopkins, and you, Matthews, lie down close together on yer sides, under the shelf and heads right up against the wall. Come on, look sharp!

"Right. Now I'm goin' to put on the manacles. No, don't move! And there'll be two hundred of 'em, all the way round. Got it?"

"What about food and drink, Jack?" I asked.

"They gets a meal and water twice a day, and it'll be your job to see to that, too."

"What about shitting and pissing, Jack?" asked someone.

"That's their business."

"What, on the floor?"

"You 'ave to scoop it up, put it in buckets and wash the floor down with vinegar in water. What's the matter with you, Townley? Turned your stomach? You took the muckin' job on, didn't yer? If yer don't do it properly, y'know, I can report yer. 'Ope I don't 'ave to."

There was a pause. Wain unfastened the manacles and the two men stood up.

"I suppose some of 'em die, don't they?" asked Wilkins.

"'Course they do. Scores of 'em. You unfasten the body, pull it up on deck and pitch it over the side.

"Now I ain't done yet. You see that shelf as runs all round; there's another two 'undred goes on that, above them what's on the floor."

We stared at one another, but no one said a word.

"And what about those partitions across, Jack?" asked Hopkins.

"They're shifted as required, to divide the slaves up. Men forward, boys midships, women and girls aft.

"Any more questions? No? All right, up yer go. Yer free to do as yer please until we reach the coast. Once we've got the niggers ready to be taken aboard, yer'll all 'ave plenty to do, as you'll now be aware. Now, one last thing. If anyone's thinking of tryin' to get out of it, yer can just ferget it, 'cos the only way out is over the side. Or you can be stripped and tied up for a taste of Lady Lash. The way that's done –"

At this moment there was a clatter from the top of the hatchway and Captain Hawkshot came down as easily as a nuthatch on a tree-trunk.

"Everyone here, Wain?" he asked.

"Yessir."

"All learned what they've got to do?"

"Yessir."

"Now listen, all of you. Anyone who wants to can back out now, or later. Any man who does will be put ashore on the African coast without food or pay."

Hawkshot broke off. As though preoccupied, he took a short, pointed stick out of his pocket and began cleaning under his nails. No one spoke. When he had finished, he looked up. "Good. Then I'm relying on all of you to do honest work for honest pay."

He climbed back on deck and we followed him one by one. I went aft and leant over the rail, gazing down into the wake. With half a mind to jump overboard, I knew well enough that I wasn't going to. I closed my eyes and tried to pray. But pray for what? God wouldn't stop what was going to happen; I was sure enough of that. If You exist, I thought, how can You let this happen? And if I did jump overboard, it would go on happening just the same, wouldn't it? There's nothing I can ask You for. Nothing.

I felt a touch on my shoulder and turned to see Townley. I had not particularly noticed him until Wain had spoken to him a few minutes before. He looked about twenty or twenty-one, big-built, and taller than myself. His expression, however, probably resembled my own, I thought, in being tense and apprehensive.

He spoke first. "Were you praying?"

"If I was, what about it? What made you think so?"

"Your lips were moving. Do you reckon we've got something to pray for?"

"Since you ask, yes, I do."

"When Hawkshot took you on, did he give you any idea of what we were going to have to do?"

"He said he wanted me to come on a voyage to West Africa for slaves, that it was perfectly legal and he'd pay me a large sum."

"It was the pay that decided you?"

"Yes."

"That was what decided me, too. I wanted – well, I still want – to support my widowed mother."

"Then you had a better reason than I had. When you came up just now, I was realising that I'm too cowardly to kill myself."

He gave a short, bitter laugh. "That's against the rules for Christians."

"And so, presumably, would be killing Hawkshot. So what can we do?"

"We can't do anything, except to pray and try to trust in God. I admit that in our position that's virtually impossible, but I suppose other Christians must have found themselves in equally bad situations before now."

At this moment Wain, accompanied by two members of our group, strolled aft to the stern rail, leant his back and elbows against it and continued with what he had been saying.

"A long way west, yer think, do yer?"

"Yes, I do," replied one of them, a man named Helm. "Only, I ain't one of the bloody landlubbers what you've took on fer this trip. I've been nine or ten years at sea, and if we're s'posed to be makin' fer West Africa, we're 'alf way across to Venezuela by my reckonin'."

"Ah," said Wain, "but then yer've never sailed with Captain Hawkshot, 'ave yer?"

"What's that got to do with it?"

"Captain Hawkshot's a deal too canny to sail along the coast of

122

Spain and the Portuguese African seaboard. We're not carrying guns, but there's plenty do – the French and the Danes and some of the Dutch as well. Captain Hawkshot has enemies, as you can guess. What we do as a rule is to sail west, then south and east and then head north for Lagos. That's where we buy our slaves, at Lekki, east of the Gold Coast."

"Takes a lot of time, that detour, doesn't it?"

"What if it does? There's always plenty of slaves: that's an inexhaustible market, my lad. Besides, Captain Hawkshot pays well for 'is slaves – textiles, cowrie shells, rum, knives, and all such things as that. Most probably 'is usual agent for the tribal kings inland is waiting for us now. They don't sell to anyone else, as far as we know."

"Are they hard bargainers?"

"'Get harder year by year. And you talk about wasting time, Helm. Those nigger dealers act as though they had all the time in the world. We make our offer and whatever it is they say it's not enough and at that rate they'll go elsewhere, find another white man, another buyer. And sometimes they really do go. Then come back four or five days later, see whether the white man's changed 'is mind. Well, yer see, it's a desperate place for illness, fever an' ague and all that. Anyone can die there easy. We don't want to 'ang around any longer than what we can 'elp. Sometimes we 'ave to give in, say all right we'll pay their price. But the boot's not always on the one leg. All the time there's no bargain struck, they're stuck with their slaves, see; got to go on feedin' 'em, keepin' 'em alive. An' of course the slaves, they die like flies, only they got nothing to live for, see? I remember one trip we lost eight men – white men – and it come to a case of payin' what they was askin' or goin' away empty-'anded. That sort of bargaining's an art in itself. You 'ave to 'ave a gift for it; and that's what Captain Hawkshot's got. He's been at it longer than some of the black dealers an' all. They mostly knows 'im by now, and knows better than try to cheat 'im."

That afternoon, Townley and I fell into talk with one of the crew, a Hampshire man named Thorn.

"How far is it from Lagos to Jamaica?" I asked.

"About 3,000-4,000 miles or thereabouts," replied Thorn.

"How long will it take us?"

"Could be three months or could be longer, according to the weather. It'll likely be fair weather this time of year. But then Captain Hawkshot'll want to go roundabout. He usually does – to keep out of the way of the French and Spanish. They won't be aiming for Jamaica, though. He'll probably make for the coast of Brazil and then go north to Venezuela. Well, I'd guess it might take us two-three months to reach Kingston; that's the capital of Jamaica. That's where he'll sell the slaves."

"What's Kingston like?"

"Hot; a lot too wet for comfort in the rainy weeks. White men run it, of course, and there's any number of niggers, mostly slaves but a few free. Whatever you do, keep away from the women, unless you want the pox. Sugar, rum and tobacco – they're what the plantation owners mostly go in for. It's all nigger slave labour, of course. Sugar – that's desperately hard work. Most of 'em don't last long at that. That's why Hawkshot sells in Jamaica. There's always a ready demand for more slaves.

"What are you two boys aiming to do? Do you mean to stay in Jamaica, buy land and set up in business?"

"No money."

"You could afford to buy land with the money Hawkshot'll pay you."

"Well," said Townley, "we'll make up our minds when we've had a look round."

"You could do a lot worse."

"We're a long way south now, aren't we? Shall we be going south of the equator?" asked Townley, changing the subject.

"Not quite so far," answered Thorn. "Was that the pipe? I must be going. Aye-aye bo'sun!" and off he ran.

During the days that followed, as the heat became more and more intense, I was overcome, preoccupied to the exclusion of all else, by the invasive knowledge, imparted by Wain, of what we were going to do and the impossibility of avoidance. In my haunted imagination, the prospect took the form of a thick, dark cloud hanging squarely across our onward progress, impenetrable by the eye but not by the body being carried closer day by day until, upon entering the cloud, it would be drawn on to a destination too hideous to foresee; beyond envisaging by my cowering, trembling awareness. Again and again in my mind's eye I approached that cloud, began to enter it and then snatched back my thoughts before they could take me farther. Whatever was concealed in that darkness was lying in wait. It would not disappear, being on familiar terms with Wain and Captain Hawkshot. In vain I dragged my mind away, trying to direct it elsewhere. It always returned. There was nowhere else to go.

Three mornings later we were still sailing westwards, under a light north wind. Basil Townley and I were leaning on the starboard rail, watching a school of dolphins curving in and out of the waves a short distance away. They seemed unaware of the ship, keeping on a course almost parallel with us until something we could not perceive deflected them, making them turn away northwards, so that soon we left them behind.

The two of us were gazing after them when suddenly we heard the cry of the lookout on the mainmast, "Ship ahoy!"

There was a general rush to the rails. Basil and I, remaining where we were, could make out nothing to starboard. The lookout, of course, had the advantage of the mast's height, but after what seemed to us a fair while, the horizon still appeared blank.

We waited. "It must be on the port side," I said, but I had hardly spoken when Basil pointed aft.

"There she is — whoever she is."

Now we could both make out the ship, approaching us on the starboard quarter. About half a mile off, however, she changed course and began sailing parallel with us, due west.

"She's a Rhode Islander," said the boatswain, behind us, closing his telescope.

"And makin' more knots than what we are," said one of the crew.

Indeed, it was clear that the American ship was going to overtake us. As she held on her way she drew level and we saw her deck more clearly. Incredibly, it was crowded with black men. At that distance I could not see what they were doing, but I could be in no doubt about their reality. At this moment we became aware of a foul smell borne on the wind, not strong but nevertheless revolting. Holding my nose, I turned to see not only Basil but almost everyone around us doing the same.

The boatswain nodded in a patronising manner. "That's the Yankee. 'Never smelt a slave-ship before, lads? Cheer up! We'll smell worse 'fore we're done."

The air cleared. Some of the sailors nearby were grinning, but to me it seemed more from bravado than amusement. Now that I knew what the smell was, to say that it was born of evil was no more than the truth. To me, it was part of all that Wain had taught us in the hold.

Two weeks later, having turned south and then east, we were approaching the African coast. Hawkshot was on deck, directing the man at the wheel. I had been expecting beaches, forests inland, perhaps mountains in the distance. As we came closer, however, all that I could make out was a line of green trees, widely broken here and there, stretching as far as could be seen in either direction. Mystified, I asked one of the sailors whether these forests formed the actual coastline or whether there were beaches too low-lying to be visible from out at sea.

"That's the Niger delta," he replied. "Biggest delta in the world, they say. There's two hundred miles of outfalls, north to south, behind those mangoes, all the way up to the Bight of Benin; that's where we're headed. There's nothing much to see, though, so long as we keep as far out as this. We've got a shallower draught than most slave-ships and we can sail closer in: that's if Hawkshot thinks there's any need to. But as long as there's no other ships to be seen, he'll probably keep this distance from shore."

By the following evening, we were well clear of the delta, and

126

headed north-west towards Lagos. Next morning I was woken by the sound of heavy surf, and having got on deck, where many of the ship's company were already gathered, saw, not far from where we were anchored, great waves breaking on a low shore. Spotting Thorn nearby, I went across and asked him where we were and what he thought Hawkshot's intention was now.

"This is Lagos Island," he replied. "And that there's the European settlement. The Captain's gone to report our arrival and pay for permission to take the ship down to Lekki. That's where he'll meet the tribal king's agent, and buy the slaves we'll be taking on board."

"Are we going to sail down close to that surf?" I asked.

"Oh, no," replied Thorn. "We'll be going through that and into the lagoon on the north side of the Island. That's all still water, right across to the mainland shore, and there's a regular chain of lagoons, best part of fifty or sixty miles, goes down all the way to Lekki."

We remained anchored until the afternoon, when Hawkshot returned and again stood by the wheel as we rounded a sandbar and came through the breakers to the lagoon. It was not only still water but shallow, with any number of mud banks, and the Captain ordered that we should sail slowly. He also put a man on swinging the lead and calling the depth.

The two days we spent sailing down the lagoon chain to Lekki passed without mishap. Here, the Captain again made himself known to the authorities, and then took the ship across the breadth of the Lekki lagoon to the north shore.

It was low-lying and desolate. Beyond the distant mangrove swamps there was nothing to be seen but dense forest. Its only feature, a little way up from the beach, was a dilapidated stone building that might once have been a fort.

Ever since we had rounded Lagos Island, the air had become more and more close and humid, and we tyros needed no telling that the place was noxious and unhealthy. The sun was fiercer than anything I had ever known. We were drenched in sweat.

Although there were several tanks of potable water on board, only a little, and that tepid, could be issued, since most would be needed for the slaves. For the moment there was no more work to be done. The only relief was to plunge into the warm shallow water, but upon coming out we were almost instantly dry.

To myself I seemed to be groping through a miasma that I could scarcely breathe, in which each movement was an effort. To go below was no escape, for the very timbers, warm to the touch, seemed to give out the heat; and though all the portholes stood open there was never the least draught.

At last, at sundown, the air began to cool and a faint breeze sprang up. The Captain ordered that the "slave conductors", as he called us, were to eat before the crew, and that after the meal we were to gather on the forward deck. Meanwhile there would be an issue of rum. Wain was put in charge of the distribution and as far as I could see he acted honestly. Since there were not enough tin cups to go round (and this was typical of the *Frisky Shark's* amenities) we lined up in groups of four, drank off our tots and returned the empty cups to be refilled for the next group.

Wilkins had been mistaken in thinking that the hold we had seen comprised the ship's entire volume, for when we turned up to keep our date with the Captain, he began by telling Limbrick to open a forward hatch in the bows. This disclosed a second, smaller hold, which was filled to capacity with wrapped packages, sealed cartons and boxes covered with coarse black cloth.

"These are the goods which are going to be exchanged for the slaves," said the Captain. "All the parcels are numbered in white paint and I have a manifest here of the contents. You're going to take them out one by one, refer the numbers to me for identification and then carry them aft and stack them on the stern deck. When you've taken one, come back here for another until we've finished.

"Right, Daniel and Townley, you can start with that carton on top."

There was no getting down into the crammed hold, and we had to lean over from above and pull the heavy carton up; a fiendishly

128

hard business that left us both gasping. When we had told the Captain its number, we manhandled it aft to the stern, stopping twice for breath. On the stern deck we found Jarvis in charge of the stacking. We put our load down where he told us and went back as slowly as we could. On the way we met Wilkins and Limbrick, staggering under a similar burden.

Our next crate was not so heavy, but it was the leaning over and hauling up which cost the effort. After Basil and I had done three lots, the Captain stood us down and told us to go and help Jarvis. Jarvis evidently knew how many heavy items there would be, for he was using these, as they arrived, to form a base. Lighter lots had been dumped all over the deck, and Jarvis told Basil and me to build them into the stack according to weight.

The Captain came down to approve the finished job, and we were dismissed. We stayed on deck, however, to watch the sailors constructing what they called a "house". They had tied a spar between the masts to form a beam and were now occupied in securing other spars to run slanting from the beam to the deck. Over this framework of rafters they laid rush-mats and lastly, they divided the interior into two compartments with a wooden partition. They told us that one of these was for the Captain, to receive and bargain with the black tribal agent, while the other was for receiving slaves before they were moved down into the hold. The place was supposed to be proof against rain.

It was raining next morning when the Captain told Wain, Basil and myself to join him in the ship's boat to be taken ashore to await the tribal agent Ushumbo and the slaves. However, although we stood in the shelter of the fort for several hours, no one appeared from the forest and finally, in the afternoon, we were rowed back to the ship for a late dinner.

"Why does the Captain feel he has to wait on the beach?" I asked Wain. "Couldn't he simply put one of us there to tell him when the agent arrives?"

"He always sees the slaves as soon as they're brought to the beach," said Wain. "He counts 'em and rejects the ones he won't accept before the rest are brought aboard. If the Captain didn't see them as soon as they arrive, Ushumbo would be quite up to sending the best ones back and substituting others he's left in the forest. The Captain don't want the bother of rejecting slaves once they've been put aboard."

Before next day the rain had ceased. Ushumbo, a big man dressed like a European in white coat and trousers, appeared about halfway through the morning with his consignment of slaves, who were controlled by three men with whips. With him were several hired Krumen fisher-folk, carrying their dugout canoes. He greeted the Captain effusively, but since they conversed in some African language, Basil and I could not follow the talk, though Wain, standing beside the Captain, seemed to be taking it in. Basil and I turned our attention to the slaves.

The mere sight of them was enough to overwhelm any beholder with shock and horror. Their drawn faces – men, women and children alike – expressed a dreadful, flinching fear, together with despair. Most were naked; a few were half-clothed in filthy rags. All looked famished and exhausted. Some clung to one another, trembling and looking about them as though expecting some further cruelty at any moment. Others had the appearance of warriors, but warriors defeated, prisoners, battered until incapable of further resistance. Several had injuries, untended wounds clearly causing them pain. There were young women who had once, perhaps, been attractive, their looks now a pitiable travesty of comeliness. A number, both men and women, had fallen prone in the mud, their heads buried in their hands. I saw aged, decrepit people, and others maimed, lacking a hand or foot. Basil, beside me, was close to weeping. "This is a picture of the end of the world," he whispered. "God forbid," I answered. I would have tried to say more, but we found Wain beside us.

"Right," he said. "Men stay here, women over there. Get on with it. Then count 'em."

Basil led a cowering, terrified woman by the hand and took up a position a short distance away, while I did my best to get the other women to join them. Some were beyond comprehending; others resisted, clinging to their men. I was struggling to pull a

130

girl to her feet when Wain kicked me from behind.

"Didn't I say get on with it?" he shouted. "'Think we've got all mucking night?"

He tore the girl from me, slapped her face and pointed to where Basil was standing. Then he used some word in their language, at which she stumbled away, crying bitterly.

Wain was carrying a whip, which he now handed to me. "Use this," he said, "and don't let me catch you buggering about again." He pointed to a woman squatting on the ground nearby. "Hit 'er!" he said. "Go on, hit 'er!"

"Jack," I replied. "I can't. I simply can't hit her. Let me pull her up."

"You stupid bastard!" he shouted. "The whole point of hitting 'er is that the others see it and don't need hitting theirselves." He snatched the whip back from me and struck the woman twice across the shoulders. She sprang up screaming and was about to run away, but he caught her by the arm, pointing towards Basil and again speaking in their language.

It worked. God forgive me, it worked. Ten or twelve women around us immediately leapt to their feet and followed Wain's victim to join Basil's group. It was easy to complete the business. Two women staggered and fell, and these Wain dragged to one side and left on the ground.

Counting the women, I totalled thirty-six. Wain, going among them, picked out two who plainly had smallpox and one who was almost blind. These he told to go and join the two lying on the ground, and took no further notice of them.

"How many women?" shouted Hawkshot, and when Wain had replied, "Thirty-three", wrote it down and told Ushumbo to make his mark on the paper.

"Shall I get the men in line now, Captain?" asked Wain. "Yes," answered Hawkshot. "Start it here, and keep the whole line clear of the mud."

With much cursing and threatening, the men were formed into line. Again there were three whom Wain rejected, one with a clubfoot and two who were deformed. "Right," he said to Basil and me, "keep 'em in line and keep the line moving." Then, joining the Captain and Ushumbo, he pulled the first slave forward for inspection.

The Captain worked slowly and thoroughly. He examined eyesight, hearing, teeth, hands, feet and private parts. The total number of male slaves was agreed as 191, but eleven of these were rejected, all on account of physical disability of one kind or another. The Captain spoke contemptuously in English to Ushumbo, telling him that he should be ashamed to have tried to pass off such rubbish on an honest purchaser like himself and that he was minded to take his custom elsewhere. Ushumbo's English was so odd that I could not understand him, but I thought that in any case there was a kind of play-acting about the whole contretemps: that is, the Captain's complaint seemed to be made almost in set terms, and the agent's reply similarly. At all events, the rebuke and the rejoinder went no further.

It was late in the afternoon before the 180 fit slaves were assembled on the beach. It was judged too late to put them aboard that night, and they and the women, together with those who had been rejected, were driven into the fort and left to themselves, with Ushumbo's three slave-drivers taking turns on guard. I never heard what arrangements were made for feeding them. Then the Captain, Ushumbo, Wain, Basil and I returned to the ship.

The Captain and Ushumbo took the evening meal alone together in the "house", and we saw no more of them until next day. Three other members of our group, Wilkins, Cooper and Hopkins, were told by Wain to join Basil and myself in going ashore.

Apparently the slaves had already been given a meal of ground maize that morning, or so Ushumbo's men assured him. Twenty men and women, selected at random – were now brought out of the fort and driven down to the beach to board the canoes.

When these poor wretches realised that they were now to be taken on board the white man's ship and that their last hope of freedom had vanished, they burst out in passionate protests and pleas for mercy. Many were hysterical and beyond responding to any threats or orders. What shocked Basil and me was the detached indifference of the Captain, Wain, Ushumbo and his men. It was plain that they were only too familiar with this kind of desperate clamour, an expected and commonplace feature of their work. At a nod from Ushumbo his three men set about them with their whips. Wain joined them. Before control was restored several had been beaten unconscious and lay on the ground with blood oozing from the wounds across their backs. Wain told us to lift bodily those who were beyond hearing orders and put them in the canoes. Together with the other members of the group, I obeyed, but Basil remained where he was and took no part in the work. When all the canoes had been loaded, Wain ordered us to find ourselves places, and then got into one of the canoes himself. When we came alongside the ship, he set us to manhandling the slaves onto the stern deck, where the rest of the group was waiting to take charge of them. We remained in the canoes as they returned to the beach.

I was surprised that neither the Captain nor Wain had taken any notice of Basil, who was still standing on the spot he had taken up when we first landed. A rod in pickle, I thought, turning to the next twenty slaves being brought out.

The loading of the ship continued all day; so did the screaming, the sobbing protests, the pleas for mercy. I noticed that Wilkins was among the readiest to use his whip. Once, when he was lashing the body of a man already beaten to the ground, Wain himself intervened, telling him, with the usual flow of foul language, that a dead slave was no use to anyone. I could see that Wilkins was enjoying himself in showing the slaves that a black man could be even more cruel than his white companions.

I felt ashamed of my cowardice, but at the same time could not see what else I could do. The alternative – defiance – I was sure would mean death in one form or another. Later that day I went over to Basil and tried to persuade him to submit like myself, pointing out that his resistance could make no difference to the brutality and wickedness proceeding round us. "I know that," he replied, "but I can't be a party to it."

"What about the money for your poor mother?" I asked.

"Thirty pieces of silver," he said. "Better go on with your work, Daniel. Your work, not mine."

As I returned, Wain met me. "Where's muckin' Wilkins got to?" he demanded.

"I don't know, Jack."

"Well, go and find 'im."

The whole shore was devoid of anywhere to hide. Not knowing what to do, I walked round to the far side of the old fort, and here I came upon Wilkins. He was masturbating. "Wain wants you," I called and went back to the beach. Wain was busy, forcing a man into one of the canoes. By the time he had finished, Wilkins had returned.

Before the day's work was done, Wain and Hawkshot went back to the ship. Ushumbo, left in charge, carried on until the last batch of slaves had been bludgeoned into the canoes. Before we followed them, leaving the beach deserted, Ushumbo satisfied himself that none of the slaves was hiding in the fort. "And a wrong dorty mess dey've left in dere," he said to me as he came out.

"Do you want us to clean it up?" I asked.

"God, no," he answered contemptuously. "What wor be point ob dat, boy, eh?"

Only a few of the male slaves were crouching on the stern deck as we climbed back on board. The rest, presumably, were already in the hold. The Captain, unspeaking, gestured to Basil and me to follow him into the waist, telling Wain to stop anyone else coming in. We stood side by side facing him. I was still holding my whip, streaked with blood.

"Townley," said Hawkshot, "you took no part in the work today. Why?"

"The work is unjustifiably cruel, sir, and against my Christian principles."

"But you were told, when I engaged you, that the ship was sailing to Africa for slaves."

134

"I didn't foresee, sir, that it would involve such terrible cruelty."

"I told you that the project was entirely legal. You were ready to join under my command and to obey my orders. I am the judge of what has to be done, not you."

"I cannot be a party, sir, to such wickedness."

"Yet you knew before you joined the ship that the slave trade is sanctioned throughout Europe and that it is not disapproved by the Church of England or the Roman Catholic Church. Do you think you know better than the whole world?"

Basil made no reply.

"Townley, this amounts to mutiny. I could hang you at once. But I will give you one more chance. Tomorrow you will work to orders or you will be condemned as a mutineer. Say nothing more. Go."

The Captain turned to me.

"As for you, Daniel," he said, "Wain tells me that yesterday you refused to whip a woman when he ordered you to. Is that correct?"

"Yes, Captain."

"Was that because you felt pity for the woman?"

"Yes, Captain."

"It's a waste of time to pity slaves, especially on the beach, where they often become hysterical. However, Wain says you've given no trouble since and I hope that will remain an isolated incident. Can you assure me of that?"

"Yes, Captain."

"I'm glad to hear it. Now go and wash that whip and put it back on the rack."

He turned away and I did as I was told.

After supper, I spent the rest of the evening talking with Basil but entirely failed to change his resolve.

"But they'll put you to death, Basil. And what good will you have done?"

"Only God knows that," he answered. "Do you suppose every one of the martyrs knew what good he or she would do? Many of them died alone and there must have been many we don't even know about; no record of their deaths, I mean."

"But Basil, you've only got to tell the Captain that you've thought it over and you accept what he said about the slave trade and its approval by the Church and State."

"Not if it means abducting and brutalising helpless women and children. Men too, come to that. What do you think Christ would have done in our situation?"

"But your mother?"

"I know. I'll write down her address and perhaps you'll go and see her, will you?"

In the course of the evening Ushumbo and the Captain, sitting together in the "house", finally reached agreement on what was to be given in exchange for the slaves, and next morning Wain assembled our group and set us to opening the various cartons and bundles and dividing the contents. Since most of the stuff had already been assigned to Ushumbo, and he needed porterage while we did not, the Captain allowed him to use the original containers, and these his men took ashore and put into the fort. He said nothing to us about where or how he meant to take them away. The Captain, of course, was not concerned; that was the agent's own business.

Before Ushumbo left, the Captain spoke once more to Basil and me. Why he included me I still don't know, but I think that he may have wanted an English witness who could, if necessary, testify to his disposal of Basil and affirm that he had not murdered him.

"Townley," he said, "I have already told you that your insubordinate conduct amounts to mutiny. Are you ready to desist from it, and to obey orders in a proper and reasonable way? Yes or no?"

"No, sir," replied Basil.

"Very well. As I told you, I would be justified in hanging you, but I have decided to exercise leniency. I shall, with Ushumbo's full agreement, hand you over to him, to deal with you as he thinks fit. The transfer will be carried out immediately."

136

Basil said nothing, but acknowledged this with an inclination, a kind of half-bow. The Captain left us, and Basil was told to collect his kit and come back to the stern deck. He had already written down for me his mother's address. There was no one to say farewell except myself. (I embraced him with tears.) Wain then told Ushumbo, who had evidently agreed to oblige the Captain, to take him away; and that was the last we saw of either of them.

I could observe no bodies on the beach, and assumed that Ushumbo must have disposed of them in some way of his own.

Our business at Lekki was now ended. Wain supervised us in returning the remainder of the barter goods to the forward hold while the ship left the lagoon.

We had not noticed it the previous evening, since the slaves had not been long on board, but this morning we had all become aware of the stench from the hold. A pervasive smell, however, is not consciously perceived after a few minutes and we were able, more-or-less, to disregard it. Now we were, in all respects, a slave-ship and would remain one until off-loading at Kingston.

Two of the group, Portway and Hopkins, were on duty in the hold. Halfway through the morning Wain told Helm and Cooper to relieve them. When they came up they said nothing to anyone, but went by themselves to lean on the forward port rails.

Earlier that day we had learned that Shergold and Matthews, together with Saunders, one of the crew, had gone down with malarial fever. "If there aren't no more than them three we'll 'ave got off light," said Wain. "The Captain ain't told me yet whether we're going elsewhere for more slaves or whether we're off to Jamaica right away. Two 'undred and thirteen's a long way below what we generally reckon to get. But if any more of us go sick, p'raps we'll 'ave to cut our losses."

After dinner, Wain told Limbrick and me to relieve Helm and Cooper in the hold. The hatches had been left open, and I preceded Limbrick down the ladder.

I thought that I had seen the most abhorrent features of the slave trade on the beach the day before, but I was wrong. The suffering that I found about me now was worse. The half-darkness was full of the sounds of affliction; intermittent cries of pain, sobs of misery, the low, spent weeping of despair. The bodies were packed close together on their sides, some motionless, others continually stirring, twitching, troubling those to whom they were manacled. All showed the effects of privation: and here the smells of sweat and ordure were intensified, and the air almost exhausted by having been breathed again and again.

Beside us was a pile of worn rush mats and dirty bolsters, and here we both lay down unspeaking. I was wondering why it was thought necessary for us to be there, when Wain called, "You all right down there?" It was Limbrick who replied. Then Wain once more, "Any dead?" "Don't know yet," answered Limbrick. "Well, get on with it."

Eyesight now more-or-less adapted, we started, half-crouching under the low timbers, on our inspection. In one way it was easy. The bodies formed roughly three-quarters of a circle on the floor, heads to the edge, feet pointed to the centre. But how to tell whether any were dead? Most were plainly alive, for under our hands they moved or muttered. Others remained still even when pinched or shaken. The way they were lying, it was often hard to tell whether they were breathing or not. However, we found the bodies of two men who were certainly dead. We released their fetters and called to Wain, who let down a kind of double-looped rope, to which we secured first one and then the other to be hauled up.

Before our spell of duty was over, I fell into an uneasy sleep, from which Limbrick woke me. We were relieved by Cooper and Wilkins.

In the early evening, Wain ordered that half the slaves were to be brought out of the hold and assembled on deck for what he called "Exercise". There was a hatch above the waterline on the starboard side, and when this had been opened a kind of gangplank was fixed, up which the slaves, their fetters removed, reached the deck. Here they were made to form a circle, facing inwards. Wain, in the middle, demonstrated a kind of hopping dance, while one of the crew beat the rhythm on a piece of iron. Having shown what he wanted, he grasped a man by the wrist and resumed his dance, while Wilkins, beside him, gestured to the man to copy him. At length, with some difficulty and with the ever-present fear of the whip, the whole circle of slaves was made to "dance" one behind the other. Those who were too weak to do it and fell down, were left where they lay. The dance went on for a considerable time, and when Wain finally gave the signal to stop, several of the slaves were close to exhaustion. Wain, having allowed a pause for recovery, told us to get them back into the hold. Then the remainder were brought out and the dance was repeated.

When the last slave had returned to the hold, I broke away, went forward and leant on the starboard rail.

I knew now that I had been carried into the very centre of that thick, dark cloud which, in my imagination, had hung across our progress, concealing what was too hideous to foresee. I knew that the happenings of the past week had changed me forever. They stood like an iron screen between my life before we had come to Lekki and the time I had lived since then. I knew, too, that it was not a matter of a few days. Henceforward, until my death, I would be a different man, the Daniel who had worked for Captain Hawkshot on the beach at Lekki, the Daniel who had been an obedient participant in that work. What I had seen was compounded by what I had done. Against my conscience and with the example of Basil before me, I had submitted, on account of fear and of nothing else, to Jack Wain, had obeyed him, possibly even gained his approval.

Yet this was not all. I had not realised before that the African slave trade, based on conscious, deliberate cruelty, was the greatest collective sin ever committed by mankind. Cruelty impregnable, all-conquering! I could never have imagined by myself the supremacy of this Brutality and its loyal followers, Torment, Grief and Misery. No wickedness so vast, no wickedness on this scale had been known in the world until now. In my mind's eye I saw the emergence into birth of this obscene, monstrous bulk, blotting out all but itself.

"By what Name are we to call Thee, Master, to worship Thy divinity?"

"I AM THE AFRICAN SLAVE TRADE."

"O Master, those are Thy flames roaring through ransacked villages, Thy foolish mothers bereft, Thy silly, defenceless victims screaming, Thy whips striking home."

"I AM ULTIMATE EVIL. FALL DOWN BEFORE ME. THERE IS NO CRUELTY GREATER THAN MINE."

"And these are our ships, Master, every cargo worth a fortune. Our reward for serving Thee. Hallowed be Thy Name."

* * *

Hitherto I had seen the slaves as simply sufferers of pain, of the whips and blows of innumerable counterparts of Mister Henderson and Jack Wain. But now I realised more. The black slaves were victims of robbery – perhaps, numerically – of the greatest robbery ever. They must, I supposed, number millions: and they had been robbed entirely: not only of their ways of life, their homes and possessions and of the familiar society, surroundings and climate where they had lived, but of their wives and children, of their traditional culture, of faith in their gods, of their prospects, of security and even of hope, for they had nothing to look forward to but unpaid, unremitting toil and death. A victim of the African slave trade could stand up naked and be seen as possessing nothing, physical or spiritual, beyond his five senses.

And I? It seemed to me that I had no option but to serve out my time with Captain Hawkshot and then – but how? – to work to deserve absolution, to feel myself absolved.

That evening, on the way back to Lagos, Hickman and Portway were taken ill, together with another member of the crew, a man named Neville. The Captain told us that in the light of these further casualties, we would not stay on the coast, but set sail for

140

Jamaica as soon as we were clear of Lagos. He told Wain to move the sick men together into the forward part of the sleeping deck, which would become an isolated "sick bay".

During the night three more slaves died and the bodies were brought up and pitched overboard. Wain made no secret of his fear that the whole ship might be stricken by an epidemic, and was continually asking one or other of us whether we felt any symptoms. Hawkshot, Wain and Jarvis now carried small bags of camphor round their necks.

On the following afternoon, the Captain again ordered Limbrick and myself to relieve Helm and Cooper in the hold. This time we started our search for dead bodies without waiting for orders from Wain. Both of us at once became aware of a dampness, a fluid thinly covering the floor around several of the slaves. Limbrick drew his fingers through a patch and sniffed.

"That's shit; and it's all over the place."

"Diarrhoea. And can you wonder? We'd better tell Wain right away."

Wain, having sent this latest information to the Captain, ordered first, that Limbrick and I were not to come up for the present, for fear of spreading the trouble; and secondly (which we did not learn until later), that none of the slaves in the hold was to be given food until further notice. (Empty stomachs, he said, would leave the malady nothing to bite on.)

The Captain did not think it necessary for Limbrick and me to remain in the hold. He ordered us to strip naked and come up, carrying our clothes. These were put at once into boiling water, while we were hosed down and each given a dose of some kind of medicine in the Captain's personal possession. It worked. That is, we did not develop the ailment we had never had.

I don't know how the hold was cleaned: no doubt with vinegar, the only disinfectant in the ship. Nor did I hear whether the diarrhoea was cleared up by the starvation imposed upon the slaves. Except for meals, I kept out of the way as much as possible, and the only news which reached me was that Shergold had died and that Cooper was down with the fever, together with two more of the crew. "That's five of us took bad, now," said Helm. "With Townley gone, that leaves only seven nigger-bashers. Jack seems worried stiff."

The ship stopped at Lagos for fresh water and general re-supply. No one was allowed on shore, probably for fear of desertion, although the prospect of Hawkshot's pay struck me as a strong disincentive.

So we sailed from Lagos, bound for the Venezuela coast and then Jamaica, with (from the Captain's point of view) a disappointing cargo, and that subject to continual depletion. Thorn told me that he thought the voyage might take eight weeks, though there was no telling. If the sea remained calm and the wind favourable, we might do it in less.

* * *

The further we went, the worse our plight became. About a week after our departure, Portway and Cooper died, and a few days later Hopkins went down with the fever, together with two more of the crew. Everyone now lived in continual anxiety. One evening in the messroom, I overheard Rawlings saying to Simpson that he believed there was a curse upon the ship, and that she was doomed to become a drifting derelict, without a living man on board. I interrupted with a threat to tell Wain if I heard Rawlings coming out with this sort of nonsense again. He answered that he believed Wain himself thought this, or something like it, more strongly than anyone else. I let it go at that.

With the number of fit "slave-conductors" now diminished to seven, the Captain discontinued his rule of requiring two men always to be on duty in the hold. Instead two of us, in rotation, had the task, every morning, of searching the hold for dead bodies and getting them hauled up for disposal overboard. This was at least better than having to remain in the hold for hours at a time.

For all I knew, the Captain might have come to think that it

142

was in the hold that we contracted the fever, although I myself believed that we had brought it with us from Lekki and that with luck it would soon exhaust its power to infect.

I still believe that I was right, for no more of us went down with the fever. Matthews and Hickman died, but Hopkins slowly recovered.

The Captain's practice of avoiding other shipping by sailing to the south of the frequented routes now turned to our disadvantage, for we might have taken our chance of enemies and reached Jamaica sooner. What we needed now was the quickest possible end to the voyage, and with this in mind the Captain changed our course from west to north west. Although we sighted one or two ships in the distance, none came near us and, with the continuance of fine weather and a favourable wind, we were at least able to make the best of our sorry condition.

The weeks passed without further illness among the white men, although the death rate in the hold remained as grim as ever. About sixty slaves had died, but as many more were ill and seemed unlikely to recover. Thorn told me that the condition of the women, who were the responsibility of the ship's crew, segregated by screening aft of the hold, was little better than that of the men. "This will turn out a bad business for Hawkshot," said Thorn. "He may not actually lose money, but he won't make anything like his usual profit."

We were in the twelfth week of the voyage when we entered the Caribbean. On the Captain's orders we made no further progress for two days. He called a meeting of the ship's officers, Wain, Jarvis and Pentland, the boatswain, together with us seven "slave-conductors".

"I must make it clear to you," he began, "that we are in a serious situation. In the first place, we're running dangerously short of water, and on this account we shall have to sacrifice some lives in order to save others. Secondly, having thought the matter over most carefully, I have been forced to conclude that all those slaves who are ill must be thrown overboard. This will be a more humane course than allowing them to linger in pain until they die."

"On this account, Wain, I must now order you to take three slave-conductors with you into the hold, and to pick out all the sick. The gangplank used by slaves when coming up for exercise is to be fitted now. The remaining three slave-conductors will remain on deck under my personal command and will take charge of the sick as they are brought up. All the sick are to be thrown into the sea."

The Captain said no more and a silence fell. I was not the only man – I am certain I was not the only man – to wonder whether he could believe his ears. If I had not spoken first, I am sure that some other man would have done so.

"Captain," I said, "I beg you to give this matter further consideration. Although the supply of water is not my responsibility, if I'm not mistaken the whole ship's company are on full rations and we can expect rain before long. Besides, we're not far from land."

"Daniel," replied Hawkshot, "I have already weighed this matter very fully. I am the Captain of this ship and the decision is for me and not for you. I rely on your loyalty and your compliance with my orders. Wain, select your men and take them into the hold."

No one else spoke. Wain, having told Helm, Rawlings and Simpson to accompany him, set about opening the starboard side hatch to the hold and fitting the gangplank. I myself felt close to hysteria. I still could not believe that we were about to commit mass murder. Surely I must have misunderstood the Captain. Yet I knew I had not. The Captain could not sell a dead slave. Likewise he could not arrive at Kingston with a ship half-full of something like a hundred sick slaves. How was he to dispose of them? The authorities would not be anxious to help him; they might even refuse to allow the ship to remain in port and compel it to return into the Caribbean to find some other destination. The Captain must indeed, as he said, have thought the matter over; and he had come up with the only possible answer. All sick slaves must be disposed of before we arrived at Kingston. I knew that the Captain had, in the past, made several slave-voyages, but in

144

all probability had never before encountered sickness on this scale; or if he had, must have done what we were about to do now.

Both Jarvis and Pentland had remained on deck. Jarvis was conversing with the Captain, but Pentland was standing by himself, filling his pipe. I hardly knew Pentland, but felt that I must speak to a person in some sort of authority.

"Can I have a word with you?" I asked. He tamped down the tobacco, looked round at me and nodded.

"This reason the Captain's given about the water," I said. "There's plenty of water, and he knows that a number of the sick slaves might recover, given the chance. And the 'more humane course' – that's all my eye, isn't it? He must have some reason he hasn't told us for drowning the whole lot of them. What do you suppose it can be?"

I had deliberately limited what I said, because I wanted to know whether he, like myself, believed that the Captain's real motive must be to take no chances, but to get rid of all the sick slaves before we reached Kingston. I wanted to find out whether Pentland would tell me this of his own accord, unprompted by anything I had said to him.

Before replying, he paused for quite some time. I had begun to wonder whether he meant to reply at all, and was about to turn away when he said, "You don't know, then, darkie?"

I shook my head.

"About the insurance?"

"The insurance? No, I don't. Can you explain?"

"If you don't know, I'm not sure whether I ought to."

"I promise you it won't go any further."

He relit his pipe. "Well, slaves who die of illness on board ship are a total loss to the Captain. He can't claim insurance for them. Underwriters won't insure against death by disease. But if sick slaves are thrown into the sea, then he can claim insurance. Insurers will pay for cargo thrown overboard in order to save the rest."

"And that applies to living human beings? They're 'cargo'?"

"Well," said Pentland, "of course the rule was meant to apply to ordinary trade goods, not to human beings. But I'm in little doubt that the Captain means to claim insurance for all slaves thrown alive into the sea, and that's his real reason."

He half-turned away and stood looking out to sea with an air of indifference. As I grasped the full implication of what he had said, my bowels loosened and I began to tremble. My feelings were less of horror or indignation, than of fear. I realised that I, an ingenuous simpleton, had been pitched headlong into a world of wickedness that I could never have imagined; a remote region, far from my humdrum, commonplace life. In this world there were no constraints whatever upon evildoing. Indeed, the words "evil" and "wicked" had no meaning here, since no distinction between good and evil was ever made. The only distinctions were between profitable and unprofitable, and between practicable and impracticable. If I protested against the Captain's orders, killing me would certainly be practicable.

This fear was well founded. The Captain was going to order me to throw black slaves alive into the sea, but I had no choice between "obey" or "disobey". The fact was that I knew I could not do it, on account of sheer revulsion. Even if morality had not come into the matter at all, still I could not have done it. At Lekki I had been involved in one piece of cruelty after another, and again and again had abandoned my self-respect on account of fear. But here, now, was the end of the road, a physical revulsion so strong that it left me no choice.

Wain was bringing up the first batch of slaves. I could avoid the sight of them but not the sound or the smell. There could be no temporising now. I made my way to where Hawkshot was standing.

"Captain," I said – and I could scarcely utter an intelligible word, but spoke chokingly, between gasps – "Slaves – overboard – I can't – d'do this – b'beyond my –"

He gripped my shoulder so hard that I winced. "What are you saying, Daniel?"

146

I was now virtually stupefied with fear. I mouthed one word, but my voice failed me.

"What?" said the Captain.

This time the sound came. "Insurance."

The Captain paused only a few moments. Then, holding my arm, he took me across to the starboard rail, out of earshot of the others.

"What did you say, Daniel?"

"Insurance, sir."

He turned me to face him, and his eyes stared intently into mine.

"I will excuse you from duty for the rest of the day. Go below now, and stay there. If I hear from anyone else that you have been talking about what you have just said, you will lose your life. Is that clear?"

"Yes, sir."

He turned and left me. I heard him call to Wain, "Take them to the stern deck." I stumbled forward and down the hatch into the empty messroom. The cook, a kindly, good-hearted fellow, came in from the galley and asked if I was feeling all right. I replied "Not too good", whereupon he gave me a tot of rum, for which I was grateful. After a while, the stupor passing off, I slung my hammock and lay pondering.

The Captain's sole motive for this voyage was to make money from bartering goods in exchange for Africans. At Lekki he had shown appalling inhumanity in the course of obtaining as many live Africans as possible. Experience had taught him that he must expect a number to die. Yet in the normal way, he could still make a large profit from the sale of those who survived the voyage – far more than the purchase value of the bartered goods plus the victualling of the ship and his employees' pay. In the present case, however, he must have lost many more slaves than usual during the voyage and stood to lose still more. Dead or ill, he could not sell them. Yet there remained a loophole. The insurance people would (he hoped) pay up for slaves thrown overboard alive, though not for those who died from disease.

Pentland had guessed this, but did not care to make an enemy of the Captain by objecting. He preferred to be sure of his pay. (And how many more? Wain? Jarvis? And I wouldn't put it past Wilkins.)

The Captain had threatened possible objectors with a horrible fate. When Basil Townley refused to do the work, he had said he could hang him for mutiny. Yet when Basil, undeterred, had persisted, he did not in fact hang him, but handed him over to Ushumbo. This was not a crime and he could not be indicted for it. I had virtually told him to his face that I knew of his cruel intention, but he had not murdered me. He had only threatened to do so, as in the case of Basil. So he must — must he not? — fear exposure if he summarily executed a white man without trial. However, he had disposed of Basil without laying himself open to any charge. Would he dispose of me? Basil had persisted in a maritime crime. I had not. It suddenly occurred to me that if I could only muster the courage, I was in a position to strike a bargain with the Captain.

After supper that evening I sought him out in his cabin, where he was apparently writing up the log.

"Didn't I tell you to stay below?"

"Captain, I have come to say something of great importance."

He frowned, then laid down his quill. "Well?"

"Captain, if you will not compel me to throw live slaves overboard, I promise you that I will not mention to anyone the matter of which we spoke this morning."

He paused. "And if it is mentioned to you by anyone else?"

"I shall say that I know nothing about it and wish to hear nothing."

"How old are you?"

I told him. "Why, sir?"

"Well, you always seem so young to me. Sort of immature."

"If I appear to you such an innocent and so uncorrupted, sir, you

148

have the more reason to trust my word."

"Wise boy, huh?"

I said nothing. His smile was like the grin of a skull.

"Very well. And this, Daniel, is entirely between ourselves."

* * *

Later that night Wilkins came up to me.

"You weren't on the stern deck this morning."

"No."

"Why not?"

"I'm not answerable to you, Wilkins. Go to blazes."

"You missed a treat. Do you know how many darkies we chucked in the drink?"

"No, and I don't want to. Aren't you a darkie yourself?"

"Fifty-four: that's how many."

I made no reply and he left me for more congenial company.

We sailed very slowly towards Kingston. Every morning Wain went down into the hold. Three days later, as Wilkins did not fail to inform me, twenty more Africans were drowned. The following week, when we were only a few miles from land, the Captain saw to the drowning of another sixteen.

It must at length have occurred to him that the longer slaves remained in the hold, the more likely they were to become ill. At all events, we docked at Kingston the next day.

As Wain had told me, the Captain had no difficulty in selling the remaining slaves, though what his net profit might have been no one, of course, knew. Of the deliberate murder of ninety diseased slaves, nothing more was said, then or ever. I personally believe that in the world of the slave-trade such cruelty was more common than is generally known.

The slaves were auctioned in the market at Kingston, some singly and some in lots. Hopkins and I went to see this final disposal of our "cargo". They were not treated as human beings. Prospective buyers were free to handle their limbs and bodies and to force open their mouths to look at their teeth – the usual way of estimating the age of a slave. All, men and women alike, had to stand passive and almost naked. Several of the women wept and might have resisted but for the white men with whips who were standing by. Yet this was not the worst. Towards the end of the business, when only a huddle of the least valuable slaves remained, the auctioneer announced that there would now be a "scramble", whereupon the purchasers were let loose among the slaves to scuffle and wrangle among themselves and their victims to seize those they wanted. For the slaves, ignorant of what might be going to happen to them, this was the climax of all the suffering and humiliation of the previous months.

We had little or no time to frolic in Kingston, for almost at once the Captain set us to cleaning out the hold with stiff brooms and strong solutions of vinegar. I am not going to try to describe the state of the hold. Suffice it to say that of all the tasks that fell to my lot during my time on board the slave-ship, this was the worst.

Once the ship had been cleansed, the Captain took on board a cargo of colonial produce (which we loaded) and then assembled us and asked whether there was anyone who did not wish to sail back to England in the *Frisky Shark*. Two of the sailing crew stood down and the Captain paid them off there and then. All the so-called "slave-conductors" remained with the ship which, after three days of internal repairs by carpenters, set sail for home.

The crossing was uneventful and upon our arrival at Bristol the Captain took all of us with him to his bank. I had been wondering what he had done with the presumably large sum for which he had sold the slaves in Jamaica. While we were all waiting to be paid, I saw him give the bank manager (with whom he was obviously persona extremely grata) a bill of exchange which I guessed to be a transfer of the slave-money.

I opened an account with the bank and paid in, all but ten pounds, the almost unbelievable sum agreed with the Captain over the whisky so many months before. Although I now knew him for a desperately wicked man, for appearance's sake I shook hands with him and wished him well. Then, after saying goodbye to Thorn, to my former companions and even to Wilkins, I stepped out into the street to embark upon what I now knew would be my true occupation.

*   *   *

As I strolled unhurriedly up into the City, enjoying the sensation of my feet being back on dry land, I noticed a church on the opposite side of the street. I was no churchman and had never had recourse to prayer. Missus Kathy had never taught me anything about it. But now I found myself thinking that if ever there had been a cause in need of the prayers of its adherents, it was surely the abolition of the slave trade. A prayer, I thought, even from a pagan like me, could not come amiss; and besides, I myself, as one about to engage in the struggle, needed to feel that God was with me. I had better ask Him.

I crossed the road and made my way up to the door. It was not locked and I went in. The church was empty; a hollow, vacant place it seemed, echoing as I shut the door behind me. I was not used to churches, but at least I knew that the altar stood at the far end. Rather timid — of what? — I went forward up the nave, into the choir, knelt down at the altar rails, clasped my hands and shut my eyes.

Then came doubt and hesitation. I had got it right so far, and if God wasn't here then He wasn't anywhere. What ought I to say to Him? The question was answered by my own spontaneous recollections. No need for words. There rose before my inward eye the black women begging for mercy on the beach at Lekki and myself taking the whip to them; the stench of the hold full of slaves; the dead bodies hauled up to the deck; Wain leading the hopping "dance"; Wilkins helping enthusiastically to throw live bodies overboard; and the scramble in the slave-market in Jamaica.

Now my tears fell. Between sobs I was uttering words. Loud and incoherent, they rose up of themselves like a spring from the rocks. "Forgive. Help. Come Yourself, Omnipotent. Fight beside me. Evil. Wickedness. Cruelty. I need You! Lord, I dedicate myself. Never forsake me. Promise, promise! Need. Help. Friend."

All my thoughts, all I wanted to tell God, everything I needed to beg for poured from my heart.

I ceased. I felt quiet of mind. In the silence there was no one but God and myself. I longed never to leave this timeless silence, this now everlastingly present.

I remained kneeling at the rails in a gradual returning. I must return to the great cause, and now I had no doubt that it was blessed. I rose from my knees, turned and went slowly down the choir steps into the nave.

"What are you doing here?"

A man – a man I had not noticed – a clergyman – was at my elbow. There was no warmth or greeting in his voice. I groped for a reply.

"What are you doing here?" he repeated captiously.

Although he spoke like one in authority, I felt undaunted. If I had been a white man, I thought, he wouldn't have spoken to me like this.

"I have been praying, sir," I replied, "about a matter of personal importance."

"That some gamble of yours may succeed, I suppose," said he. "Why were you making such a noise? I could hear you outside the church."

"I was not conscious of making a noise, sir. I am sorry. I assure you I meant no irreverence."

"Are you sober?"

"I don't have to answer your questions, sir. I will leave you."

Before he could speak again, I turned on my heel and went, taking care to close the heavy door noiselessly behind me.

Having walked on for a while, it occurred to me that I had

better get a room for the night. Looking about for a lodging house I caught sight, not far off, of a sign hanging from the first floor of some premises that had the look of a modest but respectable place.

Going in, I found myself in a small front hall that impressed me favourably, being clean, tidy and panelled to about three feet from the floor. After waiting for a short time, I was about to call out when a pleasant-looking, middle-aged woman appeared and bid me good morning in a rather reserved manner. Having replied, I told her that I would like a room for the night.

"Certainly," she said. "The first floor front's vacant, as it happens. Is it for your master?"

"No," I answered. "It's for myself."

"I'm sorry," she replied. "We don't cater for black people at all."

Feeling my temper rising, I bit my lip and searched for something to say.

"If you're going to make trouble," she said, "I'll fetch Mr. Travers to speak to you."

"No," I managed to reply. "There's no need. Good morning."

On the step outside, I trod in some dog shit I hadn't noticed before.

As I left the "No Blacks" lodging house behind me and walked on down the street, I saw for myself quite a few black people going about their daily concerns. I stopped one of them, asked him for guidance and added a few words about my recent experience at the lodging house. He replied that I was in the wrong part of the city, "full of bloody white lords of creation", and told me where to go. His advice proved sound, and I put down a deposit for the room, left my baggage and, although it was not yet midday, treated myself to an early meal.

I then set about the real business of the day, which was to find out whether Bristol contained any number of people sympathetic to the cause of Abolition.

Having learned that the Member of Parliament was in London, I decided to try the Bishop. He was away too, but his chaplain,

153

who proved friendly and talked with me for some time, gave me the names and addresses of several clergymen whom it might, he thought, be worth my while to visit.

That afternoon I managed to meet four of these gentlemen. None treated me discourteously and all declared themselves in favour of Abolition, but that was about as far as three of them went. Two plainly thought, (though they were too polite to say so), that I must be acting on behalf of some white person.

My afternoon's work encouraged me to the extent that it showed that at least the idea of Abolition was not without sympathisers in Bristol. Two out of the four told me about someone called Thomas Clarkson.

"He's the fellow for you," said the Reverend Malcolmson, a pleasant man who was digging in his garden. "I've heard he's devoted his life to the cause of Abolition. He's quite young, I believe, but he's getting talked about all right."

"Where is he?" I asked.

"I don't actually know, but somewhere in London, I suppose. That's" (with a smile) "if he's not somewhere else. He travels all over the country, speaking against slavery. Some of my parishioners think a lot of him. 'Is it right to make men slaves against their will?' That's a publication of his. Perhaps you already know it?"

"I'm afraid I don't," I said. "But I've served on a slave-trading ship from Lagos to Jamaica and I've seen a lot – too much – at first hand. Do you suppose Mr. Clarkson has?"

We parted on good terms.

Next morning I called at the bank and provided myself with a hundred pounds. Then I bought two good suits and fitted myself out with everything else I needed – shoes, underclothes, shirts, an overcoat and so on. After that I paid to hire for the day a horse and trap with a driver, a matter over which I had no difficulty when I told the proprietor that I had business with Lady Penelope Marston, of Clepton St. Peter, with whom I had been in service.

We reached Clepton in the early evening. Having turned into the

154

steep little approach from the road down to the stable yard, the first person I saw was Mr. Hodges attending to a horse I did not recognise. Looking up as we arrived, he actually broke into a smile.

"Where've you sprung from then, Dan'l? Bin on yer travels, 'ave yer?"

"I certainly have, Mr. Hodges; too far and too long." I jumped down and shook hands. "I tell you, I'm more than glad to see you again. How've you all been going on? Everything the same?"

"More or less, I s'pose. Your black friends speakin' English like a couple of monkeys but they ain't turned out too bad, 'long as I makes it plain what they 'as to do."

"Well, Mr. Hodges, I tell you, you're the best friend I've seen since I left here. I'd better go in and make myself known. This a new horse you've got?"

"No, this is one of Mr. 'ardwick's carriage 'orses. Only 'e's stayin' a few days, see?"

"Oh ah. Mr. Hodges, could you please do me a favour? This is my driver, who's brought me from Bristol. Could you please look after him, give him something to eat, see to his horse and so on? We'll be returning to Bristol later this evening."

I tipped the man, left him to Hodges and went in by the back door. Mrs. Beddoes was alone in the kitchen except for Paul Chester, who was drinking a cup of tea.

"Well, I declare," she said, "if it isn't young Dan'l! 'Nice to see you again. You going to stay with us a day or two?"

"I hope so," I replied. "But her Ladyship doesn't know I'm here yet."

Paul and I embraced and spoke warmly to each other.

"Now you're here, you'd better have something to eat," said Mrs. Beddoes. "Is Lady Penelope expecting you? No? Well, then, she won't miss you while you have a bite, will she?"

Having had nothing since that morning, I was sharp set. I was still eating when Mr. Graydon came in and greeted me with his customary reserve.

"If her Ladyship doesn't yet know that you're here, Daniel," he said, "you'd better wash your face and hands and come upstairs with me."

At the drawing-room door he said, "Wait here."

As he went in, he left the door slightly ajar, and I heard Lady Penelope's voice.

"Daniel, Graydon? Not really?"

Next moment she was through the door and shaking my hand.

"I'm really glad to see you, Daniel. Come in. You remember Mr. Hardwick, don't you?"

Mr. Hardwick, smiling, also shook my hand. "Do I understand that you've returned from travels abroad, Daniel?"

"I have indeed, sir," I answered, "and I'm more than glad to find myself back home."

At the far end of the room, a black boy of perhaps eleven or twelve, smartly dressed in uniform, was sitting in the window embrasure, knitting. Lady Penelope called him over.

"This is Philip," she said. "Mr. Hardwick found him for me after you left. He's doing well."

I shook hands with Philip and said I was happy to meet him. He was shy and tongue-tied, but I quite liked the look of him.

Lady Penelope and Mr. Hardwick sat down and Lady Penelope motioned me to a chair beside her.

"Your Ladyship," I said, "I'm sure you'll recall that I've never sat down in the same room as yourself." (This wasn't quite strictly true, but near enough.)

"Well, I'm asking you to sit down now," she said. "You'll stay until tomorrow, Daniel, won't you?" (Never mind about the booking at the inn.)

"Thank you, your ladyship. I'll be delighted to."

She sent the young page to tell Mrs. Beddoes that I was staying the night and that Hodges should be told to dismiss my driver. "And now," she said, "tell us your story, Daniel."

"Your Ladyship," I answered, "I hesitate only because I'm afraid

156

you'll find it distressing."

To this she made no reply, but only looked at me as she used to look when she was giving me an order.

So I began, starting from my first meeting with Hawkshot at Bristol, emphasising the large salary he was offering and my total ignorance of the African slave trade. I described the voyage to Lagos and then told of Ushumbo and the condition and desperation of the slaves he brought to the beach at Lekki. As I went on to speak of Jack Wain and the brutality with which the slaves were treated, I paused, feeling a growing tension in my listeners. However, they remained silent and I continued. I kept back nothing, telling how I gave in to Hawkshot and whipped the slaves myself. As I spoke of the hysteria of the naked, fear-crazed women, I saw that Lady Penelope was silently shedding tears. I asked her whether she would prefer me to stop, but she shook her head.

I recounted the heroism of Basil Townley and how he was handed over to Ushumbo. At this Mr. Hardwick broke in to ask what Ushumbo had done with him, and when I answered that I didn't know, said that Hawkshot was a villain and deserved to be hanged.

I omitted nothing about the slaves lying in their own ordure on the floor of the hold, the daily search for dead bodies and the diminution of our own numbers as the voyage to Jamaica continued. At this Mr. Hardwick jumped to his feet, crying out "No more! No more!"

"Sit down, Francis," said Lady Penelope. "If Daniel could endure it, we can hear it." She herself had become calm, although her handkerchief was clenched tightly in one hand. "You have more to tell us, Daniel?"

"The worst, I'm afraid, your Ladyship."

"Do you want to tell us?"

"As your Ladyship wishes."

"Then go on."

I spoke about the slaves thrown overboard alive but then, remembering the undertaking that I had given to Hawkshot, said nothing about his intention to claim insurance. Since it was I myself who had voluntarily initiated the promise, I felt bound to keep it. Finally I gave an account of the slave market and the "scramble" in Jamaica.

As I ended, both my hearers remained silent. I felt that I had still not told all that was on my mind, and at length blurted out, "I feel ashamed of giving in to Wain and Hawkshot. Basil didn't give in and I ought to have done as he did, but I was afraid of what they'd do to me."

Lady Penelope leaned towards me and laid a hand on my shoulder. "I don't think you've very much to feel ashamed of, Daniel. A great many people – perhaps most people – would have done as you did."

"I'm only glad you've got back safe and sound," said Mr. Hardwick. "Your Captain Hawkshot, perhaps he could be hanged on your evidence. Do you think so?"

"I doubt it, sir," I answered. "I think slave-traders stick closely together, and I'm sure Hawkshot would be able to bring Wain and Jarvis and a lot of other people to testify in his favour. Besides, sir, I have it in mind to pursue a different course of action."

"What course?" asked Lady Penelope.

"Your Ladyship," I replied, "I mean to devote myself, for the rest of my life if necessary, to the abolition of the slave trade. I've made some enquiries and I know I shan't be alone. I've been told of a man named Thomas Clarkson who's entirely committed to Abolition and speaks to audiences all over the country. I believe that my testimony – the testimony of a black man with my first-hand experience – could count for a lot with the public and also, perhaps, with Members of Parliament."

"What's your intention, then?" asked Lady Penelope.

"I mean to go and see Mr. Clarkson and offer him my full support. I shan't need pay. I simply want to work alongside him, if only he'll take me on."

"I've been told that the Quakers are strongly opposed to slavery," said Mr. Hardwick. "And that John Wesley fellow, too.

158

You might try them. I'll be going home tomorrow, and I can take you as far as Guildford and put you up for the night."

I thanked him warmly.

"And now we'll have supper brought in," said Lady Penelope.

Two or three days later, having reached the village of Croydon, I went to see a certain Mr. Charles Winter, who, I had been told, was a respected local figure in the Society of Friends. Although he could not entirely conceal his surprise at a visit from an unknown black man, he received me courteously, invited me into his sitting-room and asked what he could do for me.

I explained that his name had been given to me as that of an active sympathiser with the Abolition movement. He responded at once that he, like every member of the Society of Friends, was strongly opposed to the slave trade, and asked what I might have to tell him.

I repeated my account of all that I had experienced under Captain Hawkshot from Lagos to Jamaica. Mr. Winter listened without interruption until I told him about the slaves being thrown alive into the sea. Here he broke in to ask whether I was certain of the truth of what I was telling him. When I had assured him that there was not the least doubt, he buried his face in his hands and said nothing more for a short time. I concluded that he was praying and waited in silence until he looked up at me and nodded. As I continued, he stood up, strode twice back and forth across the room and then, facing me where I sat, said that he could scarcely believe that any man could be so wicked. I told him that my experience had been decisive in determining me to devote myself to the cause of Abolition.

We conversed for some time, and he told me about Mr. James Ramsay, who, as a ship's surgeon, had been sent aboard an English slave-ship in which the Plague was raging, and had seen appalling suffering. Subsequently he had lived for several years in the West Indies and had published an essay on the treatment of slaves in the sugar colonies. This, said Mr. Winter, was a vitally important contribution to the anti-slavery movement. Mr. Ramsay was one of the foremost figures in the cause. He had been cruelly attacked in the Press and even threatened with violence.

"He's Vicar of Teston now," said Mr. Winter. "That's a few miles this side of Maidstone. What you've told me is so important that I think we ought to go and see him, and the sooner the better. Can you come with me tomorrow?"

"But what about your own work, sir?" I asked.

Mr. Winter chuckled. "I'm a schoolmaster," he replied. "It's the holidays just now."

Making an early start and changing horses en route, we reached Teston during the afternoon and were lucky enough to find Mr. Ramsay at home. I was at once struck by his appearance. I judged him to be in his mid-fifties, and far from robust. Gaunt and haggard, he had the look of a man who had suffered, either from illness or harassment. There was a kind of preoccupation in his manner, as though we were not receiving his full attention. However, he plainly wished to make us welcome and rang for tea.

Mr. Winter said that we both wanted to congratulate him on his publication about slavery in the sugar colonies.

"I know it's had a wide circulation," he replied, "and thanks to my old friend Sir Charles Middleton I've been able to talk more than once with Mr. Pitt himself. Sometimes I allow myself to believe that one day the slave trade will be abolished. If I'm a soldier in the fight, I shouldn't complain, should I, if I'm wounded?"

"You have been wounded?" asked Mr. Winter.

"By the attacks in the press, most grievously," he answered. "The savage hostility shown to me not only by the plantation owners in the West Indies but also by their supporters in this country has been a bitter blow."

"But sir," said I, "these people have no thought beyond keeping what they are pleased to call their property – the slaves – and of opposing any change for the better. They deserve nothing but your contempt."

"That's good advice, young man. But it's always troubling to know that there are people who hate you and wish you ill.

160

However, let's forget them for the moment. Tell me the reason for your visit."

"My friend Daniel here," said Mr. Winter, "has seen the evil trade at first hand. I have brought him here expressly to tell you his story. I believe he'll be a unique witness for us."

Mr. Ramsay turned to me. "Tell me all that you've experienced. All that you've come to say."

I did so. As I went on, I was amused to realise that Mr. Winter was listening with attention not unlike that of a child hearing a familiar tale. "You've left out about Ushumbo and his insolence to you," he interrupted at one point. And a little later, while I was telling of Hawkshot's lies about the availability of water, he nodded vigorously in corroboration.

As I ended, Ramsay said, "Thank God you were spared to tell this dreadful story. Mr. Winter, in what way do you think it can best be used?"

I felt that he might in the first place have asked me. "What I have it in mind to do, sir," I said, "is to meet Mr. Clarkson and ask him whether he can make use of me when he speaks to local audiences round the country."

"Good, good," said he. "Clarkson – yes, a stout fellow. But your story should be printed and made available to the public."

"I fear that must wait, sir," I answered. "I'm but a sorry hand with a pen. If I'm to write I shall need help."

"Well, you may certainly have it from me, if you choose. You have only to ask me whenever it may suit you. Meanwhile, with your permission, I shall tell Mr. Pitt what you have told me at the earliest opportunity."

While I felt grateful to Mr. Winter for enabling me to meet Mr. Ramsay, I could not help but conclude that he was something of a spent force. He needed, I thought, stout comrades to fight beside him.

I need not tell in detail of Mr. Winter's continued kindness and help. He not only insisted on my treating his home as my own, but a day or two later told me that we would go up to London together.

"For," said he, "it's a confusing place to someone who's never been there, and to tell you the truth I'm not yet at all sure how we're going to get hold of Mr. Clarkson. All the same, you can safely leave it to me."

I certainly did find London bewildering. I had never imagined anything like the reality. In Bath and even in Bristol the noise was tolerable and the air was not polluted with smoke. London was far dirtier than Bristol. Also, of course, Bristol did not extend so widely in every direction. Walking up Cheapside with Mr. Winter, I lost all sense of direction. The ceaseless din of wheels on the cobbles half-deafened me and because of the ubiquitous rubbish, mud and horse-dung one could reach the opposite side of the street only by way of crossings swept more-or-less clean by poor boys in rags, who looked to get some sort of living with the pence for which they begged. The Cockneys (as Mr. Winter told me they were called) seemed to be forever swearing, quarrelling or beating their wretched mokes. To me this was a foreign country, peopled by unpleasant strangers, and how could any stranger hope to find his way out of it?

However, these feelings subsided somewhat as we walked through the city and came out into the green fields of Euston and Marylebone. The Society of Friends, as I was to learn, had plenty of members in the districts round London, and it was no problem for Mr. Winter to learn the address of an abolitionist so well-known as Mr. Thomas Clarkson. It turned out, however, that he was away on speaking visits in Hertfordshire and was not expected back for a day or two. It was actually the best part of a week before I was able to meet him at his rooms in Clapham.

It had been stormy all day and it was while Mr. Winter and I were looking out at the rain that the sitting-room door flew open to admit the man who was to be a decisive influence on my life – Mr. Thomas Clarkson. In one respect I was surprised; despite what the Rev. Malcolmson had told me, I had not been expecting so young a man. I guessed him to be in his mid-twenties. The first impression he made was of enormous – almost alarming – energy. As he slammed the door behind him he threw down on the table the papers he was carrying and, without a smile, looked keenly from one of us to the other. Clearly, that I was black caused him not a moment's hesitation. He was a handsome and obviously a highly intelligent man, but his features were drawn and strained as though from anxiety or overwork. I could see the pulse beating slightly at his temple. Giving each of us a quick handshake, he sat down on a hard chair and motioned us to two that were upholstered.

"I gather that you gentlemen are sympathetic to the cause of Abolition," he said, glancing at a notepad on the table. "Mr. Winter and Mr. Daniel; just so. How can I help you?"

"I rather believe, sir," said I, thinking that a direct approach would probably be the most acceptable to a man like this, "that it may be I myself who can help you. I have had direct experience of the slave trade in West Africa, of the so-called Middle Passage and of the slave market in Jamaica. Mr. Winter has kindly brought me here today to tell you all I have seen. As a black man who has served many months on a slave ship, I believe I may be of help to you – even, perhaps, a unique witness."

"You've come to tell me about it, have you?"

"Yes, sir."

"All right, I'm listening."

And so I told Mr. Thomas Clarkson – no less – about Captain Hawkshot, Jack Wain, Ushumbo, Basil Townley, my shameful capitulation and the drowned slaves.

He heard me out in silence, and when I had ended said nothing for a short while. At length he asked, "You're absolutely sure of everything you've said, are you? No embellishment?"

"None whatever, sir."

"And you want to take an active part in the movement for Abolition, do you?"

"Sir, I'm ready to devote my whole life to it, if necessary. I hope you're going to tell me what I can best be doing."

"Would you be ready to speak to audiences at public meetings?"

"With all my heart, sir. There's only one thing that makes me hesitate."

"That is?"

"Well, as I'm sure you've perceived for yourself, sir, I'm not an educated man. I haven't the command of words that you have and which I expect other gentlemen have who speak against Abolition."

"That doesn't matter. In fact it will be an advantage. You're an ordinary man, like the people we want to convince. And you're black. Frankly, I often wish I was black myself. You'll have a unique appeal. Can you join me and Denis Green this Wednesday?"

"With great pleasure, sir. Where are we going?"

"To Newbury, about sixty miles; and then to Reading on Thursday. Bring a night-bag and an overcoat. That's all you'll need. Not money; I'll see to that. Join us here at six in the morning on Wednesday. And now I'll have to leave you; I've got work to do. My thanks to you both and good afternoon."

On Wednesday morning I was punctual. I was introduced to Mr. Green and we set off in fine weather.

"I believe you know Bristol, Mr. Daniel?" said Mr. Green, evidently wishing to be friendly.

"Not well, sir. I know Bath rather better."

"Ah, a beautiful city," he replied. "I hope we'll get a chance to speak there one day."

We had luncheon at Maidenhead and changed horses. It was getting on for six o'clock as we approached Newbury and I was feeling that I had travelled quite far enough. Mr. Clarkson, however, seemed as fresh as paint. "I expect Minnock'll be waiting for us somewhere here," he said. "Yes, there he is. Pull up, Barnes. Good evening, Minnock. 'Hope you haven't been waiting too long."

"No, Mr. Clarkson, sir, thank you. I'll drive ahead of you to Reverend Slocock's."

"Slocock's a tower of strength," said Clarkson to me. "He's

organised this meeting practically single-handed. If the Church had more like him, that Wesley fellow wouldn't command so much support."

It was not far to the Rectory, where Mr. Slocock welcomed Mr. Clarkson as an old friend and extended a warm welcome to Mr. Green and myself. As we sat down to roast beef and apple-pie, Mr. Clarkson outlined to the Rector my experience of the Slave Coast, the Middle Passage and Jamaica. He went on to speak of the value he attached to me as a black witness of the horror of the trade. When Mr. Slocock tried to draw me out a little, Mr. Clarkson interjected, "He'll tell you that himself, later."

I asked the Rector where the meeting was to be held.

"Why, in the Church," he answered, "close by. No alternative; it's the largest assembly place in the town."

"Splendid!" said Mr. Green. "This is a sacred cause, no question. You had no difficulty in getting authority?"

The Rector grinned. "I'm the authority," he replied. "This is my parish and my church. If the Bishop doesn't know that by now, he ought to."

Soon afterwards we stepped outside, where we found any number of people arriving for the meeting. Mr. Slocock greeted several by name, and it was plain that he was popular. Many were clearly of the labouring class – Mr. Clarkson's "ordinary people". Most of them stared at the black man standing beside their Rector, but quite a few nodded to me in a friendly way as they turned to go into the church.

People were still coming when Mr. Slocock took Mr. Clarkson's arm and led us in, up the nave to the chancel steps. With his back to the assembly, he clasped his hands, closed his eyes and murmured "Lord God, we beg Thee to be with us this evening as we do Thy work," to which the three of us contributed a muted "Amen."

As he turned to face his audience, he showed for the first time that evening a bearing of power and authority. It was as though he had put on an imposing robe. Visibly he was the same man and yet he was not. Everyone seemed to feel this, for he commanded immediate silence.

He began by saying that we should all be glad that so many people, both men and women, had come this evening to hear about the evil of the African slave trade. In case anyone thought that this had little or nothing to do with England, he wanted everyone to know that no fewer than four-fifths of the trade was carried out by British ships. This was a dreadful sin in the sight of God, and all of us, as a nation, were collectively guilty of it. "Don't think you're not guilty," he went on. "We're all guilty. But if only enough people in this country were determined to put an end to the trade, it could be ended; and Mr. Thomas Clarkson, a distinguished public speaker, has come here tonight to tell us how. Also here to speak is Mr. Daniel, who was born a slave in America and has served on an English slaving ship. He is going to tell us what this evil trade is really like – what actually happens when black people are captured and taken across the Atlantic ocean to toil in harsh conditions and without pay until they die. In the course of two centuries millions have died. Finally, Mr. Denis Green will tell you about the harm the trade has done to Africa." He thereupon called on Mr. Clarkson to go into the pulpit and speak.

To these Newburians and to myself, who had never heard Mr. Clarkson speak, he was like a refiner's fire. His passion, his overwhelming conviction almost frightened his audience. He blazed with anger. He shed plainly unsimulated tears of grief. Not a man or woman could remain detached from his fervour. Yet it was not mere emotion, mere verbiage. He made clear to his audience the hard facts of the trade's history, of its shameful lawfulness, of the growth of public opposition and of what had to be done by Parliament. Parliament could and should be petitioned and this was something that their Rector was going to organise.

And now Mr. Daniel, who had actually served on a slave-ship, was going to tell them what the reality was like for the millions – yes, millions – of black people torn from their homes to suffer and die in misery.

As Mr. Clarkson came down, Mr. Slocock, smiling at me

reassuringly, led me up into the pulpit. I turned, gripped the edge in both hands and faced the audience.

I had not prepared myself for this. I was not talking just to Mr. Winter or to Mr. Clarkson now. Below me, looking up expectantly, were hundreds of faces; and they were all the faces of white people. I had lived for years among white people with almost no conscious sense of inferiority. Lady Penelope and her servants had all been my friends. So had Basil Townley, Limbrick, Portway – all of them. But now, as I confronted these white strangers, there rose up within me uncertainty, acquiescence, deference, standing like a wall between them and me. My forebears possessed me, slaves bowing down before their betters, submissive, obedient, waiting for permission to go. Lord above! It wasn't my servile place to speak; I wanted to go, to be among my own black people.

Looking from one face to another, I saw them becoming first puzzled and then restive. What in heaven's name was he doing up there, this black man, this natural inferior? Why wasn't he speaking? Anyway, what could a black man have to say? A few people were already getting to their feet.

"Come on, Daniel! Speak up! I've come a long way to hear you!" The voice rang out from the back and a hand was waving. Then its owner stood up. It was Paul Chester.

Instantly my true self returned. The forefathers left me. I knew my business now all right. I was essential, unique. If these people didn't hear what I had to tell them, they'd probably never hear it at all.

"I've come to tell you how I sailed from Bristol on a slaving voyage and of all that I saw with my own eyes, in Africa, at sea and in Jamaica. I promise you that every word is true."

At once my voice – my singular, black voice – regained their attention. I shortened my account of my meeting with Hawkshot and of the voyage out, and concentrated on making them see with their own eyes the beach at Lekki. When I described the condition of the slaves, two or three women, plainly upset, stood up and made as if to leave. "You *must* stay and hear me," I called to them. "The black people – my black people – you're their only hope!"

167

As I told about the slaves manacled in the hold, the killing disease, the filth in which they lay and then about the deliberate drownings, I became carried away with fury. I beat on the pulpit, shouted and was almost chanting. They still listened and no one moved. As I ended, in the slave-market in Jamaica, women were weeping and a voice called out "Well done, lad!"

Mr. Green, following, spoke about the harm done to Africa. Europe and America were progressing, were prosperous. They were developing their natural resources. Africa was not. No; it was deteriorating. For two centuries its people had been seized by force and carried off in millions. Tribal kings had been corrupted into selling their own people for alcohol and firearms. Civil wars had been fought simply to capture slaves. The continent had been stripped of its manpower, corrupted, ruined, and Britain was by far the country most to blame. Deaths on British slave-ships crossing the Atlantic ocean were sometimes as high as eighty per cent and almost never less than forty five. The damage done to Africa was almost irreparable. It would be centuries – yes, centuries – before this terrible wrong – the greatest wrong in all human history – "tell me a greater" – could be righted. This was our shame – our shame as a nation – and God saw it, if we didn't.

As Mr. Green finished, the Mayor stood up and spoke a few words. He said that he was sure that everyone had been deeply moved, as he had himself. He had no doubt that Newbury would be stoutly in favour of Abolition and would do all it could to bring it about.

The four of us stayed until the audience had gone, but when we followed I found, as I had been expecting, Paul waiting to speak to me. I introduced him and thanked him from the bottom of my heart for his help to me.

"How ever did you get here?" I asked him.

"Well," he replied, "Lady Penelope gave me leave and a friend of Mr. Hodges took me with him as far as Hungerford." He grinned. "I walked the rest."

The Rector invited him to join us for a bite to eat. Our night's lodgings, to which we were guided by one of his servants, were

168

comfortable enough, and I had no difficulty in including Paul. Next morning, at yet another parting between the two of us, Mr. Slocock secured him a place with a friend driving to Bath, while we set off for Reading.

At that night's meeting we met with hostility from a group in the audience, who opposed Mr. Clarkson as soon as he had finished his address. The slave trade, said their spokesman, was both economically necessary and humane. The slaves were well-treated. There was no improper severity. The trade was being attacked by mere busybodies, who knew nothing about it. This was philanthropy gone mad. Abolition would mean that honest merchants and ship-owners would be ruined. The French would step in and take away our trade. Worse, Abolition would be followed by Negro risings in the West Indies. Inevitably there would be bloody massacres of white people.

Mr. Clarkson replied that he had never denied that Abolition would involve a loss of trade. So it should. The termination of every evil usually brought about a loss to those who were making money out of it. Making money through the slave trade was morally unjustifiable. Let them wait and hear what Mr. Daniel had to tell them; Mr. Daniel who had experienced at first hand what they had never even tried to see for themselves.

It was at this meeting in Reading that the knowledge began to dawn upon me that my contribution to the cause of Abolition was unique and unanswerable. It constituted a complete reply against any contention that the trade was not based on deliberate cruelty, that the slaves were not ill-treated and that we were misrepresenting the truth. What I had seen, what I spoke about, had the power to defeat all attacks on that particular aspect of our case – the issue of inhumanity. Others, wiser and more knowledgeable than I, were better qualified to contend about the sanctity of property, of diseases left untreated, of early mortality from overwork and exhaustion, and of the overriding importance of Christian principles. But on the matter of cruelty being essential to the trade, of the deliberate infliction of suffering, the mere recounting of my experience was enough to defeat all

169

attempts to whitewash the hideous truth. That night, as I spoke about the whips on the beach and the slaves thrown alive into the sea, I saw our opponents put out of countenance, and when I had finished they made no attempt to resume their attack. One man alone demanded to know whether what I had said was the truth, to which I replied, "Do you think I could have invented it?"

Upon our return next day, Mr. Clarkson told me that he particularly wished me not to leave London for the time being. He wanted me to stay with him. I agreed at once and he thereupon sent a letter by his servant to Mr. Winter, asking him to let the man have my few things to bring back with him. Next day, as soon as we had finished breakfast, he told me what he had in mind.

"You've done very well so far, Daniel," he said. "I want you, if you will, to remain with me and join me in the work. As a black man you're invaluable. But I want to help you to become still better. You're a good speaker but you'd agree, wouldn't you? that at present you're somewhat handicapped by lacking a wide knowledge of words."

"Yes, sir," I answered, "I know that all too well."

"It's a handicap we can overcome," he said. "You can improve not merely your vocabulary, but your whole ability with words – your style, one might say. I'd like you to live here and put as much time as you can into reading. I'll see you get books that interest you – novels, poetry, scientific stuff, whatever you like, if only you're ready to work seriously." He gave me one of his rare smiles. "You might even enjoy it – who knows?"

This was how I came under the guidance of Mr. Clarkson, received an education in English and became literate. He was certainly exacting – very much so – but since we shared one and the same purpose, we got along pretty well. I was careful to give as little trouble in the house as possible, and his servants seemed not to resent me. Having transferred my bank account from Bristol, I had sufficient money for my simple needs.

I came to know several of Mr. Clarkson's friends, most of them principal figures in the cause of Abolition. A large number were Quakers. Among them was Mr. James Phillips, who became a good friend to me, introducing me to Richardson's novels and the poetry of Pope and Dryden.

There came a day when Mr. Clarkson told me that he wished me to accompany him to an informal meeting of Abolitionists, to meet a Member of Parliament named William Wilberforce. This Mr. Wilberforece had agreed to pursue the cause of Abolition in the House of Commons.

"He's studying the whole business very thoroughly," said Mr. Clarkson. "He's on good terms with a lot of our Quaker friends. There'll be several people there today who are all looking forward to him speaking about Abolition in Parliament. He's a close friend of young Mr. Pitt, the Prime Minister. Apparently Pitt himself is very much against the Slave Trade."

This was how I met William Wilberforce, the Abolitionist hero, the slaves' Knight Errant, the indefatigable Member of Parliament against the Slave Trade. When we arrived, a number of gentlemen were present, several of whom I had already met. They were gathered round Mr. Wilberforce, whose appearance and manner were a surprise to me. He was by no means a commanding figure. He was slightly built and short of stature, and his carriage and movements had a certain singularity; not bizarre but certainly unusual. I thought he looked too sensitive to be a fighting leader and far from robust. However, he had a handsome face, and his manner as he talked was genial and warm. He was standing near a window, and he suddenly broke off what he was saying and looked out in silence for some moments. "A goldfinch," he explained smilingly to his hearers. "Such pretty birds. At this time of year they're attracted by the seeds left on the plants, you know. But we must continue our discussion, mustn't we? 'Sorry for the interruption."

Mr. Clarkson introduced me to him, saying that my colour, and experience of the horrors of the Slave Trade at first hand, made me a valuable speaker at public meetings. Mr. Wilberforce shook hands and said he was happy to meet me, and we conversed together for several minutes. His personal attention came as a most pleasant surprise.

It was not, (so Mr. Clarkson told me), at any informal meeting of sympathisers like this one that Mr. Wilberforce had consented to introduce the matter of the Slave Trade in Parliament. First, he had had a long talk with Mr. Pitt, the Prime Minister. Then, soon afterwards, at a dinner party of several distinguished persons, a certain Mr. Bennet Langton had obtained his formal agreement. Everyone felt that this represented a marked step forward.

Hitherto, I had supposed that once we had established throughout the country the conviction, among the majority, that the slave trade was unjustifiable and evil, it would be abolished by order of the Government. Mr. Wilberforce, with a speech in Parliament, would establish an overwhelming case and Mr. Pitt, as Prime Minister, would take the necessary steps to bring the trade to an end.

I asked Mr. Clarkson how soon, once Mr. Wilberforce had spoken, Abolition would be declared.

"You mean," he said, "whether he'll be able to introduce a Bill, don't you?"

"I'm afraid I don't quite understand, sir. Once Mr. Wilberforce has spoken, won't Mr. Pitt be able to declare the Trade abolished?"

"Well, don't be silly, Daniel. Of course he won't."

"Then the King will do it? The supreme power?"

"The King's mad."

I stared, wondering whether I was mad myself.

Patiently, Mr. Clarkson explained the constitution of Parliament, the Commons and the Lords; legislation, Bills and Acts. "We've hardly started yet, Daniel, to bring about Abolition. Perhaps we'll achieve it in five or six years. Or perhaps not. The House of Lords will undoubtedly reject Wilberforce's Bill. That's if he can manage to introduce a Bill and get it through the House of Commons."

"But I thought nearly everybody wanted it."

"You thought wrong, then."

Knowing how impatient and dismissive Mr. Clarkson could be,

I desisted from further questions.

Shortly afterwards, Mr. Clarkson told me that he and I would soon be off to Bristol and then to Liverpool by way of Chester. I knew that most of our Abolitionist friends thought of Liverpool as the lions' den and I felt nervous at the idea of actually going there. A few days later, I was approached by two members of the London Abolition Committee. I felt embarrassed when they told me that they did not want Mr. Clarkson to know of our meeting. However, I thought I had better hear what they had to say.

This was nothing less than to express the hope that I might be able to dissuade Mr. Clarkson from making our intended journey to Liverpool. The Committee, they told me, had misgivings about his fitness for the task. While his zeal and activity were highly regarded, the Committee feared that he was lacking in tact and prudence. He was likely to give offence, and was not the right man to collect evidence and present it to Ministers and Members of Parliament: that called for a cooler head. I told them that my relationship to Mr. Clarkson was that of an obedient subordinate and that I hadn't got the influence over him that they were looking for. Soon afterwards, I learned that the Committee had decided to raise no objection to our visiting Liverpool, but had stressed to Mr. Clarkson the need for discretion.

I remember Mr. Clarkson telling me what he meant to achieve in Liverpool. We were walking on the city walls of Chester. It was a sunny, cloudless day in January.

"You know, of course, Daniel," said Mr. Clarkson, "that Liverpool is by far the biggest slave-trading port in England. Do you know how many slave-ships sailed from Liverpool to West Africa last year? Sixty-one, that's how many. There were eighteen from Bristol and fifteen from London. And the Liverpool ships carried more slaves per ton than any of the Bristol or London ships."

"How did you manage to get those figures, sir?" I asked.

"By persistent enquiry," he replied. "But I have my contacts as well. I'm in no doubt the figures are correct."

After a little, he went on "But what I'm sure you couldn't even guess, Daniel, is that there are a number of educated, influential men in Liverpool who are in favour of Abolition."

He paused. "You don't believe me?"

"Oh, yes, sir, I believe you. But what I'm wondering is how these men can dare to speak out."

"They can't, really," he answered. "Not in Liverpool. That's to say they can't speak out forcefully, as you and I do. But all the same, they make their views known. We're going to meet them and see whether we can't give them some help."

"Do you know any of them by name, sir?"

"Yes, as it happens, I do," said he. "I've got four names: Rathbone, Roscoe, Currie and Rushton. We'll try Rathbone for a start. I know that Mr. Barton, our Quaker friend in London, has been in touch with him for some time. Roscoe and the people around him have been talking of setting up a Liverpool Abolition Society. But that's all nonsense. Of course they daren't really attempt it; but where these fellows do come in handy is that they can give us a lot of detailed information about the African trade. Not to mention the muster rolls of a lot of the Liverpool slave-ships."

As soon as we had settled in to our lodgings at *The King's Arms*, (not a single Liverpudlian dared to offer us hospitality), we called on Mr. Rathbone.

There turned out to be two Mr. Rathbones. The elder, William, a Quaker, was in his seventies, a well-to-do timber merchant. This put him in a self-contradictory position as an Abolitionist, since for years past he had been supplying timber to the African ships of Liverpool. Lately, however, he had been gradually moving out of this business, and developing interests in West Indian and Baltic trades instead. I took to him immediately. He had a quick, shrewd intellect, and was quite without self-importance or vanity. He treated us courteously. He was, I think, the oldest member of the Liverpool Abolitionist group nicknamed "the Saints". Although the Saints had never got further than talking about setting up an Abolitionist society and although they exercised

174

virtually no political influence as a group, they were respected for their views and had never been harassed or ostracised.

William's son, who was about thirty at the time of our visit, was altogether different, an aggressive, outspoken man who enjoyed a good scrap; not only an abolitionist but a radical supporter of free trade and universal suffrage. Not unexpectedly, he had quite a few enemies, but he was the sort of man who thrives on friction.

The elder Mr. Rathbone introduced us to Mr. Roscoe, the most well-known and influential of the Liverpool Abolitionist sympathisers. For me, Mr. Roscoe (whom I guessed to be about 35) turned out to be something of a disappointment. I had been expecting a fervid, all-out abolitionist. Yet on the contrary, I soon realised that abolition wasn't Mr. Roscoe's principal interest, although he had recently done some useful work by writing anti-slavery pamphlets, which the London Committee thought well of and were going to publish. He was also, as he told us, the author of a good deal of poetry, including a long poem entitled *The Wrongs of Africa*. What he really wanted was to become famous as a poet, and to do him justice some of his poetry seemed pretty good to me. (Not that I could consider myself much of a judge.)

It was plain that he was also very much a man of business, with a sharp eye for profit. So he too was in a self-contradictory position, for on the one hand he was calling himself an abolitionist, while on the other he certainly wouldn't do anything to diminish the prosperity of Liverpool, upon which he depended for his livelihood.

Although I had these reservations about his real value to us, in fairness I ought to add that many educated Liverpudlians admired what they considered his moral fearlessness and intellectual superiority. To my way of thinking, however, he wasn't half fearless enough. "Run with the hare and hunt with the hounds" just about summed him up.

That evening at Mr. Roscoe's, we also became acquainted with two other Abolitionists, Doctor James Currie and Mr. Edward Rushton. Dr. Currie, a Scotchman from Dumfries, was about my own age, and a comparative newcomer to Liverpool. When still very young, he had emigrated to America and become apprenticed to a Virginian merchant. Upon the outbreak of the War of Independence, however, he had managed to get to the West Indies and thence back home to Scotland. He then studied medicine at Edinburgh and, having qualified, came to Liverpool, where he was successful in gaining an appointment as physician at the Infirmary. Mr. Clarkson and I both reckoned him the best intellect in the Roscoe circle. (Our judgement was confirmed when, about four years after our visit, he was elected a Fellow of the Royal Society.) I found him stiff and unaccommodating: and I was not altogether surprised to hear, later, that he had become subject to fits of depression. It was hard enough for the members of Roscoe's circle to penetrate his reserve, so there was no chance whatever for a young black man from London.

Wasn't there even one of them for whom you could feel some warmth and friendliness, the reader may ask? Yes, indeed there was. From the time of that first visit, nearly thirt years ago, Ted Rushton has remained one of my closest friends. en I go up to Liverpool nowadays it is to see Ted. During that v sit, both Mr. Clarkson and I sat and talked with him on many afternoons and evenings.

Ted, who was also about my own age, had become, at sixteen, second mate on an African slave-ship. While sailing in African waters, he befriended a black slave by the name of Quamina. One day, when Quamina and he were carrying slaves from a beach to Ted's ship, their boat overturned in a rough sea. Despite the strong tide that was running, Quamina managed to grab a barrel, which kept him afloat. But then, seeing Ted struggling desperately, he let go of it and pushed it within Ted's reach, intentionally sacrificing his own life to save Ted's. Ted saw him waving farewell as he was swept away and drawn under.

Some months later, while Ted was still serving with the same ship, ophthalmia broke out among the slaves in the hold. Not one of the ship's officers would go down there except Ted, who remained below and did all he could for the wretched victims. By the time they got to the West Indies, he was blind. Somehow he

176

managed to get back to Liverpool, penniless and on the verge of starvation.

For several years afterwards, he lived in penury.

Never forgetting Quamina, he became a committed opponent of the slave trade and, with the help of friends, expressed his views forthrightly.

For a time, he was actually editor of the *Liverpool Herald*. But an outspoken article about the press gang, which came to the attention of the Liverpool Corporation, cost him the job. However, he continued to speak out and to make no secret of his beliefs. It was only his blindness that kept him out of more trouble. He was the sole Liverpool Abolitionist who had had direct experience of the Slave Trade, and this gave his writing authenticity and a force and sharpness lacking in the articles of Roscoe and Currie. Although Mr. Clarkson obtained a great deal of valuable material from him, we never managed to persuade him to come to London and testify.

Although, as our visit continued, Mr. Roscoe and his friends did not show themselves particularly helpful, Mr. Clarkson was undaunted; he told me that he thought he would get all the information he required in Liverpool. At *The King's Arms* we were able to meet and talk to any number of seamen and captains who were "regulars" of the place. The steady flow of seamen coming off the slave-ships were ready enough to talk. What they would not do was give us the names of the captains and sailors whom they were criticising. ("Get your bloody windows smashed, 'ouses pulled down," said one of them to me.)

One day, displayed in a shop window in the centre of the city, we saw a set of tools for constraining slaves: handcuffs, shackles, thumbscrews, mouth-openers and other instruments of torture. Mr. Clarkson bought a complete set – valuable evidence to take back to London. "Do you think we might try them on the House of Lords?" he asked me.

It troubled me – though of course I said nothing – that the anxiety of the London Committee about the suitability of Mr. Clarkson was only too surely confirmed. He made plenty of enemies among the respected merchants of the city. One day, for instance, when a certain Mr. Chaffers, a member of the Borough Council and a former slave-ship captain, had introduced us to one Mr. Ambrose Lace, a wealthy African and West Indian merchant, Mr. Clarkson accused him of having been "up to the neck", as he put it, in the notorious massacre of blacks at Calabar, twenty years before. He as good as called him a dirty slaver. Mr. Lace made no reply, but walked out in haughty silence. I thought this particularly unfortunate, because hitherto, as I learned later, most of the merchants had not supposed that we were collecting evidence against them, or that we were committed abolitionists.

They supposed it now, all right. From that day we encountered any amount of hostility which, of course, cramped our style. We were harassed and had to leave *The King's Arms*. We received anonymous letters, threatening to kill us. I admit I was frightened and my fear was justified by a nasty experience.

One day the city was hit by a strong gale. Mr. Clarkson and I made our way to the pier head to observe the tossing boats and spectacular waves and spray. Upon starting back, we saw a group of some nine or ten men coming towards us. We continued on our way, naturally supposing that they would part and let us through. We were mistaken. Shouting threats and insults, they closed in on us. We were pushed against the rails and almost over them into the sea. I recognised two of the men whom we had met in *The King's Arms*.

Mr. Clarkson and I both struck out for dear life, and I admit I thought we were done for: they meant to push us into the sea. However, as hooligans they proved to be no great shakes. I knocked one down and we were able to burst through them and run, pursued by abuse and foul language.

As I have said, I found our visit disappointing. But it could hardly have been otherwise. Roscoe and his followers were only playing at Abolition. The practical effects of their so-called campaign were piffling. They entirely lacked readiness for self-sacrifice and ruthlessness of purpose. To come out into the open and declare for Abolition above all else would have cost them

178

grave financial loss and their esteemed places in Liverpool society as well, and they weren't ready to pay such a price. That was why Ted Rushton was the best man among them and the most valuable to us real abolitionists. He'd been on a slave-ship, he'd given his eyesight for the slaves and he had no place to lose in Liverpool society.

Roscoe favoured a gradual reduction of slavery, bit by bit, until it disappeared, but we followers of Sharp and Wilberforce were having none of that. Once you have realised that something is appallingly wrong and wicked, how can you agree to leave chunks of it to go on lying about for years?

As far as I remember, it was some time during the February of 1788 that Mr. Pitt set up a Committee of the Privy Council to make a formal inquiry into the conditions of trade with Africa. He meant to await its report before authorising any discussion in Parliament.

A month later Mr. Wilberforce fell seriously ill, the result of strain and overwork. Most of us despaired of his life, for a conference of doctors made no secret of their view. Although he accepted their advice that he should go to Bath and take the waters, he arrived there in a grievous state. He maintained, however, (so I was told by Mr. Clarkson) that Our Lord meant him to survive to continue His work.

It was an anxious time for all of us. Before going to the waters at Bath, he had been able to have another talk with Mr. Pitt, who promised to act on his behalf and do all that he would have done himself. Personally, I believe that this, more than anything else, was what put Mr. Wilberforce on the road to recovery.

Mr. Pitt was as good as his word. Superintending the Privy Council inquiry in person, he told Mr. Clarkson and myself that for his own part he hoped for total Abolition. Serious proceedings, however, would have to await the Privy Council's report.

It was not until November that Mr. Wilberforce was able to return to the House of Commons. During this winter Parliamentary business was seriously affected as a result of the King going out of his mind. The crisis over the question of a

Regency continued well into the following year.

That April the Privy Council Committee submitted their Report on Trade with Africa, and accordingly the Commons debate was fixed for 12th May.

I well remember, about this time, taking to Mr. Wilberforce a summary of the evidence that Mr. Clarkson and I had collected in Liverpool. He was in high spirits, and showed me a letter from Tom Gisborne, an old friend of Cambridge days.

"I shall expect," Mr. Gisborne wrote, "to read of your being carbonadoed by West Indian planters, barbecued by African merchants and eaten by Guinea captains. But do not be daunted, for – I will write your epitaph!"

"Not a bit of it," said Mr. Wilberforce, laughing heartily. "You mark my words, Daniel, I shall write his."

At this stage Mr. Wilberforce was in no doubt of success, for he had the support of Charles James Fox and also that of Mr. Pitt himself. But others were not so sure. Among them was the Reverend John Wesley, a hardened veteran when it came to urging moral principles upon people concerned with safeguarding the value of their own property. To them, slaves were "property"; chattels, not exactly human beings.

Mr. Clarkson was able to gain admission for himself and me to an upper gallery, from which we could see and hear well enough.

On the previous day, Mr. Wilberforce had told some of us that, although he knew that in their hearts, most of the Members were on his side in condemning the Trade, they felt hesitant about openly going against an essential national interest; and on top of that, he had to bear in mind the West Indian lobby. So he took care to speak courteously and moderately. Afterwards Mr. Edmund Burke who, together with Pitt and Fox, had also spoken in favour of immediate abolition, said that he considered Mr. Wilberforce's speech as good as anything he had come across in the whole field of modern oratory.

Mr. Wilberforce spoke for more than three hours, and I could have listened to him for longer. But for all his conviction and

180

sincerity, those against Abolition succeeded in postponing further consideration of the business until the next Parliamentary session. Naturally, we all felt this as a disappointing setback.

Another blow that fell upon us soon afterwards, in July, was the death of the Reverend Ramsay. His contribution to the Cause had been, perhaps, the greatest of all. His well-written, convincing pamphlets were widely read and proved of great value to the Cause. The first man of all to go into print about Slavery, for two years and more he had kept the Cause alive and borne single-handed the brunt of one savage attack after another. His death came as no surprise to me for, as I have said, when Mr. Clarkson and I met him, I had thought him in poor health. Now, I wondered only that he had lasted so long. "Poor fellow," said Mr. Clarkson, "he gave his life in the Cause. He's set us a great example. We must follow in his footsteps, Daniel, however far they lead us."

"Yes, sir," I replied. "We know now, don't we? how far they may lead us, and what we may be in for."

I believe that Mr. Clarkson, with his insatiable energy, could not convince himself that he was furthering the cause unless he was continually on the move. It was soon after the death of Mr. Ramsay that he decided to visit France, to meet as many as he could of the most well-known public figures and if possible to obtain their support for Abolition. Naturally, I begged him to take me with him, but he refused me with his characteristic abruptness. "No, no. You'd only increase the cost. You'll do more good staying here."

"But how long will you be away, sir?"

"No idea. I'll write, of course. 'Let you know what happens. I'll leave you some money. Take a good, long holiday. Then go and see Wilberforce or Sharp. They'll give you plenty to do."

I went to see Mr. Wilberforce in his dwelling at Palace Yard, opposite the entrance to the House of Lords. I found it not unlike a crowded hotel. On the day of my visit, Mr. Pitt and several of his friends were there. Falling into conversation with one of the servants, I learned that they often dined at Mr. Wilberforce's table, as did the London Committee, while those engaged in research (his "white slaves" as Mr. Pitt jokingly called them) did much of their work there. I myself had come early that morning, with the result that I (and several other early birds) was given breakfast. By ten o'clock the anteroom was more than full. There were Yorkshire constituents, Christian missionaries, people from Africa, petitioners for charity, men who had come to give their personal testimony about the Slave Trade and many more. However, I did manage to talk to Mr. Wilberforce who, after praising me for all I had done since I first joined Mr. Clarkson, told me that he thought I would certainly be of use to Mr. Granville Sharp.

I had, of course, already heard of Mr. Sharp, one of the most highly regarded veterans in the Movement. Two years before, he had been a founder member of the Society for the Abolition of the Slave Trade, and as Chairman had shown forceful leadership. On more than one occasion he had talked with Mr. Pitt, whose views on total abolition accorded with the Society's own.

Before going to meet Mr. Sharp, I thought I would ask one or two people who knew him well to tell me about his character and achievements. I sought out two of the Society's Quaker committee members, Mr. Gratby and Mr. Hayter, and asked for their advice. I explained that I had already had some useful experience, having worked for Mr. Clarkson, and that Mr. Wilberforce himself had advised me to offer my services to Mr. Granville Sharp.

They responded warmly, and asked me how much I knew about Mr. Sharp, to which I replied, "Very little", and added, "What sort of a man is he?"

"Well," said Mr. Hayter with a smile, "he was born and brought up in Durham, you know. I've always been told that's the place to look for real dogged fellows; chaps who don't give up on anything once they've started."

"And that just about fits our friend Granville," said Mr. Gratby. "He was apprenticed here in London, you know, when he was just a young chap, and I've heard that he taught himself Hebrew and Greek in his spare time. That'll give you some idea of him. He'd have been in his twenties, I suppose, when he first got interested

182

in the Anti-Slavery movement."

"Ah, and he didn't just read about it or talk about it," said Mr. Hayter. "He took it on board and lived it. 'Soon showed what he was made of. One night, going home, he came on a black man destitute on the streets, not a penny in his pocket – abandoned by his white master. Now what the deuce was his name, Terence? It's clean gone out of my head."

"The black man's name was Jonathan Strong," said Mr. Gratby. "I met him once, soon after Mr. Sharp had taken him home and was looking after him at his own expense. He struck me as an honest fellow."

"That's right," said Mr. Hayter, "and the man who abandoned him was called David Lisle. I remember that much. You never met him, though, did you, Terence?"

"No, I never did," said Mr. Gratby. "Nor I didn't want to. Didn't he get hold of Strong while he was with Granville and had him put in prison as a runaway slave?"

"That's right, and he brought an action against Granville, for unlawfully detaining his property. He said Strong was his property! But Granville fought him in Court every inch of the way and Mr. Lisle dropped out in the end. 'Found he'd 'caught a Tartar', as they say. 'Hadn't reckoned with Granville and his Durham style. Bull terrier he is, when he sees occasion."

They both laughed. "Do go on," I said. "I'm going to like Mr. Sharp, I can see that."

"You'll not be the only one," replied Mr. Gratby, taking a large pinch of snuff from a silver box. "Specially you being black. He's been a regular saint and champion for black people."

"None to touch him," said Mr. Hayter. "The great battle he won was the Summersett case. Do you know about that, Mr. Daniel? 'Changed the world, that has."

"Tell me," I said. "Who was Summersett?"

"He was a black slave until he met Mr. Sharp. Oh, it must have been something like sixteen or seventeen years ago now, I suppose. He ran away from his master and when his master

captured him and held him – held him against his will, of course
- Granville took him to law. That was when Lord Mansfield laid it
down that there were no slaves in this country. As soon as a so-
called slave sets foot on English soil, he becomes free; free to leave
his master, and free to look after himself."

"And that crowning victory was due entirely to Granville and to
no one else," said Mr. Gratby. "He won it single-handed. He had
very little money and he was entirely dependent on his job in the
Ordnance Department: he had to keep that on just to live. But
somehow he found the money and the time and the knowledge of
law to conduct the case on his own and the perseverance to see it
through to the end. You couldn't have found anyone who'd have
put a shilling on him to win."

"Ah," said Mr. Hayter. "He said God was on his side and God
was all he needed."

"That was the most important case of the last hundred years, I
reckon," said Mr. Gratby, emphasising his words by nodding
vigorously and putting a heavy hand on my shoulder. "It set
hundreds of black people free all over the country."

I told them about Mr. Grench and Lady Penelope, and about
Fahdah and her brothers.

"Ah, I've heard tell of Lady Penelope Marston," said Mr. Hayter.
"She's a servant of the Lord, all right."

"But all those freed black people have made a difficult problem,
all the same," said Mr. Gratby. There simply hasn't been enough
employment for them. I well remember Mr. Pitt himself
discussing the whole thing with Granville. Granville always had
the notion of taking them abroad to found a colony and run it
themselves. 'Need a white governor to see it go right, of course."

"And what was the name of the man who suggested Sierra
Leone?" asked Mr. Hayter.

"Oh, Dr. Sleathman, you mean," replied Mr. Gratby. "He'd lived
there himself, of course. 'Knew all about the country."

"And did anything come of it?" I asked.

"Oh, my goodness, yes. You don't know?"

184

"I'm afraid not."

"Oh, it's all of two years and more, isn't it, Ben? A whole shipload of freed black people and quite a few whites as well set sail for Sierra Leone. There were something like 80 white wives of black husbands. What I heard was that the white women were people who could well be spared."

"And have these people made a go of it?" I asked.

"I wish I could say yes," replied Mr. Hayter. "A local chieftain – King Tom as he's called - had sold them quite a sizeable area of land to start on, and they'd begun building a town. Granville Sharp (who didn't go out with them) named it 'Freedom Province'. But they had bad luck right from the start. An epidemic broke out and a lot of them died."

"Ah, and there was even worse news only the other day," said Mr. Gratby. "It takes a good deal to make me angry, but I'll tell you, I was angry when I heard this. Apparently there were some English seamen on a slaving ship who quarrelled with a chieftain known as 'King Jimmy', and they destroyed one of his villages. Well, I suppose from the chief's point of view one white man's much the same as another. Anyhow, his idea of revenge was to order his warriors to burn down everything the settlers had built."

"Destroyed all their hard work?" I asked.

"So we've heard." He took out and consulted a silver "turnip" watch. "My goodness, it's later than I thought. I'll have to be getting along. The best of luck, my dear boy. It's been very pleasant talking with you. I'm sure you'll hit it off very well with Granville Sharp."

However, before I could meet Mr. Sharp, I learned that Mr. Clarkson, after six months absence, had returned from France. It was a typically wet, grey, winter's day when I returned to his rooms and found him sitting over the fire, reading the journal he'd kept of his visit and looking none too happy.

I told him how glad I was to see him back home and then, of course, asked whether all had gone well.

"No good at all," said he, giving me a cold smile. "Might as well have stayed here."

"I'm very sorry to hear that, sir."

"Well, to start with, they're not going to join us over Abolition. That's flat. 'Got too many troubles of their own, that's what it comes down to."

"Did you meet the King?"

"Meet the King? Oh aye, and he blew hot and cold all right; hot and cold, he blew. No real interest. Anyway, I had to sit by in Paris while the mob took him and the Queen off to the Tuileries. They're prisoners there, in effect. 'Got no power at all. Anyway, the idea of Abolition in France is hopeless in the light of San Dominguez."

"San Dominguez. French West Indies?"

"Yes. Full of black rebellion, murders of white people, massacres, bloodshed. And from there the trouble's spread to Martinique. How can you talk to them about Abolition when they're up to the neck in that sort of thing?"

He poked the fire as if he hated it.

"'Declaration of Rights' my wig. 'Men are born free and equal' my eye."

"But didn't you meet any sympathisers at all, sir?"

"Oh, plenty. About as much use to us as those people in Liverpool. Abbé Sieyès, Brissot, Condorcet, Mirabeau, La Fayette. 'Amis des Noirs'. Amis des Inutiles, they are."

I did my best to give him some encouragement. "You know Parliament's reassembled, sir, and they're hearing evidence against the Trade. Mr. Pitt's on our side, and Mr. Fox and Mr. Burke too."

"I know; but Pitt can't commit his Cabinet: they're all scared stiff by what's happening in France. And as for the Lords, that Chancellor Thurlow – he'll make sure they throw out any Bill that ever reaches them."

"But Mr. Wilberforce has said they're fairly beat."

"He'll kill himself with work before he's done."

186

Of course, now that Mr. Clarkson was back and obviously in need of my support, I laid by the idea of reporting to Mr. Sharp. All through May and June the Committee for Abolition met almost daily and for a time Mr. Wilberforce sat with them, giving the witnesses every help he could. That summer his constituency returned him again with a handsome majority.

Next year the debate in the Commons was resumed. Pitt, Burke, Fox and Wilberforce all spoke movingly. But still the advocates of the sanctity of property carried the day. After a gruelling two days' debate, Mr. Wilberforce's Motion was rejected by 163 votes to 88.

"I shan't give up, you know," said Mr. Wilberforce, smiling. "I've hardly begun to fight as yet."

And now began a bewildering time, a time of uncertainty, of cross-currents in which it was impossible to tell whether the cause of Abolition was prospering or fated to be thwarted – for years, for ever? – through adversity brought about largely by its own supporters.

While Mr. Wilberforce, Mr. Clarkson, Mr. Sharp and the other leading Abolitionists had no option but to swallow the bitter medicine of our defeat in Parliament, (a defeat suffered in spite of the advocacy of the Prime Minister and the foremost politicians of the day), popular support for Abolition among electorates and the general public surged throughout the country as never before. Local meetings mobilised opinion to a degree hitherto unknown, due in many places to the advice of Mr. Wilberforce himself on how to obtain the backing of the most influential personages in the locality. No fewer than 500 petitions were submitted to Parliament and as many supportive articles appeared in local newspapers.

Josiah Wedgwood put on the market a cameo showing a negro in an attitude of piteous entreaty ("Am I not a man and brother?"), and this became fashionable, inlaid on snuff-boxes and enamelled on china. A poem by Mr. William Cowper, *The Negro's Complaint*, was widely circulated.

I know that Mr. Clarkson fully expected the submission of a

further Bill, or alternatively some direct action on the part of the Government, for our opponents in Parliament were now plainly seen to be representative of no more than a superficial minority when weighed against public opinion.

However, other influences were at work; in particular, to my unhappy regret, the characteristic forthrightness of Mr. Clarkson, the like of which he had shown in Liverpool. On more than one occasion he showed himself unashamedly sympathetic to the ideas of the French Revolution. I know that Mr. Wilberforce tried in vain to curb his outspoken candour, knowing that it could only have an adverse effect on the Abolitionist cause. Too many people thought that both of them were tarred with the same radical brush; and that Abolition would deflate English mercantile assets.

In the House there was a certain amount of support for a vagary introduced by Mr. Henry Dundas, an M.P. on friendly terms with Mr. Pitt. This man favoured not outright but gradual abolition and many Members supported him in what they saw as a rational, moderate policy. But Mr. Wilberforce was having none of that.

The next Parliamentary debate in the House took place the following April, and in spite of the best efforts of Mr. Wilberforce, Mr. Fox and Mr. Pitt himself, Mr. Dundas's amendment "That the Slave Trade ought to be gradually abolished", was carried by 230 votes to 85. "Forever and a day' that means," said Mr. Sharp disgustedly. "They're the ones that ought to be gradually abolished."

These conflicting ideas of support – compromise and total opposition – filled me with perplexity; not about the justice of our cause, but about the likelihood of its success. The King was openly against us; also Nelson and several other influential public figures. It was about now that Mr. Wilberforce was physically threatened by a certain Captain Kimber, a slave-trader who had been tried (and acquitted) for the murder of a black girl. Were there likely, I wondered, to be more attempts on our leader's life?

It was one evening in June of that summer that we Abolitionists were invited to dine with Mr. Pitt. His invitation

188

included myself, which naturally pleased me very much. I was placed on the left of Mr. Sharp, and I suspect that that kindly gentleman had expressly asked for this arrangement, to avoid my being seated at the foot of the table. (Not that I would have minded.)

I was much impressed by the unpretentious grandeur of the dining-room. Although I tried not to stare about me, I could not help being struck by the lavish number of candles, the smooth, self-effacing attendance of the servants and the excellence of the dinner.

To my mind Mr. Pitt, at the head of the table, looked every inch the renowned statesman, genial and courteous to his guests and reciprocal of all that was said to him. He was now, as I had been told, 33 (my own age), and still, after nine gruelling years in power, looking young for a Prime Minister; yet his bearing was calm and confident and no one observing him could suppose him unequal to his great office.

As usual when among my betters I remained reticent, speaking only when spoken to and as briefly as good manners permitted. I took a sip or two of each of the wines but (with deep regret) left the quaffing at that. Only when the port reached me did I allow myself a full glass; and I was still deep in the flowing tide of appreciation when Mr. Pitt tapped on the table for silence.

He began by praising us for the effort, sincerity and skill with which we had struggled against blockheaded resistance to the cause of Abolition. As we all knew, he was entirely of the same mind as ourselves – that total Abolition was the only course consistent with the principles of humanity and Christian morality. The Slave Trade now was a monstrous evil and no decent man could refuse to make use of the means that Providence had given us for wiping away our nation's guilt and shame.

He, like us, had been encouraged by the support shown for Abolition throughout the country. Yet many of our supporters among ordinary people had, without realising it, harmed this noble cause. It was both sad and troublesome that it was seen by many as inseparable from the reckless radicalism, the anarchy of the French Revolutionaries. The recent rising of blacks in San Dominguez was felt by many to be all of a piece with the disorder in France. What had happened in San Dominguez was directly attributable to the French Revolution. Many people feared – yes, reluctantly he himself feared – that to abolish the Slave Trade would encourage malcontents among the public to set about disrupting law and order here.

He was in little doubt that the French Revolutionaries were going to execute their King, the symbol of moderation and equity, and in all probability would declare war on us. He knew that they had their counterparts and sympathisers in this country. Those sympathisers must be quelled at all costs. This was why he had been forced to decide, against his own wishes, that pressing our cause of Abolition must be deferred. He would be waiting for the chance to take it up again, but for the time being, that chance was nowhere in sight.

"We mustn't pipe down, Daniel," said Mr. Clarkson, as we were going home. "If anything, we must work even harder."

I could, of course, only reply that I agreed. But in my heart I felt downcast. Our defeat in the House and Mr. Pitt's reluctant decision to set aside the Abolitionist cause, resembled, I thought, the fate of Sisyphus, condemned to push a great stone uphill, a stone that rolled back to the foot as he was about to shove it the last few yards to the top.

Next morning, at breakfast, Mr. Clarkson was silent for some time. At length he said, "Daniel, I'm going in search of a sailor."

"A sailor, sir?"

"Yes, a sailor whose evidence against the Trade I know to be of great importance."

"Have you got his name and whereabouts, sir?"

"I don't know his name, I don't know where he is and I don't know whether he's dead or alive."

"But Mr. Clarkson, sir —"

"I shall set out this morning and I shall get aboard and search through all the naval ships at Deptford, Woolwich, Chatham and

– er – "

"Sheerness, sir?"

"Oh, yes, of course, and Portsmouth. And if I still haven't found him, then I shall go down to Plymouth, too. I'll leave you some money, of course, to keep everything in order till I get back."

"And when will that be, sir?"

"How on earth should I know? I'll write to you, of course."

I am well aware that it must seem unbelievable to any normal person that an educated, intelligent man like Mr. Clarkson could formulate such a plan. It is almost more unbelievable that the plan was successful. Mr. Clarkson visited all the naval ships in all six ports, and discovered his man at Plymouth, on the fifty-seventh vessel he boarded. I forget now how long it took him, but he was convinced that what he had done was worthwhile. I never learned what the man's evidence was.

When Mr. Clarkson had left, I began seriously to consider my future. I could no longer ignore the plain truth that for some weeks past my feelings had begun to alter. At the outset of my career as an abolitionist, I had been more than happy that so distinguished a man as Mr. Clarkson should have adopted me as his lieutenant and given me my head to speak publicly about my experience of the Slave Trade under Captain Hawkshot. He had helped me, too, to educate myself, to read great literature and to improve my self-confidence and style. Hard master though he had been, I had felt glad to be his pupil. His sharp words and cutting manner had not dispirited me. If anything, they had drawn me closer to him. I had felt it a privilege to work as his colleague, one to whom he could speak his mind and be himself. He had set out to break my resolution and, finding he couldn't, had felt justified in assuming that our opponents couldn't either. And yet, without being conscious of it, I had undergone a gradual change. I had grown more experienced, knowledgeable, and able to form opinions of my own. It grieved me to find myself critical of Mr. Thomas Clarkson, the brilliant orator and philanthropist, the Abolitionist warrior whom no setback could discourage. Yet I could not repress my feelings. I remembered the London

Committee's doubts before our visit to Liverpool. They had feared that he would show himself a tactless hothead and they had been proved right. He had raised hackles. He had said things that I myself wouldn't have dreamed of saying. And he had embarrassed his fellow-abolitionists again upon his return from France, by openly commending extreme Revolutionary ideas. Furthermore, he was a man with whom one could not reason or argue with the least hope of modifying or changing his opinion. It was now my view that I could do more for Abolition without him.

In a word, I wanted to spread my wings; but this I could not do on my own account, for lack of money. So what I needed was a new, more amenable superior; one who felt he stood to profit by what I had to give him. I was black; I was not without valuable experience. Weren't those assets of worth to a man capable of recognising them?

Lastly (and less commendably) I had found Mr. Pitt's damper on Abolition disheartening. I felt I would like a change to some entirely new place and new activity.

As I stirred this bubbling cauldron, something came floating to the surface; something that I had forgotten. Mr. Gratby and Mr. Hayter had spoken of Sierra Leone, the black colony destroyed by a vengeful African chieftain. Had the very idea of such a colony been abandoned? What might be the present position?

Once more I managed to get Mr. Wilberforce's ear for a few minutes.

"Sierra Leone, my dear boy?" said he. "Abandoned? Oh, dear no; we still mean it to succeed. Our Sierra Leone Company received its charter only last year, you know. Granville Sharp's the president and I'm one of the directors. The chairman is Henry Thornton."

I thought it significant that they had elected Mr. Thornton as chairman, rather than Mr. Sharp.

"If you want to go out there," Mr. Wilberforce went on, "the man to talk to is Zachary Macaulay. He's just been appointed a Councillor to the Governor; he'll be going out to Sierra Leone quite soon now. He lives at Clapham, you know. Anyone there will show you his house."

I walked out to Clapham that evening and soon found my way to Mr. Macaulay's. I followed the parlourmaid into the drawing-room and found Mr. Macaulay and Mr. Denis Green playing chess. I apologised for intruding.

"Not at all," replied Mr. Macaulay, jumping up and shaking hands. "You're Mr. Daniel, aren't you? How d'ye do? Denis, I resign. You're too good for me."

"Nonsense," said Mr. Green. "You'll win the next game, no danger. Good evening, Daniel. 'Nice to see you again."

I was surprised (though, of course, I concealed it) to perceive that Mr. Zachary Macaulay was considerably younger than myself. I guessed him to be about 24. He wore his own hair and spoke with a noticeable Scotch accent.

"I've heard much good about you, Mr. Daniel," he said. "I'm delighted to meet you at last. Don't go, Denis. Let's all sit down and have some whisky. Have you come to talk to me about anything in particular, Mr. Daniel?"

"Yes, indeed, sir," I replied. "About Sierra Leone. Mr. Wilberforce himself advised me to consult you."

"Well, you've come at the right time," said Mr. Macaulay. "I'm sailing out there quite soon."

"Well, I want to come with you, sir. That's what I'm here to ask."

"Are you sure? You realise it'll be very demanding work, do you, low paid and possibly not without danger?"

"Well, sir, as you know, Mr. Pitt has decided that his Government will have to set aside the Abolitionist cause for the time being, but that doesn't suit me any more than it suits you. I'm not content to pipe down: my feelings about the slave trade are the same as your own. I'm told you want activity and so do I. I'm sure I could give you a lot of help – in – er – Freedom Province it's called, isn't it?"

"Have you had much experience of working for Abolition?"

We sat down, the three of us, before the fire, and I told him about my work with Mr. Clarkson. Then he told me about the cruelty of slavery in Jamaica. "I just couldn't live in the place any longer," he said, "even though I had a good job out there. It's simply not consistent with Christianity. I resigned and came back to join Wilberforce and his people – the Clapham Sect, as they call us. Well, several of us are dining with Henry Thornton tomorrow. You'd better come along. Four o'clock suit you?"

And this was how I first met the renowned Clapham Sect. That evening we were seven at Mr. Thornton's; Mr. Wilberforce himself, Mr. Venn, Mr. Grant, my literary friend, Mr. Stephen, Mr. Macaulay and – the postulant, myself. "It's heart-warming to welcome a black gentleman to our circle," said Mr. Venn. "So you're going to keep our friend Zachary company in Freedom Province, are you? I'm sure you'll be useful to him." "Hear, hear," said the others. Their approval greatly encouraged me.

Mr. Macaulay had received advice from Mr. Falconbridge, one of the Sect whom the Company had sent out as their agent when rebuilding began after the destruction of the first "Granville".

"The rains out there begin about the end of June," Mr. Falconbridge had told him, "and last till October. It won't be practicable to do much re-building until they're over."

However, earlier in the year the Company had sent out a fresh band of over 100 white settlers, and these had joined the fifty or so of those remaining after King Jimmy's attack.

The new Governor was Lieutenant John Clarkson, of the Royal Navy, younger brother of my mentor Thomas. His two Councillors were Mr. Macaulay and a certain William Dawes, formerly an officer of the Marines, who had had experience at Botany Bay in Australia.

I need not go into the details of our departure, although I must record that Mr. Thomas Clarkson was generous in speaking of what I had done for him. I think he may have been influenced in my favour by the risk I was running in going to Sierra Leone.

"You'll come across plenty of slaves there, you know," he said.

194

"Sierra Leone's the biggest slave-holding depot in West Africa. 'Makes for difficulty. Where there's slaves there's trouble."

"I shall take it as I find it, sir."

"Well, I've given young Macaulay a good account of you. I wish you luck."

In accordance with Mr. Falconbridge's advice, Mr. Macaulay and I did not set out until mid-September. Our ship was small and rolled a good deal, but was otherwise comfortable enough. With us, also bound for Sierra Leone, was a clergyman, the Reverend Nathaniel Gilbert, whom the Company had chosen to act as chaplain to the settlement. Mr. Macaulay and I found him pleasant enough and were glad to have him with us.

Accompanied by a Royal Navy schooner, we sailed well out into the Atlantic before turning south, in order to avoid the French, of whom we saw nothing.

Mr. Macaulay and I berthed together, and this was how I realised from the outset the importance to him of his Christian belief. Without the least instigation on his part and as if it was the most natural thing in the world, I found myself kneeling in prayer with him morning and evening; and then in reading, turn and turn about, a passage from the Gospels. Although, in London, despite my association with the friendly Quakers, I had never attached much weight to religion, I was content to fall in with Mr. Macaulay's practice, not only because it helped to strengthen our relationship but also, I confess, because it brought about in me a certain inclination towards the Christian faith. Mr. Macaulay never patronised or condescended to me. About religion we never conversed at all. His unselfish, considerate behaviour had more effect on me than any amount of proselytising could have had. It was easy to keep his company.

If I had only known it, the Christian faith as motivation was common to all the members of the Clapham Sect and to no one more than Mr. Wilberforce.

One morning, as we were leaning together on the starboard rail, enjoying the warmer weather, Mr. Macaulay asked, "How much have they told you, Dan, about the form of government in Freedom Province? I mean, do you know about Thomas Peters and the Nova Scotians?"

"Nova Scotians?" I replied with surprise. "Did you say 'Nova Scotians'? No, sir, not a word."

"I'll tell you as much as I know myself," he said. "I take it you've heard about 'King Jimmy' and the disaster three years ago?"

"Yes, sir; Mr. Gratby told me about that. It was Mr. Wilberforce who told me about the Sierra Leone Company getting its charter from the Crown last year, and about the new settlement they've called Granville Town. But I've heard nothing about any Nova Scotians."

"Well," he went on, "after the end of the War of Independence in America, a number of freed slaves who'd fought on our side and couldn't get a decent living where they were, emigrated to the British settlement in Nova Scotia. But they still couldn't obtain any land, and they were obliged to get their living as farm labourers on very low wages. They were in a bad way. One of them, a man by the name of Thomas Peters, came over to England last year to try to get some support for them. He met the Clapham Sect, and Henry Thornton offered to let his people settle in Sierra Leone. Naturally, Peters jumped at this.

"John Clarkson volunteered to superintend the Nova Scotians' journey. I'm bound to say he did the job well. He went over there and travelled hundreds of miles – at his own expense – to collect all the ex-slaves who wanted to go. He got about 1,200 altogether, not counting something like 120 white people. They arrived in Sierra Leone about six months ago. I'm told they've settled in pretty well, clearing the bush and putting up some shacks."

"How are they getting on with the English?"

"Not badly, I believe. Well, you see, they're almost all black people together, English or Nova Scotian. That's why you'll be such a help to me."

"Are they represented?" I asked. "I mean, is there any system of representation that extends to everybody?"

196

"Yes, there is," said Mr. Macaulay. "It's known as 'tithings'. Tithings are groups of ten families. They elect a leader annually, who's known as a 'tithingman'. Every ten tithingmen elect a 'hundredor', who has access to the Governor and the Council. The really important job of the hundredors is keeping law and order, and they've been given judicial power accordingly."

"Does it work?"

"More or less, as far as I can gather. It's not really been going long enough for anyone to be sure."

"How about land? That's what the trouble was about in Nova Scotia, you said."

"Yes; well, Sharp's idea is that land's to be equally divided among everybody. Personally, I think that if we're going to have any trouble, land's what it'll be about. 'Stands to reason, don't you think?"

The other passengers aboard were of interest both to Mr. Macaulay and to myself. Besides Mr. Gilbert, only one was white. This was Mr. Philip Watt, who was returning to Sierra Leone after a trip to England to buy agricultural tools – spades, rakes, shears and the like   with which he was returning to his property some miles inland. He told us that a few years before, he had been attracted to Sierra Leone with the idea of buying land cheap and using it partly for growing fruit and vegetables for sale and partly for farming livestock. He told us that after an initial period of trial and error, he was becoming successful. One of his assets was cheap labour although, as he said, it was "quite a job to train the natives". He paid them partly in produce – both animal and vegetable – and partly in plots of land that they wanted to cultivate for themselves.

"Sheep and cattle are no good," he said, "no good for my purposes, anyway; but goats do well and so do pigs. The black fellows are all right once you get to know their ways. You have to make them feel they're a tribe and you're the Chief. I'll make out all right if I don't get murdered first. That's the excitement, of course. They like a drink, but you have to be sure to keep it locked up and dole it out in small tots."

I made the acquaintance of two brothers – freed slaves – who had been on trial for robbery with violence; a capital crime. Their defence had been that they could get no work and were starving, and the judge had remitted the death penalty on condition that they immediately emigrated to Sierra Leone and never returned.

One group of black men and their wives said that they had been given free passage and a little money by "Massa Dornton", secretary of the Company. They had also been provided with a letter (which, of course, they couldn't read) of recommendation to the Governor, vouching for them as honest and industrious people.

The only single woman was a girl, aged about eighteen and plainly pregnant, who was accompanied by her brother. The father of her child, she told us, had emigrated to Sierra Leone, and the two of them were going out to join him. She did not say whether or not her lover was expecting them: I could only hope she wouldn't be disappointed.

A number of those on board were trained craftsmen – or said they were; I counted two cobblers, three carpenters, a tailor, a blacksmith and a metal-worker. All felt sure of finding a demand for their skills in "Freedom Province". The others hoped to find employers for their labour and also to be given land for themselves.

"They haven't reckoned with the climate," said Mr. Watt, while we were strolling on deck. "There's always a few out of every new lot who get sick and die. What the place really needs is doctors, but I doubt we'll ever get any."

"No medical treatment at all?" asked Mr. Macaulay.

"Huh! Witch doctors and gri-gri. Well, that's as much as they've ever known, most of 'em. They trust the witch doctors because they've got to trust something. A few get better simply because they believe they will."

When we eventually sighted West Africa, it recalled all my experience of Hawkshot's slave voyage and the coast of Nigeria. Jungle, matted, shaggy green, extended either way as far as the eye could see: far inland rose mountains, like another world,

198

remote and inaccessible in the evening light. The sight brought me no pleasant memories and, as we approached, the heat from the land began to feel oppressive, just as at Lagos. In my wish for a change, I had somehow contrived to forget about the humid heat and the fatal illnesses among Hawkshot's crew.

It was early evening when our ship came nearer inshore and began sailing parallel to the coast. Mr. Macaulay, Mr. Watt and I went forward and leant on the port bow rail, to avoid the crowd of other passengers further astern. Ahead lay an estuary dotted with islands. I asked Mr. Watt whether this was our destination.

"No," he replied. "That's the Scarcies estuary – the Great and Small Scarcies rivers. That's Salatook Point we're passing now and those islands ahead are the Scarcies Islands, a slave depot."

As we came closer to the islands, we could see groups of black men and women sitting or lying on the bare ground; the place was dotted with dilapidated wooden huts, several with muddy trenches along their sides.

"Those are to drain off the rain," explained Mr. Watt. "Otherwise the whole place would flood in a matter of hours."

A few of the slaves waved to the ship, but most seemed listless and apathetic. I remarked to Mr. Watt on their pitiful and dejected appearance.

"The African slave-merchants who bring them from inland leave them on the islands," he said, "and then the slave-ships come and drag them on board to cross the Atlantic. A lot of them die either on the islands or else on the voyage."

Mr. Macaulay said nothing, but I could guess what he was feeling.

"That's Barlock Point ahead of us," went on Mr. Watt. "It's about another thirty miles to Freetown."

As the sun began to set – it sets quickly in these low latitudes – we came to another estuary, but instead of entering made for its southern point, on which we saw a crowd, evidently awaiting our arrival. Country folk – I should know, should I not? – are excitable and usually noisy with it, and as we approached we saw and heard them capering and chanting. We drew in to the half-finished, makeshift moorings and as two of our sailors flung ropes ashore, any number of men rushed to grab them, falling over one another before they were made fast.

One white man, who stood out among the crowd, came forward to greet us as we tottered down the gangplank and came ashore. This I knew at once, from the family resemblance to Mr. Thomas, to be Mr. John Clarkson, the Governor. Mr. Macaulay, keeping me beside him, stepped forward to shake hands, and Mr. Clarkson bade us welcome, making himself heard as best he could in the surrounding hubbub. After a few words he turned and guided us out of the crowd towards a cluster of wooden huts standing back from the shore. The tangled grass was soft and spongy, and I could feel the water beneath my feet oozing up at every step.

We came to the only hut with a second storey and one by one clambered into the upper room. This was furnished with a wooden table, on which were lying various papers, five or six roughly-made stools and two solid blocks of wood bevelled at the top into shallow concavities to form seats. In one corner lay two or three mattresses, pillows and rolled-up bedding.

"Rough quarters," said Mr. Clarkson, "but they're all right once you get used to them. We've got two quite comfortable huts for you, Mr. Watt. Four of your fellows are here ready to paddle you up to your place, but of course it's quite a way in the dark, and I expect you'd rather stay here tonight and go up tomorrow, wouldn't you? They're unloading your tools and implements now."

"Thanks," said Mr. Watt. "That'll suit me very well."

"Bill Dawes'll be coming in a bit later," went on Mr. Clarkson. "He'll be here for the meal, anyway. Now let's all have a drink and get comfortable."

He called to the servants below, two of whom appeared with whisky, water and earthenware cups.

Mr. Clarkson enquired after Mr. Wilberforce and the rest of the Clapham Sect. When he was told of the lost debate in the Commons he said it was a great disappointment, but exactly what he had feared.

As soon as Mr. Dawes had joined us, the servants brought supper, which consisted of roast pork, bread and rice, followed by cheese and a variety of fresh fruit.

Mr. Clarkson told us how difficult he found it to live in proximity with masters of slave-holding depots and captains of slaving-ships, and to be obliged to keep up a pretence of being on good terms with them. "They could smash us to pieces if they wanted to," he said. "But now there's another threat as well. We're at war with the French. I'm half-expecting an attack at any time; and we haven't got much to hit back with."

Later, as we set off for bed, Mr. Clarkson led the way to our huts. Each of us was given a candle, which burned steadily in the windless air, but we still found it awkward going on the sodden ground. Mr. Clarkson pointed me to an open door and I saw a light inside. Going in, I was met by a black girl who had evidently been waiting for me. She wore a cheap cotton frock and little else.

"Sir," she said, "my name is Vasta. I your personal servant. I have bring your bags from ship and I make your bed here. Will you want else?"

She looked about fifteen, nervous and not sure of herself. I took her hand (which she had not offered), smiled and said, "My name's Daniel. I'm glad to meet you. I don't want anything else tonight, Vasta, thank you. Everything fine. You come tomorrow, wake me up?"

She managed a smile and said, "I bring you tea, coffee?"

"Coffee. And hot water, shave?" I gestured. "Good night now."

I felt very tired. The grubby mattress and pillow looked positively inviting. I thought about mosquitoes and insects, dismissed them from mind, kept on my shirt and trousers, wrapped myself in the top sheet and slept.

Next morning, woken by Vasta with the coffee and hot water, I had a quick shave and found Mr. Clarkson, Mr. Dawes and Mr. Macaulay breakfasting on eggs and bacon. When I had finished mine, Mr. Clarkson said he wanted to talk to us about the present

201

state of the Colony.

"This is a Council meeting," he began. "Do you want Daniel to stay?"

"Well, he is one of the Clapham Sect," replied Mr. Macaulay. He smiled. "It would be helpful to me, if you can put up with him. He's had valuable experience, working with your brother Thomas, and he's served on a slave ship, West Africa to Jamaica."

Mr. Clarkson nodded. "Good. Well, the Council will co-opt him. We have the power to do that. The first thing I've got to emphasise to you is that we've come out of the rainy season in a bad way. The truth is that we've been overwhelmed with immigrants. We weren't prepared for the last lot that arrived from England in February, and when I brought in more than a thousand black Nova Scotians – that was in April – preparations had only been made for about four hundred. The death of poor Peters has had a bad effect on the morale of the Nova Scotians and left them without any real leader. We all miss him very much.

"Mind you, they're a good lot, the Nova Scotians, hardworking, decent people, most of them. As soon as they arrived they got down to work, clearing the bush and laying out the plan for their town. They've done very well, too, in starting on a wharf and a warehouse. And they've built themselves a religious meeting-house as well as a school for their children. We have to give them credit for all that. Their women are good, too – spinning, weaving, laundering. And they've got two or three midwives – a real blessing. But the shacks they put up for themselves are mostly small – too flimsy – not really meant to last. A lot of them broke up in the rains and they're working on better ones now."

"Well," said Mr. Dawes, "all that sounds creditable. What are the problems?"

"There are two, really," said Mr. Clarkson. "First, they're all deeply religious. In one way that's all to the good, of course. But they're split up into three non-conformist groups: Wesleyan, Baptist and Countess of Huntingdon's Election. They don't quarrel, but they meet separately and sometimes make contradictory decisions. Too many people setting out to be top dog.

202

They confer among themselves and I don't get to hear what they say or think. Admittedly a lot of them are a better sort of person than the immigrants from England. The danger is of a separate body of the Nova Scotians, with a majority over everyone else, becoming a government within a government that calls all the shots. We don't want them taking the place over."

"What can we do about that?" asked Mr. Dawes.

"The answer's 'Not much', I'm afraid. We must just go on working for a balanced society. At least if I say something as Governor, they listen conscientiously. I mean, they're aware of the problem and honestly try to mix with the English. You might be the right one of us to gain their confidence, Daniel, don't you think?"

"I'll certainly be glad to help all I can, sir."

"Fine. Go among them, get to know them and let us know how you get on."

"And what's the second problem?" asked Mr. Macaulay.

"I'll give you three guesses. No, one guess. Land, of course. This is their greatest grievance – the delay in granting them farmland. They can't really be blamed for feeling resentful. Before they went to Nova Scotia from America they were told that they'd be given twenty acres apiece. But they never received any land at all. They were impoverished. And then, when they came here, they were expecting to get land at the same rate. When I arrived with them in April, we found there weren't even any houses ready for them. The administrative people the Company sent out from England had done nothing at all except put up their own houses. And they've behaved very badly to the Nova Scotians – you know, calling them 'bloody niggers' and all that, and not even trying to get to know them. The Company sent out a ship that was meant for a hospital, but the officials took it over for themselves. I managed to put a stop to that, but the Nova Scotians have only been given about four acres each – there simply isn't any more to give them – cleared land, that is.

"It troubles me to see the Settlers – as they call themselves – in such a state. Most of their houses aren't properly covered in and there's far too much illness – a lot of it's scurvy. I had a good relationship with them in Nova Scotia and on the voyage, but I'm afraid I've lost it now. Provisions are running short, too. The fact is that things are out of hand. Peters was first-class. He had the influence that was needed to make them exercise restraint and keep the peace. But now he's gone I'm afraid they may decide to take matters into their own hands. And what's at the bottom of it is their discontent about the land."

"They regarded Peters as their real leader, did they?" asked Mr. Dawes.

"Most of them would have revolted against the Company to make him Governor of an independent settlement," replied Mr. Clarkson. "But he wouldn't go along with that. He stood out for the Company; for law and order, and they obeyed him because they thought so highly of him. But they were pretty sullen about it, most of them."

There was a pause. At length Mr. Macaulay asked, "There's another thing, isn't there, you meant to tell us?"

"Yes, indeed," said Mr. Clarkson. "About our relationship with the natives, the Temne. The chief's known as King Jimmy, and he's the man with whom it's vital we keep on friendly terms. It was he who made the trouble three years ago, when his people destroyed the Colony. He took a risk there, because he had an overlord, King Naimbanna, who'd always been friendly to us. It was Naimbanna who confirmed the original treaty, making over the land we're on now. So what it really comes to is how much restraint Naimbanna can exercise over King Jimmy. Jimmy's kept pretty quiet lately. I paid him a visit soon after I arrived and he received me quite civilly; but I could see he was rather uncomfortable. The truth is, I think, that he doesn't really trust white men. We make him uneasy.

"After that visit, I took care to talk to King Naimbanna too. I sent one of our ships to bring him down from Robanna, and went aboard to meet him. We got on very well. He'd brought his queen and two of his daughters, and they had dinner with us. He speaks a little English and enjoyed airing it on me. I trust him more than I trust King Jimmy.

"So the situation's a bit fraught, and we have to take care not to do anything that might upset the Temne," said Mr. Dawes.

"That's right."

"But things have been getting better since the rain's stopped for this year, haven't they?" asked Mr. Macaulay.

"Well," replied Mr. Clarkson, "looking on the bright side, there are a few things to feel cheerful about. The Settlers appreciate the difficulty of clearing the bush, and they've agreed to the grant of four acres a man, on the understanding that we go on doing all we can to increase it. And Freetown's getting bigger and in better shape. They've dropped the name 'Granville', for some reason. There are quite a few good houses – substantial ones – and the gardens are producing a lot: rice, yams, bananas, cabbages and so on. Several Settlers are keeping pigs and poultry and I've persuaded the Company in London to award prizes for the best results."

"There seem to be a lot of canoes and small boats," said Mr. Dawes. "I've seen fishing nets drying, too."

"Yes, that's really enterprising," answered Mr. Clarkson. "They've been trading with the natives for canoes and nets. About the only thing they've got to offer is their own labour, but the natives find that quite acceptable, apparently. They trade for the canoes and nets by offering so many days' labour."

That afternoon I got Mr. Clarkson's approval to taking a walk by myself. Freetown was full of activity; carpentry, building and gardening going on at a great rate. It particularly pleased me to hear people speaking with southern accents – Virginian right down to Georgia, or so it seemed. I was walking along one of the half-built "streets" near the coast when I was plucked by the shoulder and turned to see a man of about my own age looking at me with a broad smile.

"Daniel, surely," said he. "Daniel, from ol' Massa Reynolds's plantation, ain't that right?"

"Yes," I replied. "Yes, certainly. Are you from there, too?"

"Sure am," said he. "Mah name's Jacko – 'worked in the carpenter's shop. Ah recognised you, no danger; you was a messenger, weren't you? Runnin' all over the village. And you killed that dirty Flikka fellow, didn't ya? Good riddance that was."

I shook him warmly by the hand.

"How d'you come to be here?" I asked.

"You must 'a left Massa Reynolds before the war, Ah guess."

I nodded. "Well, when the war began, ol' Massa Reynolds give it out that anyone that wanted could jine up for a soldier. On the Britishers' sahd, of course. There was abaht thirty of us, taken off to enlist by one of Massa Reynolds's sons. Ah soldiered right through the war. Ah was at Yorktown when we surrendered."

"And you went to Nova Scotia?"

"Sure did. But you didn't, did ya?"

"No way," said I. As we strolled along together, I enquired about my family, but he had no news to give me. I told him about Lady Penelope and then about Captain Hawkshot.

"On a slave-ship, were ya?" said he. "Ah've heered tell of Massa Wilberforce all right. So you've jined up with the white men for Abolition. Do ya reckon we'll ever get it?"

"I'm certain of it; only I don't know just when." We both laughed.

"Ah'm in a gang," he said. "Farv of us. We're building a house for ourselves. You'd better come and meet them."

His four friends were all Virginian, and big, strong fellows at that. The building they were putting up looked impressive and I could readily suppose that no one was likely to pick a fight with them. They took a break and sat down to talk to me.

"So ya work for the white men, do ya?" said one of them by the name of Ben. "How does that suit ya?"

"Well, in England, if you want to work for Abolition, you more-or-less have to work with white men," I replied. "The thing is that before they can abolish the Slave Trade, there has to be a law

206

passed by their Parliament, and that's what the white Abolitionists are pressing for. My boss in England was one of the leading people: Thomas Clarkson, the elder brother of your white man, John Clarkson."

"The time's comin'," said another man they called Shooter, "when black men'll order their own affairs without no need of white men."

"Well," said I, "the white men have put an end to slavery in England, and it was white men who set up this colony for freed slaves where we are now."

"Well, that's all very well in its way," said Ben, "but the white men give us all that like they'd give a bone to a dog. Who made the black men slaves, drove them from their native country, put them aboard their goddam ships and whipped them and beat them and worked them to death, eh?"

Of course, I had no answer to that; nor did I look for one, either. "We'll get Abolition quicker if we let the white men do it," I said "Your leader, Mr. Peters, isn't that what he thought?"

"Peters was a good man," said Shooter. "We all sorry he died. But even he wouldn' have been able to stop black men taking over the Government the way things are looking now. Who's your white man, anyway, Dan – the one you work for?"

I told them about Mr. Macaulay and the Clapham Sect. They'd got hold of some rum from somewhere and we all had a drink, which made them a deal more friendly.

I made a point of coming to chat with them every day, and this was how I met a good many more of the Settlers, including the five or six elders who were in authority. I attended their church services too, but never tried to join their conferences in case they should think I was a spy. What one and all of them resented was that they had been promised twenty acres of land apiece by Clarkson but hadn't got them.

For the rest of the year things remained peaceful. The building of Freetown continued and the Settlers' lives became more comfortable and productive. Many of them went into trade with the natives in rice and camwood, and about fifty, who had come to own canoes or small vessels, went in for fishing and for commerce up and down the coast. They made no trouble and got on well with the natives.

In December John Clarkson resigned as Governor and returned to England. Not only we but most of the Settlers were sorry to lose him. He had achieved a great deal in putting the colony on its feet during its difficult beginning, and he had been largely instrumental in setting up Freetown as our recognised capital. He had also encouraged the building of three places of worship and had done much to make Christianity influential throughout the Colony. After his farewell service, movingly conducted by Mr. Gilbert, a large number of the Settlers gathered round him to shake his hand and wish him well.

The post of Governor was now taken over by Mr. Dawes. From the outset I had feared that there might be friction and I was proved right. It was not easy to succeed Mr. Clarkson. He had gained a devoted following among the Settlers, beginning with his work in gathering them together in Nova Scotia. He had a natural gift for getting on with people, both black and white, and now he had gone he was greatly missed. Mr. Dawes, though hardworking and sincerely well-disposed, lacked the common touch, and in his work among the convicts at Botany Bay had come to be severe with people who opposed his will.

It was about this time that I received a letter from Lady Penelope. She hoped that all was going well with me, and that I was not finding the adverse climate of Sierra Leone too oppressive. She was writing to tell me that she and Mr. Hardwick were to be married on 25th January, and felt sure that I would wish them well. She hoped that when I returned to England, I would be sure to pay a visit to Clepton St. Peter. In a postscript she added that Fahdah, who was going on well, had asked her to send me her best wishes.

I, of course, in my reply, sent my warm congratulations; thanked her for her kindness in writing to tell me her good news, and wished her and Mr. Hardwick every happiness. I was glad to

208

hear well of Fahdah and sent her my best wishes in return.

Mr. Zachary did his best to persuade Mr. Dawes to adopt a more lenient manner in his daily dealings. Although the Settlers had forborne to challenge Mr. Clarkson directly about the land, they were ready enough to criticise Mr. Dawes, blaming him for failing to keep the promises made to them in Nova Scotia. Matters were not improved by his rather insensitive style. It did him no good when he raised prices at the Company store, and still less good when he was found to be watering the rum. After some six months of his rule, the Settlers drew up a petition of complaint, which was taken by two of them to the Company in London. The directors found their complaints unacceptable and conceded nothing. This led to still more ill-feeling and Mr. Dawes, although in the normal way a strong, active man, began to feel the strain and to find it harder day by day to endure the hostile climate, at its worst during the months of the rainy season.

Bad luck increased his difficulties. The Colony's store ship was destroyed by fire, a calamity coincident with a fall in the dark, which broke his wrist. In spite of the admirable care of Dr. Winterbottom, our medical officer, it became plain by March of the following year that Mr. Dawes's health had deteriorated to the point where he had no alternative but to resign the Governorship and return to England.

"I shall have to take over as Governor, Dan," said Mr. Zachary – as I now thought of him – while we were sorting through Mr. Dawes's residual bits and pieces. "The worst of it will be maintaining good relations with the slave dealers. They laugh at me behind my back because I can't conceal my pity for the slaves. We're surrounded by these terrible slave depots, and the evil men who grow rich from them could stamp out our Colony whenever they had a mind to."

He was right to the extent that it was impossible to avoid periodic friction between the slave dealers and ourselves. Mr. Zachary nursed a passionate belief in the future of the Colony, but he had no choice but to moderate his idealism in the face of the danger all around us. One day, for example, a certain Mr.

Horrocks sailed into the estuary to deliver some rum that we had bought in the Islands. The day after his schooner had berthed, a group of Settlers brought five of his slaves to Mr. Zachary, begging him to take them under his protection. Mr. Zachary was obliged to refuse, and to tell the slaves to return to their ship. A day or two later, Mr. Horrocks came ashore to lodge a complaint that his slaves had been enticed away. The Settlers' defence was that from the outset Mr. Clarkson had told them that any slave who set foot in our Colony automatically became free. Mr. Zachary had to tell them, albeit with great regret, that if Mr. Clarkson had really said that, he had been wrong. The Settlers were hard to convince, but yielded at last when we pointed out that if they persisted, the slave traders would unite and come down on us with fire and sword. Mr. Horrocks's slaves, however, refused to go back to him and as the Settlers had given them arms, they made it clear that they were ready to fight. Mr. Zachary's Christian conscience would not allow him to capture them and send them back to be punished by Mr. Horrocks. He said as much in a report to the Company's directors in England, but they would have none of this, pointing out that a blockade by the slave-traders would bring us to starvation. In the event, the trouble blew over and the slaves remained with the Settlers, but only after Mr. Zachary had suffered much anxiety.

Nevertheless, he achieved a considerable degree of goodwill with the slave dealers, particularly with Captain Tilley, whose depot was at Bance Island at the upper end of the estuary, and Captain Cleveland, who controlled the depot on Banana Island. This called for skilful diplomacy by Mr. Zachary, and I seriously doubt whether anyone else could have succeeded.

With one of his most successful ventures I had a lot to do. Having received a message from the Foulah people in the hinterland that they would welcome a trade agreement with us, he persuaded Mr. Watt – he of the agricultural estate – and Dr. Winterbottom to go to Timbo, the Foulah capital, and negotiate. He sent me with them, because he thought the team ought to include a black man.

We stayed two or three weeks in Timbo, and I enjoyed myself immensely; also, I played a crucial part in the agreement we drew up, because I knew a lot more than the white men about the goods the Settlers hoped to get in exchange for what they had to offer. When we got back from Timbo we found a deputation of Foulah grandees already arriving in Freetown.

One of Mr. Zachary's finest achievements was the strong support he gave to building schools and to the education of the children. Knowing also that many of the adults could neither read nor write, he called for volunteer teachers and made arrangements for them to take evening classes.

He had been Governor for only four months when he was faced with a threat of open insurrection. His reaction was swift and effective. In no time at all he arrested the ringleaders and shipped them off to stand trial in England. His courage and practical commonsense put him in so commanding a position that he was strong enough to grant a free pardon to the rest of the offenders – the best step he could have taken. Ben, Jacko and their friends were so favourably impressed that from that time forth they became some of his staunchest supporters.

The amount of work that Mr. Zachary performed personally was almost incredible. He was to be seen in the law courts, the schools and the places of worship. He was his own secretary, his own paymaster and his own envoy. He was continually writing reports to the directors of the Company at home, and, taking me with him, often visited neighbouring chiefs on goodwill missions; jaunts which, as Dr. Winterbottom remarked to me, "made up in danger what they lacked in dignity." As we had nowhere nearly enough clergymen, he preached sermons and performed marriages. He built up a fund that was used for aid to orphans, widows and people who met with accidents preventing them from working. One of his canny practices was to allot the lightest work to people who had learned to read and write. The result of all this activity by himself and his representatives was that the Colony progressed as never before.

It was at some time during late July or early August of 1794, that we received the unhappy news that Mr. Thomas Clarkson had suffered a total collapse, brought about by overwork and too little sleep. For some days it had been thought that he would die. Then we heard that although he had made a partial recovery, he still remained very weak. He had been compelled to give up speaking tours, together with strenuous activity of any kind, and had retired altogether from public life. This was depressing news for the Clapham Sect and for the whole Abolitionist cause. We knew that his forceful personality and wide influence among the public were going to be greatly missed.

After Mr. Zachary had been Governor for about seven months we had reached a new peak of prosperity, when there occurred a shocking disaster that demonstrated our vulnerability – indeed, our helplessness – when faced with armed hostility. A certain Captain Newell, a slave-trader who had come to hate our Province and its population of liberated black people, piloted a French fleet into Freetown harbour. Eight French ships, with guns, were a force with which we could not hope to contend. There was a general panic and flight. The ships opened fire and swept the streets, but killed no more than a woman and a little girl. Then the French landed, and Captain Newell led them to the Governor's house, where Mr. Zachary and myself, together with the principal officials, had stayed put.

Newell threatened Mr. Zachary with his pistol, demanding compensation for slaves who, according to him, had run away and were now under our protection. Mr. Zachary, after trying in vain to reason with him, set off with me for the French commodore's ship. As we walked down the wharf we saw the French sailors, who had come ashore in rags, dressed in our looted stock of women's clothes, and busy stealing everything else they could find. As the two of us came on board the French flagship, we were surrounded by the crew – yammering, threadbare ragamuffins, dirty and stinking beyond belief. With difficulty we pushed our way through them and found the commodore who, in reply to all we had to say, merely professed himself helpless to control his men.

When we got back to Freetown, we found the pillage in full

swing, and the labour of years being wantonly brought to nothing. The French sailors were emptying cases of wine and looting the stores, burning the houses and killing the livestock. Our citizens lost everything they possessed. We were helpless to prevent their building work being demolished. In Mr. Zachary's office, we saw telescopes, barometers and other valuable precision instruments lying about in fragments. Every desk, shelf and drawer had been ransacked in search of money, and the Company's papers were destroyed.

When I tried to intervene, the looters rounded on me, calling me a "fucking nigger" (they knew that much English) and knocking me about.

That night Mr. Zachary and I remained under guard in his house, together with several of the Company's servants. Next day he arranged for us to join the officers' mess on one of their ships. The filth and bad behaviour at meals were revolting, and our sleeping quarters were just as nasty.

Every morning I accompanied Mr. Zachary ashore and we did what we could to save something from the wreckage. All the Company's buildings, including the Church, were burnt to the ground. Freetown had had to be abandoned. The terrified people dispersed haphazardly, to the woods, the caves, the farms, anywhere they could.

Within a few days fever was everywhere; and nearly all our stocks of medicine had been destroyed. The whole colony was short of food as well.

The French remained for eighteen days and when eventually they departed, they abandoned 120 sick English prisoners on shore.

Our plight was now desperate. The slave-traders themselves took pity on us and sent in provisions, which we were only too glad to accept. If it had not been for Mr. Zachary's courage and leadership, the whole society would have collapsed. He had the fever, but refused to go to bed, and in view of the short supply would not even take quinine. I fully expected him to die and never left his side, even for five minutes. I have never seen anyone set so magnificent an example. Without him, all order would have broken down. He had no arms to compel obedience, but nevertheless he imposed his will on the seditious and the faint-hearted alike.

When we were at length able to begin the dreary work of rebuilding, he was continually among the workforces by day and night, and (although he took care to conceal it from everyone but me) often going for hours without sleep.

But even on him the strain proved at last too much. As soon as reorganisation had reached a workable state, Dr. Winterbottom put his foot down hard, saying that unless Mr. Zachary went back to England for an extended break, the consequences could be fatal. Mr. Dawes was sent for to take over, and Mr. Zachary and myself were ordered by the Company to go home.

I do not know why the route he took back to England (which I shared) did not kill him. At times I thought it was going to. What he said to me was that since he had gained expert knowledge of both ends of the Slave Trade, he now meant to experience the Middle Passage. We sailed on a slave-ship bound for Barbados. To me our journey was all-too-familiar; the dreadful "dances" of the prisoners on deck, the cat for any slave who showed resistance, the leg-irons and handcuffs, the iron collars fastened with chains to ring-bolts on the deck; the daily pitching of dead bodies into the sea. One night I spent in the hold, watching over a crowd of sick slaves huddled together; the stench was worse than anything I remembered.

We came home and remained eight months in England. For Mr. Zachary, and for myself, they were momentous.

When I told him that I meant to visit Lady Penelope and her husband, he replied that he was going to look up an old friend at Kelston, a village not far from Bath, and could drop me near Clepton on his way. We stayed the night at Sonning and reached Clepton early the following afternoon. Before going to see Lady Penelope, I took a fancy to look in on Mr. Hodges. Thirteen-year-old Marian opened the door to me and after telling me that her mother had gone to Bath for the afternoon, took me into the garden, where we found Mr. Hodges weeding on hands and knees.

214

"Well, I never!" said he, getting to his feet and giving me a grubby hand to shake. "'Ain't seen yer in a long time. Very near give y'up for lost. 'Ow yer bin gettin' on, then?"

"All right, Mr. Hodges. How's yourself?"

"All right, Darkie."

"Black people still here?"

"Oh, ah. But those young chaps, they goes out to work nowadays, down old Farmer Leeson's. He seems 'appy enough with 'em. Well, they can work all right when they wants. 'E pays 'em reasonable, mind. 'Er ladyship seen to that."

"And Fahdah? She still here?"

Mr. Hodges paused a few moments.

"That there Fahdah. You know what 'er Ladyship bin and done? She bin and made 'er a bloody parlour-maid, that's what. And you better not say a word, 'cos accordin' to 'er Ladyship, she's just about the greatest what ever smashed a plate."

"And she's taken to that, has she?" I asked.

"Gor, like a cat to cream." He paused. "Well, 's'pose she ain't too bad at the job. Lady Penelope's got 'er up like a bloomin' Queen of the May. She looks all right, I'll give 'er that. Bit different from when she first come. Still, that wouldn't be too 'ard, would it?

We chatted on for a while, and I gathered that he seemed to have no great objection to Mr. Hardwick. "Mind you, there's times when 'e wants 'itt'n on the 'ead 'eavy 'ammer, like, but then I says nothin' and does it the right way be'ind 'is back, see? E ain't a bad sort, all things considered."

As I had expected, I found Lady Penelope reading in the garden. She greeted me warmly, and I thought how well she was looking, despite the lapse of eight years. Mr. Hardwick, she said, was away in London until next day.

She told me she was still visiting prisons, and that the almshouses she had built at Guildford were happily filled with deserving cases. I told her at some length about Sierra Leone and our problems with the Settlers. I told, too, of the wicked harm done by the French sailors and of Mr. Zachary's heroism as Governor during the exhausting task of reconstruction.

After a time the sun clouded over and the garden became a little chilly. She led the way into the drawing-room and as we sat down said that she thought a fire would be nice. That being her inclination, I agreed with her.

She rang the bell, which was answered by Fahdah. As she came in I felt an involuntary tremor. Her dress, as a parlour-maid, was entirely correct yet neither black nor brown, but a clear pink which complemented perfectly her African skin. Her appearance – her whole demeanour – had changed so much for the better that she seemed almost a different person, unrecognisable as Grench's wretched victim who could not even sleep in peace. Her face had lost altogether its former look of apprehension and disquiet. A happy self-assurance informed her whole bearing. The hollow cheeks were gone and it seemed to me that even her lips were fuller. Her skin, which had been sallow and blemished, was smooth as dark satin. Her very step had altered. It dawned on me that I was seeing the real Fahdah for the first time. This was how she was meant to look, beyond argument a beautiful girl.

I sprang up, shook her hand and kissed her on the cheek. She smiled and her eyes met mine with friendly confidence. No words passed between us but for me it was more than enough to see her so wonderfully improved.

She lit the fire and then, at Lady Penelope's bidding, left to bring us a pot of tea. Soon after, Lady Penelope having told me that I was welcome to stay for as long as I liked, I thanked her and went downstairs to report myself to Mr. Graydon and Mrs. Beddoes. I certainly meant to stay, but I was not going to impose myself further on her ladyship.

I joined the servants for the evening meal. Of course, Paul and I greeted each other warmly, and in response to Mrs. Beddoes' request, I once more gave an account of my work in Sierra Leone under Mr. Zachary, emphasising his heroic courage and resolve in all the work of restoration necessitated by the French. When I said that if he meant to return to Sierra Leone I should certainly

216

go with him, some of them pressed me to think better of it, stressing the danger from hostile Africans and the risk of fatal disease. I explained that my motive was to play my part in the struggle against the Slave Trade, but then, just to please them, I said I would think it over.

Throughout the meal and the conversation, I remained involuntarily aware of Fahdah listening intently but saying very little. When we were speaking of the Slave Trade, she unexpectedly interjected that anything I could do to help to bring about its destruction would be entirely right. During the talk I had gained the impression that by no means all the servants had given much thought to the Slave Trade or felt consciously opposed to it. Fahdah, however, had plainly been driven to speak, no matter what others might think of her, and even went the length of silently shaking her head when Mr. Graydon remarked that when it came to Abolition, there was room for differing opinions. Since by my reckoning it was all of ten years since Lady Penelope's rescue of Fahdah and her brothers from Mr. Grench, there were probably several of the servants who had either forgotten or never known of it, so that they would not have her personal feelings in mind. She must know this, but had been ready to incur their disapproval of a mere girl putting her oar in.

Next day Paul, of course, had his work to see to, but it so happened that it was Fahdah's half-day off, and when I asked her whether she would like to join me in a stroll by the river, returning by way of Clepton St. Mary for a cup of tea, it seemed to me that she accepted with pleasure.

I need not describe that happy walk in detail, except perhaps to mention that for some time we watched a kingfisher flying to and fro, feeding minnows to its squeaking chicks in their nest down a hole in the opposite bank. We found plenty to talk about. Fahdah asked me to tell her about the campaign for Abolition, and when I explained the rôle of Mr. Wilberforce and the necessity of a Bill in Parliament, despite knowing little or nothing of the world of affairs, she showed herself extremely bright, hitting several nails on the head most accurately. I thought how much my friends would like her, but then dismissed them from mind, thinking only how much I liked her. That she was black, of course, played its part in my feelings, but it would have been all one to me if she had been sky-blue pink. Sierra Leone was full of black girls, but none of them had meant anything to me.

Once or twice that afternoon she teased me a little, and while I clearly remember her happy laughter I have no recollection of what prompted it. She had a beautiful voice, and I found myself thinking that whatever she might say, I would enjoy listening.

She was in no hurry to leave me; that was plain. We didn't go home for supper. We had ham, cold beef and beer at a farm, the farmer being one of Darkie's friends. Out of Fahdah's hearing, he said to me, "Doin' a bit of courtin', are yer?" I replied "Could be." He wouldn't take my money.

From that day on, I spent as much time with Fahdah as I could. Her afternoon's work included listening for the front door bell, and also waiting for a possible summons from Lady Penelope. While she knitted or plied her needle, I sat in the kitchen with her and Mrs. Beddoes. Some of the time I spent reading, but she could tell plainly enough that where she was, I liked to be.

Lady Penelope used to receive *The Spectator* as well as *The Times*. These came down on the coach from London to Bath, where they were received by the stationer and sent out to Clepton. When Lady Penelope had finished with them, it was one of Fahdah's duties to clear them away. They didn't become rubbish, however. They were retained and read by Fahdah, Paul and myself, and now and then by Mrs. Beddoes. They always gave rise to any number of questions from Fahdah, which I used to answer as best I could.

I recall one Sunday afternoon, when we walked through Clepton St. Mary and up onto the hills beyond. Fahdah seemed spellbound by the marvellous northward view. She stood gazing into the distance, quietly singing and swaying rhythmically from side to side. Then, turning, she embraced me and kissed me again and again with her broad, soft lips.

As one week followed another, it became clear to everyone, both

218

above and below stairs, that although I took care never to show it in my behaviour, I was in love with Fahdah. Of course Lady Penelope was too kindly and considerate to ask me about my feelings. On the contrary, she never alluded to the matter at all, either to Fahdah or to myself. Yet we could both tell that she had no wish to discourage us. She was content to leave the outcome – whatever it might be – to ourselves. This was entirely in accordance with her principles. As far as she was concerned, Fahdah was a girl whom she had rescued from miserable slavery and had helped and encouraged to grow up with a mind of her own. To Lady Penelope, it was an essential part of her rôle to stand aside now; to release Fahdah from her influence and leave her to make her own decisions. If anyone's ideas were not far from those of Mr. Wilberforce, it was Lady Penelope's. In all actuality she regarded herself and Fahdah as equal in the sight of God. This was not sentimentality. She did not relinquish her authority as Fahdah's employer, but she was not going to step beyond it. Many ladies in her position would have felt themselves fully justified in influencing their personal servant to do what suited themselves. Lady Penelope's philanthropy, however, did not stop short at building almshouses and visiting prisons.

I never made a formal proposal of marriage to Fahdah. As our affinity grew, we both knew that we wanted to marry as soon as we could. What stood in the way?

Nothing less than my deep sense of loyalty to Mr. Zachary. Initially, on the advice of Mr. Wilberforce, I had asked him to take me with him to Sierra Leone. When he felt that in the public interest he had no option but to become Governor, I had played a full part in furthering his work. When almost all he had achieved had been destroyed by the French sailors, I shared his bitter disappointment and came to admire him more than anyone I had ever known, as he led the daunting work of restitution. Without him, the colony would never have been restored. In all probability the entire population, Settlers and all, would have become victims of the slave traders, those predators who hovered at his back night and day, withheld only by his skilful diplomacy and their respect for his courage. His resolution had all but cost him his life; and I was one of those who had been with him in everything that he had achieved. If he was going back to Sierra Leone and wanted me to go with him, then for my very self-respect I had no option.

It was Fahdah herself who decided the matter over which I myself had put off speaking again and again. As the happy weeks at Clepton were drawing to a close, we were strolling one evening through the meadows when she stopped at a stile, turned to me and said, "Daniel, Abolition's the most important thing in our lives, isn't it?"

"It means everything to me, ever since I got back from that slaving voyage with Captain Hawkshot. Like Mr. Wilberforce, I'm going on until we win."

"And I'm going on with you. Now tell me; is the Sierra Leone colony a crucial part of the work?"

"I'd say yes. I know that what we're primarily aiming for is a Bill in Parliament, but Sierra Leone has been a real victory along the way. Almost the entire population consists of freed slaves from England and America. Mr. Wilberforce, Mr. Thornton and several more of the leading Abolitionists are directors of the Company. Four years ago, Sierra Leone looked likely to collapse, but Mr. Wilberforce wouldn't let it. And it was Mr. Wilberforce who sent me to Mr. Zachary in the first place. If Sierra Leone broke down now it would be a heavy blow to the cause of Abolition and do us a lot of harm."

"Then if your Mr. Zachary means to go back and if he asks you to come with him, that's what you must do."

"But I couldn't take you to Sierra Leone, dearest. The risk's too great. Apart from disease there are a whole lot of unpredictable dangers, such as the French sailors I've told you about."

"I know. But if you and Paul go for two or three years, don't worry. I'll still be here when you come back. I shall love you just as much and more. And you'll be able to feel for the rest of your life that you did what was right."

As I've explained, Fahdah didn't care to be embraced. I put my

220

hands on her shoulders, kissed her and replied "I shall write to you. Every other day if I can."

To leave Clepton and so many friends, was hard. Lady Penelope and Mr. Hardwick told me that I was always welcome to come back, but when I told them that in all probability I would be returning to Sierra Leone with Mr. Macaulay, Mr. Hardwick looked grave and said that he hoped I wouldn't stay there for any longer than my duty required. He had always understood it to be an unhealthy place.

Mr. Hodges drove Paul and myself into Bath to take the London coach. Fahdah, of course, came with us, and parting from her would have made me shed tears if she hadn't managed with an effort to restrain her own. "When you come back," she whispered, "I shall be even more proud of you. My dearest love, you'll find my heart unchanged, and our true happiness will begin."

We found Mr. Zachary already arrived home and preparing for his return to Sierra Leone. I introduced Paul to him, explained that we were close friends and that if he approved, Paul wanted to come to Sierra Leone with us. At this Mr. Zachary paused, and then asked Paul whether he realised that the climate was unpleasant and the job not without danger. Paul left him in no doubt that he was serious and intent on coming, and Mr. Zachary, after questioning him closely, finally said he would be glad of both of us and that he'd already ascertained that a ship would be sailing in two days' time.

That evening I began telling Mr. Zachary about Fahdah. I had not got far when I perceived that he was apparently suppressing laughter. Naturally, being well-acquainted with his normal sensitivity and kindliness, this rather upset me and I paused, bewildered. Mr. Zachary immediately apologised and, begging me to continue, said that everything would shortly become clear.

When I had ended my tale, Mr. Zachary said that his great experience during our holiday had been almost uncannily, though most happily, the same as my own. He told me that he had made a visit to Hannah More, the well-known Blue Stocking and philanthropist. At this time Miss More was at the centre of a group of young lady pupils and disciples among whom was a Miss Selina Mills. Miss Mills and Mr. Zachary had formed a close attachment, and become engaged to each other. Miss Mills's family, while entirely approving of Mr. Zachary, had made so downright an objection to her going to Sierra Leone that he had given in.

Naturally, Mr. Zachary had been "struck all of a heap", as he put it, by our almost exactly similar fortunes. His initial reaction of laughter had been due to incredulous wonder – to being scarcely able to believe his ears. The whole affair was the happiest of coincidences – "or should we say 'a phenomenon'?" said Mr. Zachary. "Yes, that's it: a most propitious phenomenon." He opened a bottle of claret and we toasted each other, while Paul toasted us both.

We sailed to Sierra Leone with Mr. Zachary in March of 1796. Mr. Dawes, during his ten months as Governor, had managed to avoid trouble, although I had the unspoken feeling that he was relieved to hand over and return to England.

It was plainly with enjoyment that Mr. Zachary took up the reins. One of his first steps was to install artillery batteries sited to command the seaward approach to the river. On and off, throughout the next three years, there were rumours of another French invasion; but nothing came of them.

Once the rains were over, a militia force was raised, and Mr. Zachary set out to instil in them a proper degree of martial ardour. Although this did not extend as far as enthusiasm for drilling in the heat, they enjoyed swaggering about in their uniforms and drawing attention to their (unloaded) firearms. On one ceremonial occasion Mr. Zachary made them a memorable speech about defending wives and children, safeguarding the liberty of the subject and upholding law and order. They were never called upon to go into action, but this did not stop them having an excellent opinion of themselves, a true esprit de corps; and at least the slave traders knew they were there, armed and ready.

Later in the year, Mr. Zachary took Paul and myself with him on a visit to King Jimmy. The old rascal seemed positively glad to renew his now-less-wobbly relationship with Mr. Zachary, and I had the impression that during the interim he had come to the conclusion that, from his point of view, he could have worse Governors.

One night, about two months after our return, I was woken by one of our night watchmen, (recruited from the Settlers), who seemed too much excited to speak. I made him light two more candles from his own and then sit down and pull himself together. At length he panted out "Slave-ship, sah, English slave-ship, Bance Island depot – bad trouble – I wake Governor, sah, he say wake you –"

I immediately went to find Mr. Zachary. He was outside on the piazza, gazing down at the estuary in the light of the half-moon. "Trouble, sir?" I asked. "Yes, Dan," he said, "a whole lot of trouble, as far as I can make out. But the light's too poor to see much."

At this moment Paul came running up the slope and joined us. "Well?" asked Mr. Zachary.

"What's apparently happened, sir, is that an English slave-ship went up to the depot on Bance Island to load up with slaves. It was on its way back when the slaves broke loose and overpowered the crew. They've either killed them or thrown them overboard and now they're controlling the ship themselves – to go out into the ocean, I suppose. We're a good twenty miles from Bance Island downstream here but this happened some little time ago. We should see the ship pretty soon now."

Mr. Zachary merely nodded. "I see. Thanks."

"Shall I take a boat out and intercept them, sir?" asked Paul.

"No," said Mr. Zachary. "We haven't got a big enough boat and we haven't got enough manpower."

"But sir –"

"Do you seriously think we could stop them?" said Mr. Zachary impatiently. "They've got the ebb tide for a start."

After about half an hour we heard the clamour on board the ship before we could see her. As might have been expected, the slaves were vociferous. Soon we were able to make her out in the uncertain light. She was coming downstream with the tide and yawing wildly, mainly, as far as I could see, because a crowd was scuffling round the wheel, with each man trying to steer her as he got control. While the uproar grew louder with the ship's approach, spectators were gathering along the shore below us, while to our left Freetown was evidently awake and showing interest.

"Excuse me, sir," said Paul, "but if they've thrown the crew overboard, oughtn't we to take a boat and try to pull out as many of them as we can find?"

Mr. Zachary turned to him with a sardonic smile. "I was afraid you were going to ask me that. Yes, I'm sorry to say we'll have to, because it would look bad afterwards if we had to admit we hadn't. I shouldn't try too hard, though," he added, and with this resumed watching the ship.

Paul and I went down, took a boat each, recruited four assistants and set out into the estuary. We knew we were miles below Bance Island, near which the crew had presumably been jettisoned, but nevertheless we did our best to go upstream. However, with the tide against us it was hard work. After a time, when both of us felt that for the moment we had done as much rowing as we could, two of our crew took over, but they were no oarsmen and we made little headway.

Looking ahead and steering, I suddenly caught sight of some sort of bundle or pile of stuff floating down towards us. "What's that, can you see?" I called to Paul, who was nearer than I was. "Are they people?" After a pause he called back, "If they are people they're not moving. We'd better go and have a closer look."

I shouted as loud as I could, "Who are you? Can you hear me?" but there was no response. As the strange object drew nearer we both put ourselves directly downstream, so that we were bound to intercept.

"My God!" cried Paul. "They're black bodies!"

"Dead?"

"They're either dead or insensible. We'd better grab them as

224

they reach us."

We waited in silence while the river flowed on. They were indeed black bodies, face down and somehow fastened together. As they drifted between us I grabbed the shirt collar of the nearest and pulled up the drooping head against my arm.

The next moment I cried out in unrestrainable horror. The black face I recognised before the head fell forward again, out of my grasp, was the face of Wilkins.

For – how long? – My mind was swirling in chaos. I had no power of thought. I believed myself the victim of a dreadful phenomenon: a repressed obsession had been projected as a palpable image. For months I had done all I could to suppress, to dismiss Captain Hawkshot and the ultimate cruelty, the slaves thrown alive into the sea. Now, rejecting my feeble suppression, they had formed for themselves a semblance so real that I had touched and seen it. Someone was leaning across, shaking my shoulder. I turned my head. I saw Paul. So I could see. "Are you all right?" His voice. So I could hear. I bit my finger. I could feel.

"We'd better get them in to the shore, Dan. Give me a hand, will you?"

"I won't touch them."

"What?"

"Won't touch them."

"Why on earth not?"

I didn't answer and after a moment he let go my shoulder, took the oars of his boat, turned it, followed the sodden mass and made his men grip it while he struggled shoreward across the current.

Meanwhile, as I still did nothing, my boat was drifting downstream. "Sah, sah, we go too?" I nodded. He took the oars and his companion steered. I don't know how long we took to reach the bank. They got out, moored and ran upstream to Paul. As I remained in the boat, he came down to me.

"Dan'l, for God's sake, what's the matter?"

I had a sudden visitation of commonsense. Of course it wasn't

Wilkins at all. It only looked like him and I, with my ineradicable memories, had allowed myself to be scared silly. "Nothing; I'm all right."

"What d'you think we should do?" said Paul. "D'you think we ought to lay them out decently and then find some stretchers and take them down to Zachary?"

I nodded, and stood aside while his men cut the bindings. I saw that at least one of the bodies was horribly wounded and supposed that for some reason they must have been fastened together after being murdered.

Paul and the men dragged them apart and laid them side by side, face upwards. I forced myself to look. It was Wilkins. I could be in no doubt.

But now I was further away from the face and had Paul beside me. "Look, just give me a minute or two, Paul, there's a good chap. I must explain; it'll put me right."

He heard me out, showing no impatience. "Poor old Dan'l. No wonder you took on. And it really is Wilkins, is it? You're sure? Well, that's better than if you'd had a hallucination, isn't it? Perfectly natural reaction. But whatever was he doing here, for God's sake?"

"Wilkins? Bashing slaves? Why, man, he did make love to this employment. For him, the more cruelty the better. Nothing more likely than he'd be on a slave-ship. It's simply a nasty coincidence – him and me, I mean."

By a paradox, our four black companions understood the occurrence with no scepticism at all. There was no need to convince them, one way or the other. They were familiar with the supernatural, and in the account they spread I was not in the least to blame for having been afflicted by a devil.

We never heard what happened to the ship that the slaves had taken over.

*   *   *

226

Freetown expanded steadily and the new dwellings were built to unprecedentedly high standards of comfort. Cultivation also progressed. That year, for the first time, we achieved a self-sufficiency of rice, as well as producing gratifyingly good crops of tapioca, ginger, cinnamon, pepper and bananas. Several new fishing-boats were built. Weather permitting, the fleet went out three or four days a week, and usually came home with a good catch.

There was a certain amount of attempted sedition, but Mr. Zachary was upsides with that all right. On one occasion, having got wind of a plot to murder him, he gave out that he would hang anyone who could be proved to be implicated. Nobody was; the threat was sufficient to scupper the conspiracy.

Not infrequently Paul and I, just the two of us, were employed on further goodwill visits to local chiefs. I won't say that initially we didn't feel nervous, but Mr. Zachary's confidence in us proved sounder than our confidence in ourselves. Among the Foulahs at Timbo I was always sure of a welcome, for they were kind enough to credit me with having contributed a lot to their trade agreement with the Colony. Visiting King Bill was a more ticklish business; but we managed to bring off what Mr. Zachary wanted and to come home in one piece. Of the second King Tom – a nasty bit of work – I was frankly afraid and almost went the length of begging Mr. Zachary not to send us. However, we survived, although I had the impression that King Tom spared us only because we were fish too small for his net. On our return I warned Mr. Zachary to expect an armed attack by King Tom; and this in fact took place in less than a year after he and we had finally left for home.

The diplomatic mission that remains most strongly in my memory is the one which Mr. Zachary told the two of us to make to a certain King Afreera, whose realm lay in the further interior, well beyond the neighbouring tribes with whom we had more-or-less friendly relations. This King Afreera was notorious as an avid slave-trader, not only making war on his neighbours for no better reason than to take prisoners for slaves, but even selling his own people when he thought he could get away with it. Mr. Zachary wanted to know more about King Afreera's subjects and his régime, about the economy, the approximate size of the population, how his men went about his dirty work, his contacts with the still deeper interior and so on. He was wondering how much minatory pressure the king might be able to bring to bear on our friendly tribes.

We were provided with an interpreter – a freed slave, formerly a subject of King Afreera who, he told us, wouldn't want to try to sell him twice – and an armed party of twelve men from the militia. We took along twenty bottles of indifferent whisky as a present for the king.

Well, we got there in three days, just about; smartened ourselves up as best we could, and next morning had an audience of King Afreera, a burly, rough-looking man aged about forty, who wore a crown of silver set with rubies and emeralds; and was attended by some twenty or thirty warriors, plus about a dozen quite attractive women, some of whom looked like Arabs and others like people from India. We didn't take to him. He was not even trying to be friendly, but was chiefly concerned to impress us with his wealth and power. He said he had no use for coinage, either from the Arab merchants or from anyone else. What he would like to acquire from us was whisky, fine cloth, e.g., silk, velvet, satin, etc; artefacts made from brass, copper, iron and silver; guns, shot and gunpowder; women, and white slaves.

We replied that since our country lay beside the sea, we had ready access to wealth brought by ships from Europe. Whatever the King wanted could be brought by our ships, provided that he paid us generously and fairly. I asked him whether he had ever seen the sea. When he replied that he was so rich and powerful that he did not need to, we unrolled for him a painting on cloth, depicting Freetown, the estuary, the sea and the ships. This certainly caught his attention, and he asked a number of questions that showed that he was not lacking in shrewd intelligence. I told him that our King Zachary would be glad to receive him as a royal guest, and that if he thus honoured us, we

228

would take him for a sail on the sea in one of our great ships; a hundred miles if he liked.

To this he replied that first, he would send a party from among his most exalted subjects to visit us and report back to him. We told him that they would be welcome, but that the actual details of a trade agreement would be best worked out between our principal merchants and his own. Merchants, I said, were the best people to discuss assets, artefacts and the relative values of trade goods. Why not let some of them come back with us, to get acquainted with our people and our products? We had only one reservation: we would not deal in slaves. (I wanted to make this clear, because if he sent us slaves Mr. Zachary would, of course, free them immediately, whereupon they would become a dead loss as merchandise and not representative of any value to us in weighing up a trade bargain.)

King Afreera thereupon said that in his experience the white men's demand for slaves was inexhaustible. He could not imagine what they did with them all. I repeated that for the time being, at any rate, slaves must be left out of any trade agreement between us. The king, with the air of someone playing the ace of trumps, said what about white slaves? White slaves? I asked. Had he any white slaves? Yes, he replied: about nine or ten. They were scarce and thus very valuable and worth a great deal simply as possessions. Would we like to see them? I replied Yes, very much; whereupon the king came down from his throne, took Paul and myself by the arms and led us out of the presence chamber.

We came to a mud-brick building, the front of which consisted mostly of a row of doors. The king explained that behind the doors were rooms, each of which accommodated one of his white slaves. They were not like ordinary slaves, he said. They didn't have to work. Simply by being his possessions, they were of unique value, and accordingly were well treated and looked after. They were, of course, guarded night and day.

At this moment one of his warriors came running up to us and told the king that an important tribal deputation had just arrived to speak to him. Would he wish to see them immediately? The king thereupon excused himself, ordered the head guard to look after us and went back to meet the newcomers.

We still had our interpreter, who conversed with the guard at some length and then told us that we could be admitted to individual rooms and were free to talk to the occupants. We nodded our assent, whereupon the guard opened one of the doors and gestured to us to go in.

The small room we entered was certainly well appointed by African standards. It contained a plank bed and a wooden chair and table, together with a free-standing cupboard, a row of hooks along one wall, a wash basin, a towel and a pail of water. This certainly bore out the king's assertion that his "white slaves" were comfortably accommodated. On the opposite side of the room a half-door gave onto what looked like a fairly extensive garden.

On the bed a bearded white man was lying on his side, naked except for a loincloth. I could see that he was not asleep but his eyes were closed and he took no notice of us as we came in. The guard called to him "Barz, barz," at which he opened his eyes, looked at us but did not sit up. He seemed entirely apathetic, so that I wondered whether he was ill. I sat down on the edge of the bed, took one of his hands in mine and said in English, "What's your country? Can you understand what I'm saying?"

At this he sprang up into a sitting position, so quickly that I myself reacted by jerking backwards. He said slowly, "Angleesh? Are you - Angleesh?" I replied, "Yes. But are you?"

He said "Yes, but no speak, long time."

Now, looking into his face – the face of a man more-or-less my own age – I was visited by a vague, here-and-gone feeling that I had seen him before. I could make nothing of this, however.

"What's your name?" I asked.

"Basla Towneelo," he replied.

"But you're English, aren't you? You have an English name?"

Then, in a flash, I recognised him. I put my hands on his shoulders and cried out "Basil! You're Basil Townley!"

He frowned, shook his head and buried his face in his hands.

230

But now I was in no doubt. I pulled his hands down and raised his face with a hand under his bearded chin. "You're Basil, Basil Townley, aren't you? I'm Daniel! Don't you remember Captain Hawkshot's slave-ship?"

He replied slowly, "Yes. I'm – Basil – Townley – 'course. You're – you're Daniel?"

I turned to the interpreter and said, "Will both of you please leave us?"

He spoke with the guard and then answered, "Absolutely not. He must not leave you."

"Then please remain silent while we talk."

They plainly did not like this, but I took no notice of them and continued talking to Basil. He was groping for English, and as we went on, it returned to him more and more easily.

He said he had lost count of time and almost forgotten that he was English. He recalled being taken away by Ushumbo. He recounted – here a stumbling phrase and there another – how Ushumbo had degraded and brutalised him until he had become as crushed as any subjugated slave could be. He had been bullied out of any trace of self-respect and had virtually lost all sense of himself as a man. Ushumbo used to show him off to people as a fine example of a white man, and would often starve him; after which, to entertain his associates, he would withhold his food until he had first performed tricks, like a dog, many of which were disgusting and obscene.

He knew vaguely that Ushumbo had become rich through slave-dealing and had travelled to many coastal countries, always making money. He could not remember when they had arrived at the court of King Afreera. King Afreera had told Ushumbo that he collected white slaves and after a lot of haggling had bought him. He had lived here ever since and had accepted it with a kind of contentment, since at least he was not ill-treated. He looked for nothing more.

I began speaking about getting him back with us to Sierra Leone and then to England, but found that I had said too much too soon. He replied that he had no wish to be released. Release would mean a return to a life he had long forgotten, a kind of previous incarnation that he had finished and done with. If he were to return to England he would not be able to cope with life – with strange people, with the situations and demands made on him, with the necessity of getting a living. Here, there was none of these things and he was glad to have lost them.

I thought, he's like someone with frozen hands and feet who dreads the pain he will have to suffer as they thaw out. And then Yes, but once he has suffered it, the pain will stop and he will be back to normality. I said "You must agree that you're living here in a kind of prolonged trance; a stupor; a dream. And you don't want to wake up and come back to reality." He answered that he was, indeed, happy to remain in the dream until he died.

Suddenly another idea came into my head, and for this, I thought, I had Mr. Zachary to thank, even though he didn't know it.

"Can you remember the slaves on the shore of the lagoon at Lekki?" I asked, "and how you and I refused to obey when we were ordered to whip them?"

He said, "I think I remember."

"And do you remember how the two of us were browbeaten by Captain Hawkshot? He asked us whether we would obey in future, when Jack Wain told us to whip the slaves."

Basil said nothing and there came a pause. At length he said, "Yes, he asked us whether we'd obey orders."

"Right. And I was a coward and said I would obey, and you said you wouldn't. So he let up on me. But you he handed over to Ushumbo and that was when your terrible suffering began."

Basil again remained silent.

"And why did you tell Hawkshot you wouldn't obey if you were told to whip the slaves, Basil? It was because you had to obey God, wasn't it? What was His Name?"

He whispered, "Jesus Christ. I was a Christian then."

"And you're still a Christian, Basil. I know you're probably going to tell me that you forgot Jesus Christ during those years of

232

suffering and humiliation. But He didn't forget you. He never forgets anyone. You were suffering for Him, from the moment Hawkshot handed you over to Ushumbo. And now Christ wants you to come back to your own country and your real life. He wants you to come back with me. You can't say He doesn't."

More silence. At last he said, "But I don't think I could manage the journey, Daniel. My health –"

"He'll be the judge of that; and I promise you shall have all possible help from me and my friend Paul."

At this he shook my hand, smiling rather like a loser congratulating a winner at the end of a contest.

"Well, Daniel, you've persuaded me, God bless you. I'm ready to come, but the king will never let me go."

"Yes, he will," I replied. "Just leave it to me."

I wanted him to come at once with me and Paul, but this the guard would not allow, so we had to leave him. I need not recount the rest of that day. The next morning Paul and I, with our interpreter, again presented ourselves before the king.

After a lot of pondering, I had decided that no invented tale would carry conviction; plain truth would be best. I told the king the whole story, from my first friendship with Basil on the slave-ship and among the slaves on the shore, to the extraordinary occurrence of finding him here among the king's "white collection". I said that Basil's mother in England was still alive and praying for him, and then did my best to persuade the king to imagine what he himself would do in my situation; and in conclusion, begged for his generosity and mercy.

To my astonishment the king was sympathetic. (He may have been superstitious, too.) He said that he was certainly disposed to believe our God wanted Basil to be taken home. But there was one proviso. He had bought Basil at great expense and now it was only right that we should give a fair price in exchange for him.

This fairly floored me. I said I could only agree with him, but to my regret I had no goods to offer. Yes I had, he replied: my men's firearms. He would exchange Basil for all twelve of them, plus their powder and shot.

I reminded him that we had a long journey home, much of it through wild country, and that our very lives might depend on our firearms. Would he accept six of them?

At this he became impatient and less friendly. No, he said. We were lucky to have received such a generous offer from him. It was all twelve or nothing, take it or leave it. And he stood up as if to go.

This was Basil's life, I thought, or as good as. Without more hesitation I told the king that I accepted his offer, and we shook hands on it. End of palaver.

Next day we were ready to go. In spite of the near mutiny of my militiamen, I had handed over our firearms. The king's people had given Basil a pair of what they were pleased to call boots as well as a travelling cloak. Paul and I had rigged up a sort of hammock slung on poles for Basil in case of need. Food (of a sort) we had and full water-bottles. The king himself graced our departure; I had feared that he might go back on his word, but although (as I thought I could perceive), he was rather regretting the loss of his white slave, he confined himself to wishing us a safe return and said that before long his people would be coming to talk to our king about trade.

Our journey was less irksome than it might have been. The militiamen had had second thoughts, being spared from carrying the weight of their firearms, and were in good spirits to be going home. Basil, though for the most part walking in a kind of daze, did better than I had feared. He didn't spend much time in the hammock and seemed to improve day by day. He was slow, of course, and cost us an extra day's journey, but once the militiamen had grasped that this white man had, in effect, been rescued from King Afreera after much suffering, they bore patiently with him and even became quite solicitous.

Reporting back, Paul and I got a distinctly rough ride from Mr. Zachary. Had we really given away twelve firearms – which were not even ours to give – to a suspect, untrustworthy, slave-dealing despot, in exchange for a half-barmy man who was a plain

234

liability and no good to us whatever? He wouldn't have believed it of us. It was inexcusable. He had a good mind to send us both home in disgrace. When I pleaded that what was at stake was a man's life, he disagreed. By our own account the man had been living quite comfortably and to begin with had even said that he didn't want to come back with us. And twelve good firearms in working order! Did we think firearms grew on trees? Had we any idea how much it would cost to replace them? And this man — what were we supposed to do with him? Ship him home at our expense and dump him on the Clapham Sect as a useless encumbrance? That was about the size of it.

I replied that for years the man had suffered appalling torment and misery as the result of his courageous refusal to act against Christian principles; alone, he had stood up for the right, in a slave-ship, a devil's realm of terror and cruelty. I asked Mr. Zachary what he would have done in my position. "Nothing," he answered. "I would have let well alone, and you should have done so."

"I'm sorry, sir," I said, "but I'm afraid I can't believe you. You would have acted as I did. Apart from anything else, I had a moral obligation to purge my own cowardice; my cowardly submission to Captain Hawkshot."

Mr. Zachary paused. "Did you honestly and truly believe that you were doing what was right in getting this man released and bringing him back here with you?"

"Yes, sir, I did. And I still believe that."

"Well, if that's really what you thought, we'll say no more. But next time I send you on a diplomatic visit, don't do anything like that again, do you see?"

Basil remained with us for a month or two, gradually regaining the ability to live naturally, to make friends in an English-speaking society and — as he put it — "to do a day's work like anybody else." Yet Paul and I were compelled to realise that he was by no means free from the effects of the cruelty he had suffered for so long. When he had told me that he was well off in King Afreera's "white collection", he had said nothing of his epileptic fits and his terrible nightmares. Dr. Winterbottom gave him every attention, monitoring the beneficial effects of regular treatment with laudanum and morphine, but gave his opinion that the case resembled that of Lady Macbeth, "More needs she the divine than the physician." Rev. Nathaniel Gilbert spent much time with him and did all he could to "cleanse the stuffed bosom". He told me, however, that he thought that Basil would be to some extent mentally scarred for the rest of his life. He needed a regular occupation and sympathetic companionship. The latter he certainly received from Paul and myself and at Mr. Zachary's suggestion I wrote to Mr. Thornton, explaining what had happened and asking whether it would be possible to keep an eye on Basil as well as finding him some suitable employment. I might have known that Mr. Thornton would be supportive. He arranged for Basil's case to be put into the hands of the Quakers. Mr. Gratby's eldest son, George, took ship from England for the express purpose of accompanying Basil on the homeward voyage. Having met George Gratby and talked with him, I felt that Basil couldn't be in better hands, and the two of them departed in excellent spirits.

Mr. Zachary remained as Governor for three more years. Although he continued to be not only active, but approachable and courteous in his dealings, particularly with the Nova Scotian Settlers, they were years of dissension, with the society hovering on the brink of revolution; a revolution involving loss of control by the Company and the assumption of rule by the Settlers. The two prime factors of dispute were Land and Trade.

The same vexation remained unredressed, which had been at the heart of the Nova Scotian grievance ever since their arrival four years before. They had been promised twenty acres of land per man and they had never got them. The plain truth was that they were simply not there.

The Clapham Sect – and particularly Mr. Wilberforce, Mr. Sharp and the Clarkson brothers – had had a vision of Sierra Leone as a prosperous country, its economy based on agriculture. With a society consisting largely of freed slaves, it was to become an agricultural Eden providing produce for Europe and happy

236

lives for its inhabitants. This was really an unduly starry-eyed concept; at bottom it was not realistic. There was not enough fertile soil and not enough informed knowledge of tropical agriculture. The Nova Scotian Settlers, a group conscious of themselves as a strong, united body, hanging together within the larger society of Sierra Leone, found that in effect they had been deceived. They had been promised land that wasn't there. But they were "stuck" with Sierra Leone. They couldn't go anywhere else and somehow or other they had to make a living. They possessed two assets – their religious unity and their numerical majority over any other group in the country. When Mr. Zachary tried to introduce Quit Rents they simply failed to pay them and he had to drop it.

During this last decade, Freetown developed as an entrepôt for goods from Europe. This became for the Settlers a firm economic foundation for Trade. Within a year of their arrival, they had gained approval and respect by growing produce in their own gardens. Some successfully farmed hogs. Their fishing boats went out regularly; some of the fish was consumed locally, but a good deal was traded to neighbouring societies up and down the coast. Another commodity in which they dealt was rum, which they sold in Gambia and the Bunce Islands. A number of them ventured up the inland rivers to the indigenous, tribal people, trading European commodities in exchange for agricultural produce from those more fertile lands (such as Mr. Watt's) in the interior.

The gradual demise of Mr. Granville Sharp's dream of an agricultural Province of Freedom was really due to the Nova Scotians' developing something more workable and profitable, namely, Trade. True, in many of their trading activities they were no more than middlemen; but they were shrewd; they made profits nonetheless and in so doing superseded Mr. Sharp's original concept.

In his dealings with the middlemen for the Settlers during these last three years, Mr. Zachary was troubled by that very system of local representation that he had described to me during our first journey out. In their meetings with him, the locally elected "tithingmen" continually beset and criticised him, and behind their troublesome carping lay always the black shadow, the unspoken threat of insurgency; a threat expressed in plain words by my adolescent Virginian friends. "We don't need your Mr. Zachary, you know," said Shooter to me one afternoon. "We could run the place ourselves better than that chartered company or whatever it calls itself in London."

And this was what became clearer and clearer during the first decade of the new century, after the days of Mr. Zachary's Governorship. The chartered company in London gradually went bust. From the outset, its policy had never really had a future. The Settlers paid it lip-service and more-or-less ran the economy themselves. Finally, in 1808, the Company wound itself up and begged the Crown to take over, which it did. Sierra Leone became a Crown Colony.

During the last years of the old century, Mr. Zachary became more and more disillusioned with his appointment. He was not furthering the cause of Abolition as he had once hoped. He wrote almost every day to his Selina, and naturally his impatience for marriage, like my own, occupied his thoughts more and more strongly.

It was one day in March of 1799 when he invited Paul and myself to dinner and spoke to us confidentially and frankly.

"You've supported me loyally," he said, "and you deserve to be told what I have in mind. The plain truth is that we're wasting our time here. Granville Sharp's idea of an agricultural Colony of Freedom hasn't worked and the economic prosperity of the country is in the hands of the Nova Scotians. I honestly don't think there's much more we can contribute. You came out here, didn't you, Daniel, with the idea of helping to destroy the Slave Trade, by making a financial profit for the Clapham Sect, to help them in the cause of Abolition by creating a society of freed slaves? Well, in effect it is a society of freed slaves, but they're not ours; they're black people from the southern States of America. The prosperity is due to them, and that's to their credit. But meanwhile, the Clapham Sect – the Company - are losing money hand over fist. So what it comes to is that I'm clearing out and going home. Apart from anything else" (and here he smiled, passed the port and gestured to us to refill our glasses) "it isn't fair to keep Selina and Fahdah waiting any longer. Selina's impatient and so am I. When we came back here, Daniel, after our extended leave, I made up my mind to carry on as Governor for as long as I reckoned I was still useful. Well, I don't think I'm doing any more for the cause of Abolition by staying here. What do you two think? Do you feel the same?"

We said we did.

"Right," said he. "We'll resign forthwith."

On 4th April 1799 Mr. Zachary, (who was only thirty), handed over the Governorship to Mr. John Gray and we sailed for home. Our ship's destination was Southampton, and upon our arrival we separated – Mr. Zachary to join Miss Mills, while Paul and I set off for Clepton. It was an awkward journey of more than 60 miles and took us three days, stopping overnight at Salisbury and Warminster. We reached Clepton late in the afternoon. Paul surprised me by going straight to Mr. Hodges's cottage, while I went to Mrs. Beddoes's kitchen. Here, as I had hoped, I found Fahdah, who wept for joy as she took me in her arms. I thought she had never looked more beautiful, and I kissed her again and again until Mrs. Beddoes sat me down to a large bowl of stew from the stockpot. I was still dealing with this when Lady Penelope's bell rang. Fahdah, of course, carried her joyful news upstairs, and Lady Penelope told her to bring me up to the drawing room.

"Have you finished, Daniel, with Sierra Leone?" asked Mr. Hardwick. "You haven't got to go back, have you?" I told them about Mr. Zachary's resignation and forthcoming marriage, whereupon Mr. Hardwick said he was relieved on my account and added that he supposed my own marriage was not going to be delayed. Lady Penelope enquired whether we had left all well in Sierra Leone and when I told her that I feared there was likely to be another attack by the natives before long, said that she was glad that Mr. Zachary, Paul and myself were safely out of it. Then she excused Fahdah from duty for the rest of the day, leaving us free to enjoy the fine evening. Going into the stable yard, we met Paul and Marian Hodges, who seemed almost as happy as ourselves.

Paul told me that three years before, when we were about to set out with Mr. Zachary for Sierra Leone, he and Marian had become engaged. At that time her parents had thought her too young to marry and had told him to wait until he returned to England. Marian had that very evening received their consent.

Fahdah, being in Marian's confidence, had known of her engagement but Paul himself had preferred to say nothing while he and I were in Sierra Leone. I thought his reticence perfectly understandable, and not in the least out of keeping with our friendship.

As Fahdah and I were sitting in the meadow by the pool, she said, "Do you remember, Daniel, how I told you that when you came back our true happiness would begin?"

We were married three weeks later. Mr. Hodges drove us to Bristol, and here we stayed for two weeks in a welcoming district of black people, where we made several good friends. One evening two of these asked us about our plans for the future. I told them of our commitment to the cause of Abolition, and said that we meant to rejoin Mr. Zachary Macaulay and Mr. Wilberforce in London. They replied that we were lucky to work in such distinguished company, and wished us every success.

Before Fahdah and I left Clepton, Paul told me that he hoped I wouldn't be disappointed if he returned to service with Lady Penelope. I gathered that Marian didn't feel altogether happy at the prospect of life in London. In the event, they have remained at Clepton, and for good reason. Some time ago Mr. Graydon, with Lady Penelope's recommendation, was successful in gaining the post of butler at the country residence of Lord Nailsden in Wiltshire. Upon his departure, Paul became Lady Penelope's butler while Marian, aged seventeen, also joined the household. They have a boy and a girl, and are entirely content.

Although in a way sorry to be leaving Lady Penelope, to whom she owed so much, Fahdah was excited at the prospect of going to

240

London. As soon as we arrived, we went to see Mr. Wilberforce, and found awaiting us a letter from Mr. Zachary in Suffolk. He and Selina, he told us, were married and had taken a lease upon a house in the village of Marylebone. He gave us the address and hoped that we would join them whenever it might suit us.

We went there the same evening. Mrs. Selina Macaulay made us welcome, and I told Mr. Zachary that I wished for nothing better than to resume work for Abolition under his direction.

Fahdah and I found Selina charming. I guessed her to be in her early thirties, about the same age as Mr. Zachary. She seemed by nature full of gaiety and high spirits, and (as it seemed to us) perfectly complemented Mr. Zachary's rather more serious character. That impression has turned out to be altogether correct, and I have never seen a happier marriage.

Mr. Zachary told us that he had already been in touch with George Gratby, to enquire after Basil Townley. He had learned that things were going on as well as could have been hoped. George, having first found out that Basil's mother was still alive had then, to her indescribable joy and elation, brought him home. She had long given him up for lost. Before leaving them together, he had gained from the vicar and the local doctor assurances that they would keep a watchful eye on Basil and give him all the help he might need. Apparently the vicar, when told of Basil's refusal to give in to Captain Hawkshot, had been deeply moved and said that he had never heard of a finer example of Christian courage. Basil was all but a martyr. He had written to the bishop, who had replied that now that Mr. Townley was safely home, he deserved the fullest support that the church could provide. While George could still not help feeling some anxiety about poor Basil's intermittent mental troubles, he thought that at least his future was in the best possible hands.

Mr. Zachary went on to say that to the opponents of Abolition, Mr. Wilberforce now seemed almost a laughing-stock. In 1798 and again this year, he had put forward his regular Motion for leave to introduce the Bill. On both occasions he had been defeated. We knew that he had told the Commons that the prospects for

241

Abolition actually seemed weaker now than they had been when he had first raised the matter twelve years before. Yet, he said, his heart was still in the cause and he meant to fight on until he won.

At this time we had at least one consolation; namely, the recovery of Mr. Thomas Clarkson. After nine years as an invalid, he now returned to the fray with all his former energy and commitment. He resumed his speaking tours, on one of which – to Birmingham and Worcester – Fahdah and I accompanied him. He addressed both the large audiences with all his old ardour. He had not changed, but the audiences had. On each occasion he met with the greatest enthusiasm and strong support. At Worcester he was loudly cheered and the audience were virtually unanimous in their support for Abolition. I saw to it that Mr. Wilberforce received a full report.

Mr. Zachary's subsequent career could not have been more honourable and distinguished. Upon his return, with his wife, to London, he learned that he had been elected to the Anti-Slave-Trade Committee. Soon after, he was chosen as a member of the Royal Society. He became well known as an active member of the Church Missionary Society and was one of the founders of London University.

At the beginning of the new century, most of the members of the Anti-Slave-Trade Committee felt sure that the Bill would soon be introduced and would undoubtedly succeed. Yet if they had only known, eight more years of hope deferred lay before us.

The times were full of trouble. Parliament was facing discord up and down the land, and there never seemed to be a favourable occasion to introduce the Bill. Ireland was in open rebellion. Lord Nelson's stupendous naval victory in Aboukir Bay had not brought about the eclipse of Napoleon. The devil took care of his own, and the Corsican brigand managed to sneak back to France, where he was given command of an army to campaign against Austria. Mr. Pitt, although he had rejected French overtures of peace, was almost at his wits' end for resources to meet the cost of the war, and incurred outraged condemnation for introducing an income tax of ten per cent. He was also faced with widespread dissension among workmen and labourers, whose combinations (or "unions") to gain higher wages he felt constrained to prohibit by law.

In a cold, dark February he resigned office and his place was taken by Mr. Addington, of whom all we knew was that he was no supporter of Abolition. "Doesn't do us any good, does it?" said Fahdah. "He won't help Mr. Wilberforce."

Next month there followed a negotiated peace that no one could believe would last. And neither it did, for just over a year later the war was resumed.

Yet there seemed little or no prospect of the defeat of France. Napoleon assembled an army on the opposite side of the Channel, intending to invade England in a ridiculous fleet of open craft. For a whole year our regiments kept watch on the south coast from Kent to Dorset, but in the event Boney plainly didn't fancy a set-to with our Navy, for he gave up the idea and marched his men away to try their luck elsewhere in Europe.

"Still dreaming of Abolition, are you?" remarked Mr. Thornton's porter as he opened the door to me one fine morning.

"Aren't you?" I replied. As he shook his head I added "Then you've got no business in that job."

When, late in October of 1805, the whole nation rejoiced to learn of the almost total destruction of the French fleet at Trafalgar, they also mourned deeply the death of Admiral Nelson in the battle. Yet we Abolitionists could not join wholeheartedly in mourning for the man who had pledged his word to the burgesses of Liverpool that so long as he possessed any power or influence, he would continue to support the "valuable and necessary Slave Trade", upon which the prosperity of Liverpool depended. Although we didn't, of course, say this publicly, we felt he was an obstacle out of our way.

Three months later, Mr. Pitt died, aged only 47, worn out by his long years of leadership of the nation throughout the greatest danger it had ever faced. He had always been a true supporter of Abolition. The Clapham Sect grieved for him, yet if we had only known, our battle was already as good as won. Virtually the whole country was now in favour of Abolition.

It seemed strange that the Bill – the great Bill for which we had worked and struggled for so long – should be introduced first in the House of Lords, the once invincible castle before whose walls Mr. Wilberforce had so often been repulsed and humiliated. Yet in a way it was fitting, too, for the Bill was presented by none other than Mr. William – now Lord – Grenville, the third man who, together with Mr. Pitt and Mr. Wilberforce, had sat under a tree at Holwood twenty years before, and pledged themselves to defeat the Slave Trade. Mr. Charles James Fox, during this, the last year of his life, gave his fullest support in the Commons: and all went forward like a charge of cavalry.

It was on the afternoon of the 23rd February 1807 – a day to be celebrated forever – that Mr. Zachary sent for me to join him at dinner. Upon my appearance he told me that if he was any judge, the evening was going to turn out a memorable one in the House.

"I thought I'd take you along," he said, "as a well-deserved reward for all the loyal good work you did for me in Sierra Leone. With any luck we may be able to get places in the Strangers' Gallery, but we'd better be there in good time."

As soon as we arrived, we felt all around us an atmosphere of mounting excitement. Mr. Gratby and George were among those present, and I caught sight of one or two more Quaker friends. Mr. Zachary, who was, of course, well-known as a leading Abolitionist, had little difficulty in gaining admission, and although our view was somewhat restricted, we felt more than happy to be there at all. Mr. Granville Sharp, now an old man, had, of course, been placed in the best seat, and beside him sat Mr. Wilberforce's brother-in-law, Mr. Stephen, the distinguished lawyer and author of the widely-read pamphlet *War in Disguise*. Not far away were Mr. Thomas Clarkson and Mr. James Phillips, to whom I owed so much for my literary education.

The House had been taking a short break, but now they began to reassemble by twos and threes. Among the first was Mr. Wilberforce, escorted (one might almost say "guarded") by Mr. Thornton, who kept at bay the many Members who wanted to speak to him. Mr. Wilberforce nodded and smiled about him in his usual kindly way, but I could perceive that beneath this lay a more-than-normal tension and expectancy. When Mr. Fox appeared, he glanced across to Mr. Wilberforce with a broad smile and a silent clapping of his hands.

Business was resumed. I was wondering whether Mr. Castlereagh, one of the foremost adversaries of Abolition, would speak, or Mr. Rose, who had been so devoted a friend of Lord Nelson. But they remained silent, and only three or four die-hard Members, whose names I did not know, put up the bravest display they could. I'm ashamed to say that my attention wandered for a time, but I was jolted back to proper alertness as the Solicitor General, Sir Samuel Romilly, began to speak for the Government. We all felt the atmosphere of the House rising to the highest pitch of excitement as Sir Samuel spoke of the persistence of the indefatigable Mr. Wilberforce during long years of scorn, ridicule and disappointment; and of how he had, almost single-handedly, impelled the nation's conscience to its present, virtually unanimous condemnation of the cruel and evil Slave Trade. At this point Mr. Clarkson turned in his seat and whispered, "You fought for nearly as long as he did, Daniel."

At this tears sprang to my eyes, but they were a mere trickle in the flood from Sir Samuel's audience. And as he spoke of Mr. Wilberforce's Christian heroism and final triumph, of the innumerable voices that would be raised in every quarter of the world to bless him and of the incomparable felicity he must enjoy in the knowledge of having preserved so many millions of his fellow-creatures, the remainder of his speech was drowned in the outburst of an ovation such as the House had never given to any living man. All order was flung to the winds. Total uproar prevailed. Hardly a Member but was on his feet, cheering, and shouting his congratulations. I had never seen Mr. Zachary shed tears, but he was shedding them now all right, and so were Mr. Clarkson and Mr. Sharp.

As for Mr. Wilberforce, he seemed insensible to everything about him, the still centre, sitting bowed in his seat, his head in his hands. From time to time he gave an almost imperceptible nod. I believed – and still believe – that an archangel was speaking in his ear.

After the clamour had at last died down, the House divided and the second reading was carried by a majority of 283 to 16. A month later the King's assent was given and the Bill became law.

One morning afterwards, in early April, I was told that Mr. Wilberforce wished me to call upon him at three o'clock that afternoon. It seemed strange that he should be thus precise, for almost always there were so many people, crowding one upon another, in the hope of gaining his attention, that it was usually impossible for him to say at what time he could make himself available to anyone in particular. Today, however, almost as soon as I had joined the usual throng outside his door in Palace Yard, (these being the overspill from the reception-room and the corridor), a servant came out and asked whether Mr. Daniel was present. Following him upstairs, I found Mr. Wilberforce alone in a little sitting-room overlooking the sunny garden. As we shook hands he said that he was most pleased to see me, since there had been so little opportunity lately for us to talk together. Mystified, I sat down in the chair he placed for me beside the fire and waited as he settled himself in another opposite.

"Daniel," he said, "I owe you a great deal and I'm very happy to thank you for all that you've done for Abolition. I know you've been at it almost longer than I have. More than that, you endured something like two years on a slave-ship; you sailed to West Africa and crossed to Jamaica on the Middle Passage. So you were able to tell the public the truth at first hand. Your evidence couldn't be refuted; it was one of the strongest weapons we had. It was unique; the authentic voice of a black man speaking of what he'd experienced himself.

"And then you joined Tom Clarkson and went to Liverpool with him. That took some courage, as I know well. And you got him out of a bit of nasty trouble, didn't you?"

"Then you went to Sierra Leone and worked with Zachary Macaulay in one of the worst climates in the world. He's told me

246

how you stood by him when the French sailors destroyed everything you'd built. I doubt whether Zachary could have survived without you at his elbow.

"I'd like to tell you about an idea I've had, Daniel. A few years ago I bought a house out at Clapham. I had thought of living there myself but as things turned out I had to stay at Palace Yard. Availability – pressure of business, you know. So I let the Clapham property to an American friend. He's just told me he's returning to Delaware, so the house has fallen vacant. If it suits you and your charming wife, I'd be only too happy to see you living there as my tenants. Now the Bill's been passed, there'll be any amount of work for experienced Abolitionists like you. We've got to enforce the Act and move on to our next battle – the prohibition of Slavery throughout all British-controlled countries.

"There's no hurry to decide about the house. I'll write down the address for you. Why not take Fahdah to have a look at it, and let me know in a day or two's time? I can guarantee you won't find the rent excessive; not for someone who's contributed as much as you have.

"I know Henry Thornton's hoping you'll work for him; and young Zachary's of the same mind. I'm in no doubt they'll pay you what you're worth. If you do decide to take the house, you'll be living quite near Henry's place. Most convenient."

That was six months ago, and the yellow leaves are falling in the little copse opposite our front windows. Fahdah and I are watching our children playing in the garden: William will be eight next birthday; he was born in the year we were married; and Penelope will be six. Henry, the baby, is just beginning to walk.

The other day, not far from London Bridge, I happened to see Jack Wain in the distance; but I was careful to avoid him. Fahdah and I may not be rich, but we're very comfortably off and feel we want for nothing; except an end to Slavery throughout the world.